SISTERS

Other Works Available in English
by Brigitte Lozerec'h

The Temp

SISTERS

BRIGITTE LOZEREC'H
TRANSLATED BY BETSY WING

DALKEY ARCHIVE PRESS
CHAMPAIGN / LONDON / DUBLIN

Originally published in French as *Trait pour traits* by Éditions Belfond, Paris, 2009

First edition, 2013

Library of Congress Cataloging-in-Publication Data

Lozerec'h, Brigitte.
[Trait pour traits. English]
Sisters / Brigitte Lozerec'h ; translated by Betsy Wing. -- 1st ed.
p. cm.
ISBN 978-1-56478-798-9 (paperback : acid-free paper)
1. Sisters--Fiction. 2. Women artists--Fiction. 3. English--France--Fiction. 4. Paris (France)--History--1870-1940--Fiction. I. Wing, Betsy. II. Title.
PQ2672.O97T7313 2012
843'.914--dc23

2012033682

Published with the support of the Josef and Anni Albers Foundation

Partially funded by a grant from the Illinois Arts Council,
a state agency

www.dalkeyarchive.com

Cover: design and composition by Mikhail Iliatov; illustration by Vera Iliatov

Printed on permanent/durable acid-free paper

For Jean-Jacques Pauvert
As devoted to books
As Manet was to painting

"Giving order to chaos—that is what creation is."
Guillaume Apollinaire

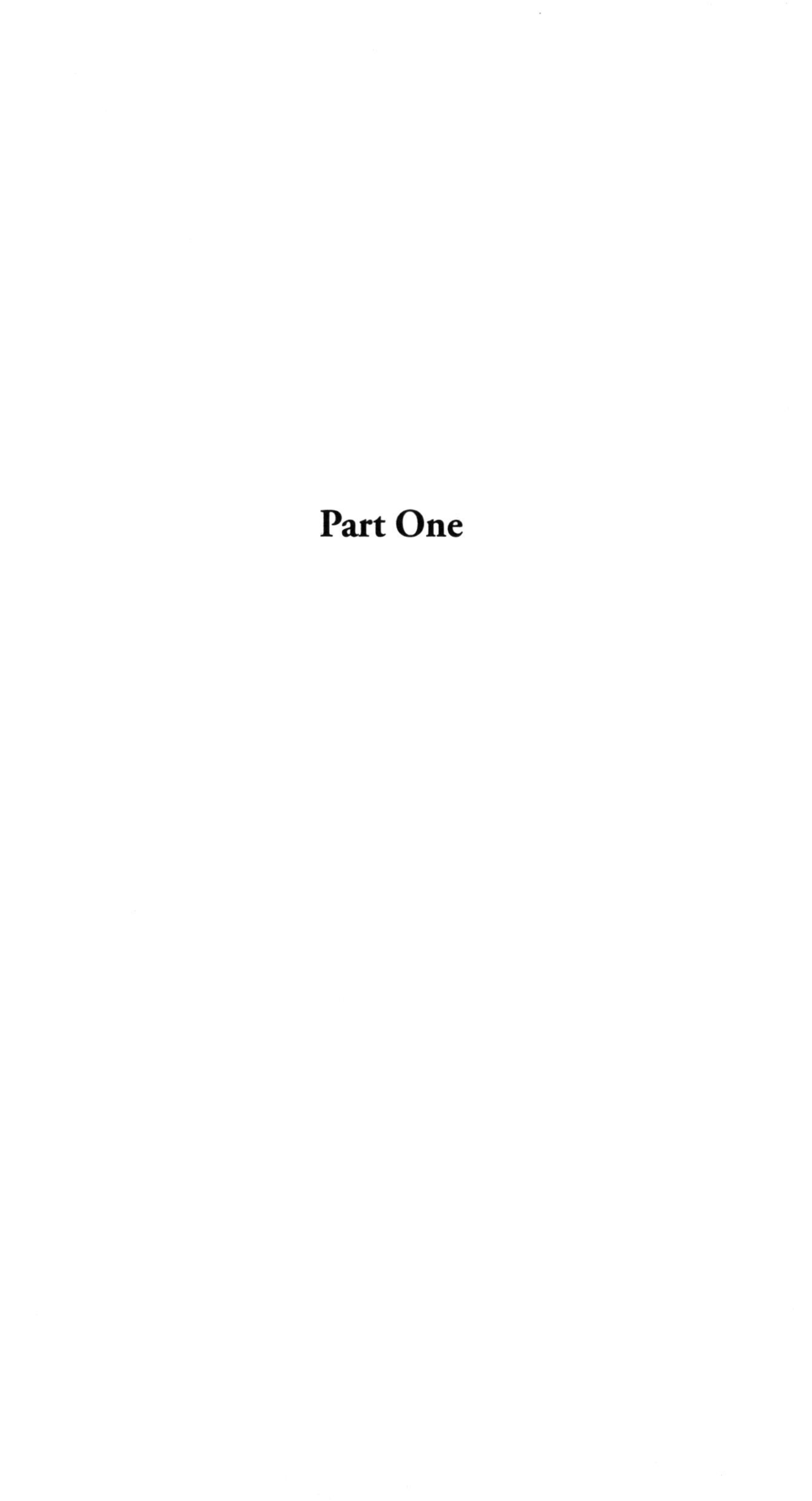

Part One

1

I ended up feeling at home there. And, actually, I've been calling it "our studio" for a long time. Frédéric completely rearranged it shortly before our marriage.

It wasn't considered proper for me to visit him there alone during our engagement. My chaperone's presence kept us from having any real familiarity at all, and made us all the more impatient. He slipped the ring on my finger in August 1904, a few days before my eighteenth birthday, but it took me a long time really to relax in his space, into our new life. The fear that I was just passing through never went away.

Our plan was that, from then on, we each would have one end of the studio to ourselves. Located on the ground floor, in the rear of a courtyard on rue Chaptal, our work space is a few streets over from place Clichy. Our glass window is closed off from any passing apartment dwellers by a privet hedge perfuming the air when summer comes. With the large doorway open we can hear hoofs and the wheels of horse-drawn carriages clattering on the stone pavement, as well as loud voices: the man selling newspapers, the vegetable man, the one selling rabbit skins, the knife sharpener and other peddlers, occasionally an automobile motor . . .

For ten years now I've been privileged to work on colors and patterns in a place reserved for that purpose alone. Slight shudders of anxiety, unexpected and incongruous, still take me by surprise, as if someone were about to tell me, "Pack your bags again, you have to leave." I keep fate at bay when this happens by closing my eyes and whispering, "Never again will a train or boat be loaded with my bags . . ." Anxiety has made me sedentary.

Being shut up, though not a prisoner, in the studio makes me happy. It's the place where I'm able to love Frédéric, able to be myself.

The arrangement hasn't changed since I got here and its stability suits me.

Frédéric put his easels, his trestle table, and his wardrobe next to the door, and my workbench and storage cabinet are set up in the back, near the steep staircase leading to the attic. In the front of the building there's a workbench running the length of the glass window, just beneath it. It's stained in some places and polished by the years in others because of the artist's habit of putting the finishing touches on some detail by daylight. Jars of powdered pigments are lined up here, along with plates for mixing them, penholders, candles, paraffin lamps, bunches of paintbrushes, rags, and any number of other things. We work there with our feet on the cans of linseed oil and turpentine stored underneath.

At either end of the studio, we have each organized our own spaces, each with a screen close at hand in case one of us feels like being more alone. Disorder prevails on Frédéric's side; at my end I've meticulously organized my cabinet so it holds all the boxes of pencils, pastels, tubes, and piles of old cotton fabric cloth. I've also sorted papers according to size and whether they're smooth or coarse in the drawers of a low chest. Three easels and the folding equipment I need for working outdoors stand waiting where I can reach them, like good servants always ready to go to work. A sofa for visitors, two armchairs, as well as a console table and a stove stand between Frédéric and me, like a little boudoir separating us.

We exchange glances at a distance, smiling or looking annoyed, depending on what we're producing. There are hours when we're both completely given over to our work, ignoring one another. But sometimes we'll emerge and invite ourselves to take a break "in the parlor," a steaming cup of tea before us, pipe and tobacco ready and waiting. We're rarely in the same mood at the same moment, but if one of us should despair, that same fear of failure gnaws at the other's inspiration and can poison it. Creation is an act of love constantly threatened by impotence. This sort of failure for an artist or a lover is like a foretaste of death. To fight it when you feel it quietly constricting your breast, chewing at your heart, and paralyzing your brain and hands, anything goes: a snack, taking a walk, hopping over to Café Prosper where maybe we'll find some friends as full of doubt and fed up with work as we. It doesn't matter what we do, we just have to get moving before smearing our anger all over everything; it's a little like fogging up a mirror to avoid seeing the pimples on your own face anymore. I understand people who tear up their paintings. Maybe my turn will come to do this. There are certainly some I've already locked away, never again to see the light of day.

Sharing the same space, I have to keep from falling into Frédéric's utter confusion. That's not easy. Nor is it easy sometimes to keep from falling into each other's arms, coming together as lovers when it's what I want, in spite of myself, because facing my work makes me feel all dried up inside. That's even worse. I envy Frédéric when I see him battling his picture, palette in one hand, brush in the other, as if he knows that he'll come out the winner. I'd like to steal his energy, breathing in the strength of his will from a distance. No. I force myself to unfold the screen or turn my back on him to protect him from being invaded, protect him from the vampire deep inside me. It's never completely asleep. I need him. When I have problems I might cry out for help, scream for him to come and save me from drowning. I mustn't do that. But there are other times when we drown together, our bodies caught up in love, then resurfacing, both of us enriched by our passion. After the welcome of the sofa, we can go back to work. I see my canvas through new eyes. It doesn't seem like the same picture as before, or else now I can see its problems clearly. Sometimes, after exhausting ourselves on the sofa, when I see my tubes and pots of powder, my pastels—in short, all my colors—I even dream that the hand of some genius might pick them up, mix them, and put them side by side on a canvas to produce a masterpiece. Any other hand, using the same materials, would create nothing but a worthless canvas . . . And my own? The thought makes shivers run through me. How strange it is to devote yourself to a passion that inspires doubt as much as it fuels one's need to create. I'm still afraid, despite all my years of work, that I'll be categorized as a mere dauber. M. Jacquier, who used to be my teacher, often told me: "Work, yes, but talent isn't something you can develop, you either have it or you don't. It's a way of looking, feeling. No one can teach you that."

The studio's tools are eloquent in their silence. Visitors are unable to decode the messages they're always sending—but I can. I know that there's nobility in each object's acquiescence, its faithfulness, its discretion. The very fact that a particular something is in one place rather than another suggests an intention, a specific movement and even thought—or absentmindedness. Objects know how to wait, they're never disapproving. They tell stories. Permeated with their masters' obsessions, they confirm for me at every instant that Frédéric exists and that I exist. Sometimes they make me laugh, even when I'm struggling with a project.

One day, Frédéric was mixing colors in a plate to get the blue he wanted, not just any blue but the one he had in mind, the absolute only blue, the one that was to give his canvas an extraordinary depth. He'd just spent hours doing it, after having added further hues to the ones he'd put in the day before. I was watching him from a distance, distracted from my work by the aura of brilliance surrounding him, and also, perhaps, by the grace you recognize in people who are experiencing a moment of fulfillment. His passionate stare gave his entire body a new weight, which I loved; and his hands, mixing the thick paint from his tubes the same way a careful cook works the ingredients of a sauce, fascinated me anew. The colors he was obtaining provoked such feeling in him that it permeated his entire being and emanated a wonderful sensuality. My jealous body, feeling the vibrations of his emotions, was spellbound. Abruptly I saw him stop stirring this blue soup with its pale gray and slightly purple tints. He brushed some of the color onto his canvas; then he dropped his three brushes and palette knife haphazardly onto the plate and, triumphant and full of the desire to lift his spirit up beyond every quotidian plane, turned toward me. My senses, permeated by the caresses that he'd lavished on his preparation, were in turmoil; I was weak in the knees, my lips greedy for his skin. For years now he has taught me about his pleasure and mine.

Trembling, without taking my eyes off him, dropping the soft lead pencil and the tracing paper where I'd copied a sketch I'd made the night before, I went to the sofa where he joined me. I looked at the bluish scar he'd smeared across his forehead with the back of his hand. As he kneeled close to me and reached for my blouse with fingers still stained with the colors he'd mixed, I was already unfastening my corset to give him my breasts and already he was lifting my skirt with one hand. I learned then that seconds can last forever, because this memory still moves me deeply whenever I conjure it up. I recognize our communion in it. Our glances, our caresses, our increasingly frenzied outbursts summoned fantasies, unfurled grandiose landscapes filled with sublime shapes. Together we suddenly experienced a glorious, exhilarating fall that left us exhausted and still locked in our embrace. Bit by bit we regained possession of the place, sweeping our eyes around what were, after all, our everyday surroundings, but as though we'd just landed there from another planet, changed by the incredible voyage in each other's arms. The three brushes and the palette knife still awaited their master in his blue mixture; my tracing paper and my soft pencil called to me from the cabinet. I considered them our most faithful friends. A tool, any tool, inspires me with respect for the hand that can tame it despite the demands every tool makes on its user in the beginning—the limitations it imposes.

We have an undeviating ritual before we can move on to our "outside" life, the life with our flesh-and-blood friends, strolling around town, visiting shows and galleries—always the same, immutable rite of cleaning all our brushes to cleanse the spirit after hours of work, to prepare it for the outside world. A slow and necessary transition.

When I first met the man who became my husband, I lived with the sense of being under an invisible bell jar that separated me from the world and protected me. How was he able to break through? That's a question I still ask myself.

2

I owe our chance encounter to the birth of my half-brother, when I was just about seventeen; I'd been living for more than two years at my grandmother's, at the corner where rue Moncey and rue Blanche meet.

Grandmother was bustling around after getting a telegram early in the morning. Later I found out that M. Versoix, my mother's second husband, had sent word that the first pains had begun and that she should come to the rue du Four on the Left Bank. My grandmother told me none of this; she would have had to put words to things about childbearing that couldn't decently be revealed to a young girl. All I knew was that my mother was "in a family way," since she could no longer hide it, but I didn't know when the "event" was supposed to take place, and I'd always been taught that it's indiscreet to ask personal questions. Unaware of what was happening, but seeing that Grandmother, in a state of great excitement, was preparing to leave the house, I took advantage of the situation to ask her permission to go to rue Amsterdam and buy some tubes of paint and other art supplies. My mother had opened an account for me there so I could replenish my stocks whenever I wanted. Actually, this was itself a pretext. I needed to get out and escape the pent-up feeling that I sometimes had in my room, where the alcove had been turned into my studio. My mother had lived there during the years preceding her remarriage, and it had also once been the room of my little sister, Eugénie.

"Well, child, Madame Chesneau can't go with you!" Grandmother fired back, giving the impression that I should know it wasn't the moment to ask her anything at all, no matter what.

Young girls don't go out on the streets alone—that was something I'd known as long as I could remember. What would happen if I disobeyed? Would attackers suddenly leap out from porches and alleys or from the entrance to the metro to menace me? After six years in a convent and two years under the surveillance of a grandmother and her lady companion, I lacked all instinct for the outside world and knew nothing about the habits of what I took to be society at large.

Flanked by my family when I was out walking, I deeply wanted to feel something of the real city, something of the intense excitement that never touched me because I was so thoroughly insulated. My world consisted of what I could see of the few people, the workers and servants of whom I knew only their public face, and then the few things I thought I knew of a life that was more refined, revealed to me entirely through how certain people dressed and carried themselves; I could sense subtle differences in their behavior and was curious to know more, but everything outside apparently threatened some invisible danger. What was I being protected from? That's what I hoped to find out, if with a slight rush of apprehension.

Which brings us again to that day which began with a strange disturbance in the house, when something told me that I might take advantage of my grandmother's panic.

"I'll just run out and come right back, Grandmother! I promise I'll hurry."

She'd known for a long time that if I didn't draw or paint every day I became impatient and aggressive, thanks to all manner of anxieties even I wasn't quite aware of. So, with a wave of her hand, as if to brush away some flies, she murmured as she went down the hall, "Don't take forever—I trust you! Just this one time, Mathilde!"

I raced down the staircase as fast as I could go, my coat still half-buttoned and my gloves in my hand, without even taking time to put my hat on straight—either driven by the fear that she might change her mind, or perhaps in my haste to know who I was once I was alone in the midst of strangers on the boulevards. On my way down rue Blanche the idea came to me of going to immerse myself in the lively crowds at the gare Saint-Lazare, where I'd feel life swarming around me. I laughed, lighthearted and alone, looking at the stores and cafes as if they might have changed overnight, weaving my way through the onlookers, the peddlers, the horse carriages, the junkman at the crossroads. On the other side of the road, on one of the buildings that I thought I knew very well, I was amazed to discover caryatids standing on either end of a porch and holding up a broad stone balcony. "I'll have to come back some day and sketch them in pencil," I thought. Just as I was about to set out to cross the congested street, I hesitated . . . If I didn't muster my courage all these strangers would see the slight anxiety unsettling my euphoria. I might have been unaware of where the danger lay, but these strangers all knew for certain. The women all seemed happy to me and the men good-natured in spite of the overcast skies of early March. Free in their midst I'd have liked to run the way I did as a child, until I was almost out of breath and dizzy, in the lane along Marble Hill Park, where our house was next to last before a bit of meadow began, hidden by a hedge. The Thames flowed down below.

On the steps to the station, a crowd of travelers was going up and down, a rhythmic stream of people. Suddenly an invisible hand pulled me back to my childhood, to the time I'd just been thinking about. An arrow stuck in my heart made me stop short, there on the Cour de Rome. I was looking at the stone arcades, the clock, the station's large windows, all with a fascination that was becoming more and more painful. We'd just arrived in Paris, right here, in the spring of 1895—my twin brother, William, was holding my hand, and our little sister, Eugénie, still an infant, was asleep in the arms of our mother who was dressed in mourning. It seemed to me that it was at the bottom of these stairs that happiness got away from us forever—though we didn't know it at the time. William and I weren't quite nine years old, and now, at almost seventeen, I saw that nothing had changed about this station or this crowd. The only thing different was that now, ever since the turn of the century, a few automobiles were mixing in among the horse carriages.

Yet how long ago that all seemed! I was there at the foot of the stone steps both in the past and in the present. As if I were arriving there to greet us. I remembered that my brother and I had been beside ourselves with the joy of our adventure when we left London. After crossing the gray swells stirred up by a north wind, then an interminable train ride, we'd arrived at this very spot. Fatigue, perhaps, had added to the excitement we felt as the children we were then, in this noisy, crowded Cour de Rome—simultaneously huge and too small. Our father, buried two months earlier in Twickenham, wasn't really dead for us yet. We were still expecting to see him emerge from the crowd, with his arms open for us to leap into them so he could hug us and murmur "my lovely twins." The feeling of his absence had not yet eaten into our souls, attacked our memories, gnawed away at our existence.

Dazed, I'd have stood there indefinitely, enduring the pain of standing at the frontier separating me from a lost happiness, at the foot of the steps leading to the gare Saint-Lazare. This boundary felt so real, I could almost touch it. I'd have liked to cross over it, go back in time the way I did in my incoherent dreams, and catch hold of the harmonious years spent in our home with its pretty name: Swann House, our beloved place at the end of Montpelier Row in Twickenham. All those names still sing inside me like the notes of a nursery song that might once have rocked me to sleep.

Intimidated and traipsing along behind our mother, we were approached by two women, one of them more refined looking than the other, who were waiting for us in the throng. The more I stared at them, the more I heard them ask us about our crossing, the more I knew that I knew them, but when and where had I seen them before? Which one was my grandmother? The driver, with the help of a porter, tied our baggage down on a carriage, while the horse tossed his head and pawed the ground, making me feel very sorry for him. How unhappy he must be so far from fields and forests! As for myself, lost in this crowd, all of them speaking French, laughing in French, I was sure I was the only one paying any attention to the creature. His loneliness and submission broke my heart. I hadn't yet said hello to the two women lingering over my little sister with worried looks on their faces.

I'd willingly embraced one of the two women after she'd said "Hello, dear child," but five months later, at the end of August, she was the one who, with her daughter, my mother, would exile me to the Sacré-Coeur convent.

Though I'd come out now with the notion of melting into the bustling city, with no thought of digging up old memories, it became obvious that it was here on the steps of the gare Saint-Lazare that our little unit had come undone, and not at the English cemetery where our father, Frank Lewly, lay at rest.

I now know that stones have memories. I looked at that façade as if I could decipher all the layered palimpsests, inscribed there ever since men and women began to arrive here to experience moments of life that were full of despondence or hope, the throes of love or abandonment as the trains went on coming and going . . . That day I discovered that streets have memories too, as do monuments and bridges.

Leaving the Cour de Rome I was unaware that I was on my way to a meeting arranged by fate on the pont de l'Europe—a meeting that was to determine the course of the rest of my life. I set out for it at a brisk pace.

3

I was brought back to the present by the cold gripping my feet and legs. I knew that the moment of freedom Grandmother had granted me couldn't last, but the sketch pad in my pocket kept pulling me on.

It was my guide.

Stamping my feet to get them warm, I went up rue Amsterdam, then I turned left into rue de Londres to make a pencil sketch of the pont de l'Europe. Again. It's an endless source of study. Its metal beams crisscrossing the entire length of the superstructure reminded and remind me of the Eiffel Tower's meshwork. The confusion of horizontal lines supported by diagonals and a few curves just above the railway was something of a trap for an apprentice like me. I'd already spent hours there while Mme Chesneau, shielded from the sun by her wide-brimmed hat, did needlework on a little folding chair close by.

At the top of the rue de Londres, on the part of the sidewalk overlooking the rails, I had an interesting view through the grills of the junction of the six roads meeting in a star shape above the railway traffic. I wanted to render the complexity, the contrasts of the parallel rails running under the complicated bridge structures. It was a challenge; I was only a beginner, sixteen and a half years old.

Frequently a train would come in or out of the station causing an incredible racket, loud enough to cover the din of the streets. Each engine created vibrations underfoot. The locomotive's plume of steam enveloped the great metal network of the bridge. Cars and passersby were absorbed in its coils and then emerged as the steam dissipated. That was where life was. My fingers numb with cold, having only just scribbled a few first sketches in my notebook, all I could think of was going home. My escapade had lasted long enough. Then a young man whom I hadn't noticed came up to me with a smile on his face. He didn't introduce himself—just started up a conversation:

"May I suggest a few changes, Mademoiselle?"

I didn't know what to think. It was my fault, caught without a chaperone. It's not proper to speak to a man you don't know. But I was flattered by his visible interest in my work. He had a straightforward look, kind, slightly amused. Could his criticisms be of some help to me? How could I know?

"So, you were watching me, Monsieur?"

"It's not just anybody who'd stop in this kind of cold to draw a few lines on a pad . . . Besides, this isn't the first time I've seen you working on this bridge. That intrigues me. May I?"

A hand with strong, slender fingers took careful hold of my pencil. The young man's self-assurance encouraged me to let him do it. With an air of great concentration, his gaze focused inward, he changed my lines with a few strong, controlled marks that gave the tangled framework of the bridge some density and balance. Then, lightly, almost caressingly, he drew a few diagonals coming together in the distance.

"That's where the vanishing point is, Mademoiselle, you see . . . It changes things a lot, doesn't it?"

I smiled to show I agreed.

"You can draw, I see," I said. "But do you also paint?"

"My studio is in rue Chaptal. You're welcome to visit . . . Are you studying at some academy?"

"I take private classes with M. Jacquier, yes, but I only started last year. Granted, it's not an academy, but it suits me."

"He makes stained glass windows and paints signs, if I'm not mistaken. Indeed, he's beginning to be known!"

"Watercolors and oils as well . . . Portraits, landscapes, pictures of the docks . . . I asked my mother if I could take classes with him. His studio isn't far from here."

"Work, work, work. Your hand will end up moving with confidence. If you have talent it will show. Love colors, love lines, feel what you want to see on your canvas with every fiber of your being. No doubt, M. Jacquier must tell you this again and again . . . Fill the colors and shapes with your own life."

"I have to go home, Monsieur."

I certainly felt a bit silly; what he'd just told me was beyond me. What did it mean to "fill the colors and shapes with my own life"? I guessed it was meant to sound encouraging. But my need to paint wasn't something I'd really thought about—I'd never analyzed it. It had been essential ever since the days when I'd spent hours with my friend, Alice, looking at illuminations in the convent library.

"Do you live in the neighborhood?" he went on.

When we realized that we were neighbors—his place was on rue Chaptal and I lived at the corner of rue Moncey and rue Blanche—we went down the rue de Liège together. We introduced ourselves to each other, if briefly. As we went along he repeated the invitation to his studio. I promised I'd go there with Mme Chesneau. Mentioning my chaperone reassured me and made it possible for me to regain some of the dignity I'd lost by allowing him to converse with me all the way to No. 1, rue Moncey.

We only had time to exchange a few scraps of information about our lives, almost nothing, and especially not the fact that I was living at my grandmother's. I was ashamed of it. I'd have liked to be able to say that I'd go back to my parents' home soon, that I was going to find my twin brother and little sister there, that we lived in Twickenham and were only visiting Paris. Flattered that he'd been drawn to me as an artist, I chose, however, to be silent. But what kind of artist was he? My curiosity would have to remain unsatisfied for the time being, because in a moment he was going to vanish. He was preparing to veer off for the boulevard de Clichy as I stood at the bow of the stone steamship solidly anchored at rue Moncey and rue Blanche. Then I left this stranger and climbed our stairs rapidly in order to conceal what I was feeling. I wanted to shake off all the things this encounter had stirred in me, things I couldn't have analyzed but that made me want to visit Fréderic Thorins in his studio as soon as I could. I needed to hide how excited I'd become; I needed to hide my fear that someone would notice how I was buzzing, full of both hope and distrust, and likewise the fear that I'd been wrong to allow myself to be seen on the street with a strange man.

When I pushed open the apartment door, only the cook was there. Grandmother had gone to be with her daughter on rue du Four, on the Left Bank. Mme Chesneau had accompanied her in the fiacre because Eugénie would have to be taken for a walk while my mother was giving birth.

I then understood the panic caused by the morning message. My half-brother, François, was born in the afternoon of that unforgettable

March 6, 1903.

No one could ever have imagined that I was meeting my future husband while my mother was in labor. In fact, as I climbed the stairs to the first landing, I was thinking of him as an old man. But he was only ten years older than I, and, now that our lives are bound together, I don't see the least difference.

4

Curiosity was behind my asking Grandmother for her official permission to go with Mme Chesneau to visit the studio of M. Thorins; then came the interrogation: Who was the young man? How had I met him? What was his background? She reluctantly agreed but made it clear that it had to be "A short visit, of course! Mme Chesneau will tell me what she thinks of him!"

In Frédéric Thorins's studio I found the same spirit of work and the same love of silence as I'd felt at M. Jacquier's. But here an old sofa and two slumping armchairs invited one to rest or daydream. Behind them a screen served to camouflage very poorly the long room overflowing with bric-a-brac. Everything about this studio, except for the artist's work, seemed to me an invitation to idleness. The old sofa brought shameful things to my mind, questionable situations, but then also animated conversations, joyous get-togethers among friends—altogether, the sorts of thing you heard about artists. None of which had ever occurred to me at M. Jacquier's.

I liked the atmosphere in my teacher's studio. Tall and solidly built, he wore a shirt fastened at the collar with a bow tie to work, all of a piece with this space where I was struck by the vertical lines of the furniture—very straight and upright: tall easels, armchairs with straight backs, a high table, a narrow chest of drawers, and a cupboard that seemed immense to me. You could see it was home to a spirit that was constantly seeking. Pictures hung side by side on the walls and invited you into little harbors, the marshes of the Vendée and the lives of peasants. And then, in unexpected contrast: posters for seaside resorts, spas, casinos. Elegant women wearing cumbersome hats that were wrapped in light veils that made you imagine how pleasant it would be to be driven by automobile along the twists and turns bordering the Mediterranean or on snowy mountainsides. Bold lettering, visible from a distance, spelled out the names of cities for wealthy vacationers.

M. Thorins invited us to sit down next to the stove. At that point I experienced a strange confusion. I glanced quickly at Mme Chesneau and felt reassured by her round silhouette, her skirts bouncing around her hips, her hands with their large palms and the short fingers I knew so well. Still, what was alarming about sitting here? Why did obstinate visions of little seamstresses or laundresses posing on that sofa keep bothering me? Why would it upset me to imagine the bodices that were just slightly too low cut, skirts lifted to show petticoats and tight-laced little boots displaying a delicate ankle? I imagined merry, uninhibited laughter. What had come over me? Was I remembering scenes I'd seen on the walls of the Louvre, where I frequently went with Mme Chesneau? Why should I suddenly feel warm all over? I couldn't manage to continue the sober conversation interrupted in front of Grandmother's house a few days earlier. There was a good chance that all sorts of inappropriate, possibly indiscreet words would pop to the surface of whatever I said, and then be reported to my grandmother.

A tin kettle on the stove soon began blowing steam through its spout. Frédéric Thorins served us some tea. His nervous laughter and the way he kept running his fingers through his short, thick, straw-colored hair showed how uneasy he felt. As if giddy with fatigue he told us that he wasn't ready for his exhibit next month, that he still had a great deal of work to do. Though he'd seemed so sure of himself on the pont de l'Europe, I could feel his anxiety now. Today of course I know how to name the anguish of an artist afraid of losing his touch, his sense of color, the originality of his perspective and composition, or worse, an artist deserted by inspiration, an artist drowned in doubts—one whom, in this case, our visit had perhaps disturbed, or, to the contrary, rescued from his distress. Without this knowledge, I was consumed at the time with my desire to talk about the pangs I could see he was suffering. Were they the same as the ones I'd experienced? But we were only exchanging meaningless banalities. Mme Chesneau's teacup was empty and she was already suggesting that we should go home.

I was hoping, however, to see some of the paintings by this artist. He vanished several times behind a huge curtain that covered the side wall, the entire length of the studio. After having taken five pictures from their hiding place, one by one, he turned to face me; the smile on his face was kind and distant at the same time. The same smile I'd seen a week earlier. "Here are a few I did last year . . . I'm not showing you the most recent, two or three of them will be shown at the next exhibit at Willon's, sometime around mid-May."

He was watching to see my reaction, but I didn't have one. It was impossible for me to think at all, beset as I was with so many questions, and maybe also disappointed to feel how foreign his work was to me. People, still lifes, monuments, and landscapes had all been taken apart into geometrical shapes, blended with each other by means of more or less contrasting, monochromatic shades and unceremoniously juxtaposed, I might even have said flung up against each other. I'd already seen pictures of this sort, but they belonged to a world remote from mine. I didn't think I'd be mixing with anyone who made paintings like these.

"It's rather odd, don't you think, that you're the person who corrected my perspective," I said jokingly, my only comment.

"True, it might seem peculiar. But I also know how to paint academic landscapes and even portraits—it's just that I chose Cézanne as my master, you see. You don't have to like them. It is how my eyes dissect the light and shadow. There's much to be explored in this new mode."

"I'll probably never get used to it. I must lack a certain openness," I stammered.

"Turn your sense of appreciation loose, that's all. Set it free! Come, will you, to the opening of the exhibit on May 13!"

When I left, my mind was abuzz. I had a lot to learn in order to earn the right to walk the path I'd been determined to choose for myself ever since M. Jacquier had begun working zealously to teach me. Few women devoted themselves to painting, which made me very ill at ease, because I would never have dreamed of doing something that might make me conspicuous. Nonetheless, the idea of having to put my paintbrushes away forever in order to please a husband seemed to me a mutilation that was intolerable. Ever since Grandmother began talking to me about marriage I'd been wondering what sort of suitor would put up with this need of mine.

When I'd entered the convent at Sacré-Coeur, in the old Biron mansion across from the hotel des Invalides, invisible prison bars had grown up like tall trees around me. The only way I could forget those bars and come in contact with my contemporaries was through line and color . . . How could I make this happen?

5

I'd been full of joie de vivre, even sensuality as a child. But for what are called the pleasures of the flesh, for vice, I think, I had to wait for convent life to contract the infection, if imperceptibly. The countless prohibitions governing our life, all the suspicion, the prying eyes, the obsession with sin, the penances inflicted by our confessor after we'd listed our pitiful little misdeeds, all that and even more—if you take into account the agony of the martyrs we were given as models for our behavior—were bound to throw our souls and senses into a turmoil of over-excitement, duplicity, and secretiveness, thanks to the familiar, detestable routine of constant inquisition.

In a convent one quickly learns to see and feel everything that's beneath the surface, all the while looking as though you are studying, praying, or embroidering. If the nuns hadn't checked every night to make sure we'd sleep with our hands on top of the sheets and not underneath, so we wouldn't get any bad ideas, I'd never have thought of trying to discover what was wrong with it. It took me a long time to figure out and even more time to reach the conclusion that for those ladies to hound us like that, they had to be obsessed with it . . . I'd never been quite able to think of those women, almost completely hidden beneath their veils and long black robes, as human beings. Ugly, shameful images kept coming to mind, where they were concerned; as if to bring them down from their inaccessible heaven: the headmistress on the toilet or completely naked in her bathtub washing her "unmentionables." Did she even have those? If she did, then did she think it felt nice to touch it with her soapy fingers? I wondered if the hidden bodies of the nuns were different from those of secular women, if they wore underpants and corsets, if they had hair. I watched them as closely as they watched us. There couldn't possibly have been eyes less discreet than mine.

We weren't allowed to favor one friendship over any other. My forever-frustrated need to snuggle up in someone's loving arms was making me ill. How much I needed to feel a hand touch mine, warm lips slip along my neck as they whispered tender words as our mother used to do before she turned out the light in our first life. It had not been long ago that I'd fall asleep with the smell of her perfume in my hair and on the sheets. I also wanted to sniff the milky smell of my little sister who used to burst out laughing in her cradle when I mewed like a cat as I kissed her. Any demonstration of friendship was forbidden to us boarders; I felt alone, different from my fellow students who were almost all from noble families and who proved to be well versed in the duplicity suitable to the mind-set of the place. Obsequious attention was paid to the girls who were of noble birth, especially in the parlor, where each family would gather around at a separate, round table to give the impression of being in a private salon.

I was ashamed of how insignificant I was in their midst, with my bourgeois origins, lacking a fancy family tree. I could tell that I was only tolerated there out of Christian charity because my grandmother, as she'd also done earlier on behalf of my mother, had asked for the support of the bishop, Monseigneur Gallois, to whom she was distantly related. At first I'd thought that it was only my language that kept me apart, despite the fact that I'd been speaking French for as long as I could remember. But I didn't get the puns and local jokes, though playful language came naturally to me in English. It wasn't a big thing—but it was huge.

Of course, to develop a real passion, there's nothing like being forbidden to love.

I devoured Alice with my eyes; she was a girl in my class who wore her hair in long braids wrapped around her head like a fairytale princess or a saint, and I always managed to sit beside her in chapel. In the silence and cold of the stones, nothing escaped my senses during the daily service. We were supposed to read the sacred texts with visible enthusiasm, but were still half-asleep. Still, I recited each word of love composing the hymns intended for God, the Holy Trinity, or the Virgin Mary with a heart so full of joy that I thought it might crack. I thought I'd die every time, and I imagined with delight how much attention I'd get as they tried to bring me back to life. Alice would be leaning over me then, and in the moment I opened my eyes, I'd be able to see how upset she was. That would be bliss. Without Alice I wouldn't have been so ardent in chapel. Religion, garnished as it is, most plentifully, with words otherwise intended for secular love—so delicious to say or just to hold in your mouth—filled the vast emptiness into which I'd sunk when I'd arrived. It was my guilty pleasure to contemplate Alice's profile, like some holy image. What was it she radiated that was able to inspire in me a sort of inexpressible hope? The line of her high forehead, her slender nose, her mouth, her well-formed chin, and her crown of braided hair made my pulse erratic. These surges felt both so good and yet so painful that I could sense that I was in a state of sin without knowing why.

Now I wonder if having to get up at six o'clock in a building with no heat and being made immediately to wash ourselves quickly in cold water—by dampening our ardent desire to just let things go, be comfortable, not to mention all sorts of other lascivious temptations—didn't have the opposite effect from the one intended, in the long run . . . In the end, convents often return girls to their families entirely depraved. All their frustrations during the years they were pent up have fed their desire for luxury, for wild extravagance, and those pleasures of the flesh. Some women try to realize these dreams when they're returned to a worldly life, while others remain immured in themselves, as obsessed as the nuns who brought them up. The marriage of my mother to wild Frank Lewly stands as an example of the first scenario, and my life among bohemian artists as another instance of the same. I hope it doesn't take an entire lifetime to expurgate one's soul of the perversions with which it's been impregnated during one's youth. How many times, as an adult, in the midst of delirious ecstasy, have I had visions of Frédéric and myself locked in an embrace on the tiled floor between the font and the confessional of a chapel lit by stained-glass windows . . . I've tried and tried each time this happened to get rid of the image, because I still have the notion that some things are sacred, but back it comes, against my will, as if I still needed the place that had first inspired my secret passions in order to reach the heights of pleasure as an adult.

When finally I ended up dissolving into the mentality of that establishment, it was the workings of the outside world that came to alarm me. I would have liked to stay shut up inside, hidden beneath the veil, and when I was twelve I thought I'd made the mother superior like me when I confided to her that I wanted to become a nun when I was older. “Continue to pray, my child, and we’ll talk about it later,” she said, looking me in the eye with her hand on my shoulder. It was almost pleasant. I was moved for a moment. I felt I really existed.

Deep inside me, however, there was something else, welling up as though determined to humiliate me. I could feel it coming, and, with all my might, refused to accept it.

6

If I'd known when I was young that it was because my father had died bankrupt that our house in Twickenham had been sold just before our return to France, I'd have been even more miserable among those wealthy heiresses being brought up with the sole purpose of making good marriages and prolonging a respectable lineage. I did indeed feel that the death of my father had caused a great disruption, but I certainly didn't want to listen to my intuition, especially if I might discover that my fears were well-founded. I would then have lost him for a second time. Still, a little voice inside kept whispering that, despite the fine lifestyle I'd experienced, despite the loving atmosphere at Swann House, I was worth nothing. Occasionally, I'd have bad dreams in which I saw myself barefoot, begging for a living. Clearing my mind of those images took a long time; they felt like a premonition. Though I wouldn't have known how to put it in words, my entire being was permeated with my mother's shame. Ruined after paying off all the debts by selling our home in Twickenham, she was forced to move back to Grandmother's—this time with a baby in her arms and two other children in tow. She had barely any income at all, as I found out later. Though she'd been affectionate and free at Twickenham, now at the house on rue Moncey she had to stifle all rebellious instincts and, too weary to argue, consent to her mother's strict requirements; for one, she hadn't been able to prevent William and I from being sent to boarding school. I sensed something broken deep inside her, something collapsing with each hour of distance between England and us, as if her life were ebbing away. The day must have come when she'd had to renounce some essential part of herself and I realized that we were losing her.

She herself had been sent away to Sacré-Coeur after the death of her father, and she still had bad memories of being shut up inside the convent. There were always two or three less wealthy and less well-born little girls who were tolerated there "out of Christian charity"—as we were rather disdainfully reminded. Was it out of revenge that my mother, at the age of twenty, had married a very rich thirty-year-old man who loved parties, horses, and gambling?

Luckily for William, he was blossoming at the Lycée Lakanal. Whereas I was moping, he was playing sports and bridge and chess and studying the arts and mathematics, all with equal verve and with fascinating teachers. He formed strong friendships in this brand new institution with its revolutionary methods of education built on furthering the boys' development with lots of outdoor exercise. And, above all, something it took me years to understand, he had escaped the exclusively feminine milieu of our family. An unspeakable distance gradually grew up between us—a loss I suffered like a mutilation.

Imprisoned as I was, I could feel memories floating back to me of the first weeks we'd spent in Paris before going out to Grandmother's property along the Seine, near Meulan, for the summer. Every night when I was trying to go to sleep, these images would emerge one after another to fill my heart; day by day I was growing more aware that they marked the real end of our childhood. I didn't know that, in consequence, I was cultivating an incurable nostalgia for the days when our house held only two children and two parents.

Scarcely had we deposited our trunks at the rue Moncey in April 1895 than our mother had established a new ritual—one that lasted until June. The moment we'd swallowed our midday meal she would exclaim: "Get ready, children, we're going to citify!" and then, in a fiacre she'd engaged, we'd take off—my mother, my brother, and I, leaving the baby with her nurse for the afternoon. It was as if we were prolonging the adventure we'd begun at the station in London, after which we discovered the docks of Southampton and the train station at le Havre. I liked that expression: citifying. I didn't know she'd made the word up; I still and will always use it to describe aimlessly strolling around the city, whether on foot or in an automobile. Much later I understood that it was a form of escapism for Jeanne Lewly and her twins, all three of them concealing their mourning deep inside a horse-drawn carriage. Our mother kept us as long as possible in a world of illusion, prolonging the complicity that had bound us so tightly together up to that time. Was she hoping to impress upon our memories forever those hours stolen from the rules of our new existence? We drove around Paris a lot that spring.

North, south, to the Champs-Elysées or the Faubourg Saint-Antoine we drove, staring open-eyed at the city. They were carefree hours when we would speak our father's language and sing the songs we'd always sung; we also listened to our mother as she told us the names of monuments, streets, and parks, which, compared to the great gardens of London, seemed so meager. We weren't old enough yet to appreciate the architecture and situate it in its proper period and culture. Notre-Dame didn't seem as impressive to us as Westminster Abbey. It sat there on its island like a stone sphinx pricking up its ears and surrounded by the river flowing past in its narrow, fortified bed. What were we to make of the pathetic yet charming Seine with its elegant bridges when our eyes were accustomed to the broad Thames that it took forever to cross in the great capital of England? In London as in Paris there were quays and embankment roads piled high with crates, barrels by the hundreds, enormous piles covered with tarpaulins, unrecognizable cargo waiting to be loaded into the bilges of deep barges or onto the decks of flat ones. But in Paris there weren't any proud three-masted schooners setting sail and leaving onlookers behind to dream! Never any tide. William and I became aware then of the sea's influence in London . . . In Paris what we liked to see were the carts full of old books lining the parapets along the quays shaded by plane trees and poplars, and also the café terraces on the sidewalks that filled with people the minute the sun was up. So, how Paris revealed its charms to us, and likewise its hideousness, was determined by the horse's pace, sometimes walking, sometimes at a slow trot . . .

Everything about our life was different, even our mother who'd already changed in the first few months after our father died, and had changed even more since we'd arrived at her mother's house. Taking us out on carriage rides was a way she'd invented to fill herself with the intoxicating spectacle of the streets, all the while remaining seated safely inside a fiacre. The façades, avenues, and gardens of the city of her youth unfurled before her and it gave her obvious pleasure to show them to us. But every now and then we'd see her become strangely languid and despondent. William and I would glance at each other, worried. As soon as she became aware of this, she'd quickly reassure us: "Paris, the city of grace, the city of harmony . . . You'll find that you love it, my children!"

One day we paid a visit in Passy to one of our father's cousins, whom she called by her first name, Dilys. She welcomed us beneath an arbor of wisteria in full bloom. For an instant our mother rested her cheek on the shoulder of this elegant woman in her forties, then she closed her eyes as if she wanted to fall asleep right there on her feet. Her acting so familiar with someone I didn't know caught my attention, but I saw also her thin-lipped smile: I felt she wanted to cry but was holding it in. William and I instinctively moved closer together. Seeing that we were petrified, our mother forced herself to lift her head and speak. "So, Cousin, will you treat us to some nice tea with some of your wonderful fruitcake?" Then, almost immediately, there were the charming sounds of porcelain and silverware on the garden table with its embroidered tablecloth, and we spent a merry, completely English afternoon that remains preserved for me perfectly, because it was my first contact with the woman who would come into my life, years later, as though she were a guardian sent by my father.

In two years now I'll be thirty, my mother's age at the time. I'm trying to get a real sense of the depth of her bewilderment in those days, even though I have no children. Right then, no matter how hard I tried to imagine her utter grief, I couldn't see how alone she was—because *we* were there! I'd not yet noticed that she no longer sat down at the piano; it had been months . . . Only quite recently have I realized that she'd given it up in the months when she was expecting Eugénie.

I also remember having caught sight during our interminable carriage rides of a dark opening between two apartment buildings in a very populous suburb. The passageway plunged away toward dilapidated houses from another century. Was it over by the Bastille? Toward the fortifications? Or maybe near Montmartre where, all in the same slow but steady rhythm, men in wooden shoes wielded scythes to cut the tall grass in the square below the basilica then under construction? In that alley that I've never forgotten, children in rags shared the pavement littered with rubbish, with geese and scrawny dogs. They were playing in the mud. A little blonde girl stood there and followed us with her eyes; her arms were wrapped protectively around some other little ragamuffin as if she feared we might snatch him away from her. There was just time enough to catch sight of them and then we'd gone by. But I saw them. I remember being gripped by a fear impossible to describe because I could see that she was more or less my age. I was struck by the feeling that something similarly catastrophic was threatening us as well. I'd read it in the eyes of this child standing there, motionless and dignified with that chaos of blonde hair heavy on her shoulders. She stared straight at us without hatred during the few seconds it took us to go by, and the dark brilliance of her eyes alarmed me. If I'd known the word "destiny" then, that's the one I'd have applied to the way she stood there with as much swagger as resignation: this was some sort of omen of our destiny. For a moment, remembering the sale of Swann House, I'd thought it possible that we might ourselves arrive at such destitution. An unpleasant shiver ran through me. As soon as I looked at my mother, her head held high beneath her black hat, the feeling went away, but not the fear—the fear of a fall. Yet none of these emotions and reflections kept William and me from our puns and laughter; the woman in black accompanying us played along, but was no longer the happy person we'd known.

The crowning moment in our outings was always a visit to the Café de la Paix where a glass of juice or sherbet would be set before us. My mind would race ahead then to the end of our jaunt. I thought how I'd be back with baby Eugénie before the hour was up. She'd have finished her nap and would greet us with little chortles that clearly showed how pleased she was to see me again. I'd put my dolls away in a trunk the day she was born because I was so happy to have a real little baby in the family, a doll baby in the flesh that I could hug and examine and love as much as I wanted. I made puppet shows for her with my fingers; I sang; I could see the tiny changes from one day to the next on her jolly face, so pale, so alive, and so mysterious. I'd never imagined a lovelier miracle. I didn't like being away from her for more than a few hours, and so the sound of the horse's trot as it went back up the rue Blanche was a joyful noise soothing my impatience to see her again.

We spent the summer after we'd come back from England at

Sainte-Coulombe, Grandmother's house on the road out of Villennes-sur-Seine, downstream from Poissy. This prolonged our carefree days but didn't lighten my mother's burden of grief, which could be seen in her eyes and the way her body seemed to crumple when she didn't know she was being observed. She was well aware that our fate was already sealed. We'd hardly celebrated our ninth birthday when my brother and I were each led off to our respective boarding schools. How can I ever forget that terrible autumn of 1895?

As for William, yes, he blossomed at Lakanal.

7

In the well-regulated life of the convent I performed whatever gesture I was ordered to undertake, though without ever really understanding what they meant. What I did know was that they weren't leading to the love that the nuns kept going on and on about, describing it as "divine." Sometimes I didn't even hear people speaking to me, haunted as I was by beloved voices from my past, letting them resound to fill the emptiness inside me. All the nuns' rules and regulations continued to seem foreign to me. Still, I'd have liked to be satisfactory. Their criticism of what they considered my provocative attitude was enough to make me feel terribly guilty. In England we'd never gone to school. A tutor came to Swann House to teach us how to read and write and do arithmetic; he told us about distant lands that he then showed us on our globe, and recounted stories of wars waged by kings and princes. From this point on, however, my youth was going to be conducted within high walls. We'd only go outside once a month and for the holidays. I could have visits in the parlor on Thursdays. Feeling terribly abandoned, I told myself over and over that our father would never have put up with that situation.

The lavish words of adoration in the sacred texts were like honey soothing a sore throat. Through them I entered into a world of thought, unreal and magical, experiencing moments of elation that lifted me into who knows what fictional, harmonious upper reaches of reality, into flowery feelings filling the emptiness of my heart with their syrup. I became a star, or a cloud, maybe even a single longed-for raindrop on an earth that was so dry it crackled under one's foot . . . And my self became diluted in the violent beauty of the stained glass in the chapel. Depending on the time of day and the sun's intensity, the reds and blues in particular made me want to dissolve away into them. The dream drew me up and away to a timelessness outside of the quotidian matters of existence.

My friend Alice took me to the library where the only books to which the students had access were sacred texts, antiphonaries, or bibles. Gilt-edged volumes full of sleeping miracles: the illuminations. People, plants, and animals scrambled up the opening letter of each verse, coiled inside their curves, likewise separating chapters and running around the borders of the pages. I never got over my astonishment at these discoveries. My passion for illuminations remains intact.

We tried to copy them or invent new ones in our notebooks. I rediscovered the pleasure I'd once taken in drawing fruits, birds, rabbits, and flowers to compose a farandole of color and motion. My eyes transformed everything into miniature form, which I set down in multicolored garlands in the margins of my pages. My guilty obsessions showed up here, but you'd have had to know what you were looking for to recognize them. Who could have guessed that the leaves folded across the central vine represented hands under the sheets placed exactly at the intersection of two other stems, there, in the forbidden spot? I alone knew it, and it was wonderful not to be scolded or judged when I showed people my drawings. Nor did anyone know that when I drew a family or rabbits or a nest of birds I never was able to put the young in alongside their parents. Each member of the family had its own leafy branch or teetered on letters that were far away from each other. I was the only one who knew that they were from the same litter or the same hatching and that they were waiting for someone to bring them together again . . .

I never let go of my colored pencils. For my twelfth birthday I asked for brushes and tubes of paint.

8

My mother took the family as well as Aunt Dilys to the opening of the show at the Willon Gallery on May 13, 1903, scarcely two months after the birth of little François. This was a chance for her to meet Frédéric Thorins and decide whether or not he had any talent in her eyes.

She arrived looking quite haughty, with Eugénie hanging onto her gown and Grandmother, despite having her cane for support on one side, leaning on her arm. M. Versoix, my mother's second husband, whom I still can't call anything other than Monsieur, brought up the rear with his son from his first marriage, Alain, a fourteen-year-old boy who meant nothing to me but who had the same little brother as I. We looked at each other with a certain mistrust. We were polite when we spoke, but quite reserved. I would have liked to have William there with us at the opening, but he was preparing for his baccalaureate exams.

The personal history that I had with painting, and that I had now with this artist, whom I'd met a few weeks earlier, was turning into my mother's business, and I had a strong sense of watching these private connections be taken away from me. Her little group, attentive to her words, followed her from room to room. She analyzed the construction of the works and went into raptures over a particular color, or, whispering to her family what they *ought* to think, rejected a certain style. Where did she get this knowledge? Was it profound or superficial? I had no memory of having heard her discuss painting when she was at Grandmother's; rather, all she talked about were things she'd read, or concerts and plays that she went to with our English cousin. Had she gone with my father to art exhibits in London? My memory was completely blank on this point, but I had a question: was it because of this familiarity with art that she had not stood in the way of my taking classes with M. Jacquier? Or had that kindness been, instead, an attempt to make recompense for my abandonment in the convent?

I saw Frédéric Thorins coming toward us in the crowd and had a sinking feeling, as though he represented some wrongdoing in my life and all these people were now going to be exposed to it. Besides, I wanted to protect myself from my family's judgment concerning the work of a person whom I hardly knew but who belonged to the world that I wanted to enter. A person who knew how to talk about things I felt passionate about. The worst of it was that their point of view might possibly influence me and I was ashamed of this in advance. As soon as he'd greeted me the reflexes instilled in me by my education came to my rescue and provided some guidance. I introduced him to my family, despite how much I regretted having brought these two opposite poles of my existence face to face when they shared no point in common.

How proud I was, however, of my mother's natural elegance, the gracious yet haughty way she held her head . . . Since her marriage to M. Versoix, she had regained her panache. In another life I'd adored her, and perhaps I still adored her, but in a way that was more reserved, even stifled. She intimidated me, seduced me, crushed me. She still had power over me, while her own mother held all the authority. Which reminded me that I belonged to them. It was at once reassuring and appalling. William, even though he too had been shut away, seemed free to me, by contrast, simply because, being a young man, he was able take the train from Sceaux by himself, get off at the gare du Luxembourg, and hop into an omnibus to come to Grandmother's, if he didn't saunter instead along the streets of the Latin Quarter on his way to the home of our mother and her husband on the rue du Four . . . That's the stuff dreams are made of! Occasionally, without the least concern on his part, he'd even *give up* his monthly permission to leave school in order to take part in a game of sports or go riding with his fellow students. No one even commented when he decided to do this. The entire family knew he'd begun riding lessons with our father and still was passionate about it. William, less supervised than I, took life head-on.

As I watched my mother at the Willon Gallery, she seemed larger, wiser, and more triumphant in her new existence. Her name was no longer Jeanne Lewly but Jeanne Versoix and I couldn't get used to it, even though it was almost as though M. Versoix were giving me back the happier woman of before. Still, I couldn't help but think that now she owed her triumphant air to him, and that it was with him and her new family that she shared it above all. We, the twins, belonged to another life that had led briskly and joyously to bankruptcy, the sale of Swann House, and our return to Grandmother's.

Feeling the need to build up my self-confidence in the midst of this crowd, I moved toward Frédéric Thorins, who was busy talking with a man. When he caught sight of me, he waved me over and introduced me to the visitor in a manner that I found quite surprising: "Take a good look at her, she's going to be my next pupil, and I think people will be talking about her some day!" The man, a journalist, turned to look at me, full of curiosity, then he gave Frédéric a knowing wink, which made me very uncomfortable indeed. But at the same time, because the artist himself was watching me so steadily, with eyes that were so warm, so protective, eyes shining with a gleam that was unique, a burst of joy quelled my anxiety. Not only had I just learned that he was thinking of having me for a pupil and that he believed I had a future, he'd also made me conscious of feeling something very pleasant that I was savoring for the first time—something I wouldn't have known how to encourage. For a brief moment I saw that he thought I was pretty, and I was flattered by that and felt alive.

I had no time to enjoy my happiness. My little sister slipped catlike close beside me, fishing for compliments with a smile and a glance. Her slightly auburn hair, her green eyes, and her voluptuous lips, which were so skilled in the arts of pouting and laughter, formed an adorable mélange that would always be the perfect temptation for portrait painters. In her smocked dress and large collar she was flirtatious and stylish with all the arrogance of her eight and a half years. I'd have liked it better if she had stayed with our little brother.

Eugénie was never able to see any member of the family conversing with someone outside of our circle without forcing her way in. She talked charmingly about herself, about how her music teacher had recognized her gift for the piano, even predicting that because she was so gifted, she might have a career. Eugénie was careful not to mention that this attentive woman had added that one had to work on it every day, if one wanted to be great, which my sister didn't do. She was always looking for compliments, but, in order to avoid provoking a tantrum by reminding of her obligations, she was left alone to practice her music however and whenever she pleased. A quick glance in my direction made her certain that I wasn't going to contradict her in front of these gentlemen. I recognized her way of saying "See, me too!" or maybe "Me most!" without actually putting it into words. The two men, charmed with her audacity, smiled and congratulated her on her ambition. We'd interrupted their conversation, so I took the little one by her hand and led her off to our grandmother, who was sitting on a sofa. She'd been keeping an eye on us the whole time.

When our family left the exhibition, Eugénie voiced her challenge: "And what if I painted with you?"

"Would you like that, dear?" my mother replied, giving us an encouraging look.

"Yes, I'd like to learn."

I had to say something. "If you don't work at your piano lessons, why would you work on painting, which you've always found boring? You've always said so, even at the Louvre, not too long ago."

"With you it would be different," she replied.

"What a good idea, Mathilde!" my mother decided.

M. Versoix put in his opinion: "A very good idea!"

And Grandmother went them all one better: "The little one could come to my house once a week."

9

This exchange completely knocked the wind out of me, right there in the street. For years I'd been hearing: "The eldest has to have the grace to give in, Mathilde—don't make her cry . . ."

I was perfectly aware of a fact that eluded them: my little sister had simply glimpsed a door opening upon a world she didn't know. Sensing that I wished to go through it, that I was standing on the threshold, she'd been stricken with panic. I could see it in her worried expression: she wanted to come with me, or else, barring that, to stand in my way. When M. Thorins let it be known that I might take classes with him, I'd seen it in her eyes: "Me too!" It's possible that it occurred to her that, if I was a painter, I'd no longer be available the way I'd always been whenever I was allowed to leave the convent, from the time she took her first steps until our mother's marriage.

Before she could even walk I used to turn up in her world every time I could get out. I had a wonderful time playing with her, I cuddled and kissed her, and then I'd vanish for another month. Soon enough she'd toddle after me, chasing me down the hallway that was canted at an angle running along the façade of the building. She knew I'd hide myself in the cupboard at the end, that I'd shut myself into it and make noises like jungle animals and she'd punctuate her delighted terror with bursts of laughter. "More, more!" she'd demand, her eyes wide with excitement. My brief visits became a celebration for us both. Thanks to Eugénie, I had happy memories with which to fill that apartment, where I had nothing save an extra bed set up in what had been our late Grandfather Nolès's study. Eugénie lived in the large room in the alcove—the room she'd shared for several months with the English nursemaid who'd gone back to London as soon as the child was toilet-trained. It was the room they'd given me after our mother got married.

But I'd discovered reading; I began to draw; I enjoyed working on embroidery—the only thing I did with Grandmother. I still played with my little sister but now I also kept some time for myself. And I was constantly trying to find some way to make my mother less listless, trying to reach her in the tenebrous lands of sorrow or imagination she'd inhabited since the death of my father. Anything just to get her back again! She'd smile like an invalid, staring off into the distance as she stroked my cheek. In order not to annoy Grandmother, we no longer said the words "Swann House" or "Twickenham," and certainly never spoke of our father, Frank Lewly. Making even the slightest mention of any corner of England made me feel I'd committed a sin as bad as keeping one's hands warm under the covers.

Whenever I wasn't devoting my time to her, the little one watched my every move. What an extraordinary thing it is to see darkness imperceptibly overtake a pair of eyes! Beneath the fine golden lianas hiding her face, my sister's eyes could give the impression of turning black. And yet, they were still green and always would be. A remarkable, subtle phenomenon would intervene: the pupil grew larger, encroaching on the iris and engulfing the yellow specks that made for its unusual sparkle. Even if I wasn't looking at her, I could feel her staring at me all too often, the same way as, in a small town, you can sense the inhabitants watching strangers from behind their window curtains. There was a silence deep down in Eugénie's staring eyes. The silence of a waiting animal hidden in its burrow, making not a sound, senses on the alert.

I sometimes wondered what this child still remembered of the tribulations following the too sudden death of our father, as if there might be, perhaps, some link between her inquisitive attitude and that absence. How could one grow up without having deep inside the memory of a father so full of life, a man who loved the hunt, who would take us on great picnics in Kent or Cornwall with other families, and play card games that lasted so long that we'd go upstairs to bed long before they'd finished? I had thought grownups didn't sleep, that they lived on a different plane in the cloud created by their cigars. Was my little sister still invisibly imprinted with the few weeks during which she'd seen our father, had heard the voice of that man who loved the great outdoors, who continued to exist so powerfully in the lives of her older brother and sister? Had she heard his voice? What did she want from me, spying on me like that? Her silent, intense observation gave me the sense that I was entrusted with memories that I had to pass on to her.

Animal-like, she gradually set herself to protecting the place that she considered was rightfully her territory in the rue Moncey apartment. In a few months I saw by the way she looked at me that she considered me an intruder. All I had to do was use Grandmother's sewing basket for an instant and she would grab it, screaming and putting it back into our grandmother's old hands with their brown spots. It did no good at all for Grandmother to tell her to give it back to me—she'd refuse. And if she saw me paying attention to my embroidery, or, worse, absorbed in reading, she'd hit the book until I'd seize on any game at all to distract her. Only then would I find my cheery and cuddly little girl again. The worst for her was hearing me speaking English with William on the rare occasions that we had the pleasure of being under the same roof. The child would start screaming "No! No!" blindly punching at both of us. Our need to rekindle and relive our complicity could only be fulfilled in the language of our early years. We refused to forget. She couldn't stand it—any more than she could stand seeing me in conversation with our mother and our grandmother. I knew her less with every month and felt her searching eyes begin to weigh me down with accusations. It was only in her earliest years that we were really close. And always, coming from a room opening onto the hallway or at the entranceway rotunda, there would be a voice reminding me that "the eldest has to give in to the littlest, Mathilde!"

Like so much else, I wouldn't have been able to put words to the anxiety I felt in those days. I think that it frightened me and I chose to repress it. My only role in the apartment was to entertain the child. Avoiding her upset her and consequently upset the grownups. But it was what I really wanted to do. "Go take her a cookie!" they'd say, "Go see why she's crying!" and I'd dash to the end of the hall where I'd find her leaning against the cupboard door as if she were counting to twenty, as when we played hide and seek . . . But she wasn't counting, she was sniveling pitifully just loud enough for us all to hear. Sometimes our mother's voice spoke more firmly: "Take her into the parlor or go in her room with her!" I'd soon be dragging a recalcitrant little girl by her arm and she'd be screaming as if I'd beaten her black and blue.

How hungry I was behind the convent walls for someone who would focus sweetly and tenderly on me alone. But I found out that, on my monthly visits home, I was the one who had to do just this for the baby. In my first life, when I'd been younger, this attention had been there for me and somehow I fervently hoped that my mother would give it to me once again. I began, however, to doubt that I'd ever really known happiness. Were my memories only a dream? Even my brother was finding fulfillment somewhere else, as if disavowing our past—the past that I was huddling around like a miser bent over his treasure. William talked about how much he liked his multifaceted life: he got to spend as much time outdoors and playing chess and bridge as he did in the classroom. Had my mother not remarried, had my grandmother not stopped eating because she was driven to despair by the departure of her daughter and little granddaughter, I'd have remained in boarding school. For who knows how long? It wasn't for my sake that they took me out of the convent, but for Grandmother's well being. This thought brought me up short—and it hurt. It's only now that I understand where this unceasing nostalgia comes from, and why an invisible hand draws me firmly back to the past as soon as I put down my pencil or brush and lose touch with the life that Frédéric offered me. I leapt right into it however; I know that I was destined to be with him.

The true gathering place for the three Lewly children was Sainte-Colombe, the house in Villennes. A two-story stone house overlooking, though not too high above, the slow, twisting riverbed of the Seine downstream from Poissy. It was set on the nearly flat portion of the meander, on the bank facing the limestone hill where the river came up against it to flow back in a curve. The meadow gently curved inward to the embankment below the terrace. We each had our own room and we'd always find the same atmosphere of reassuring habits there when we returned, which dated back to when Grandmother was herself a child. For decade upon decade the house filled, spring and fall, with every sort of preserves; as soon as the weather was nice the linens were spread out on the meadow on the other side of the hedge, while herds of cows used to be led, morning and the evening, by their herder down the sunken lane behind the outbuildings to be milked in the stable. All this permanence gave me a sense that existence was coherent after all, and that I had a real connection to it.

When we were there, I spent my time drawing and painting. Soon now I'd be joined by my little sister, since that's what she'd said she wanted. Our departure was planned for mid-June.

10

Nonetheless, I found that being surrounded by the people I loved was wonderfully exhilarating.

We all arrived, mother, grandmother, lady's companion, and children, just as the cherries and strawberries came in season. Eugénie and I picked basketfuls of them to make into preserves; one of us would perch on a ladder and reach for all the mouthwatering "earrings," while the other crouched down, lifting the leaves in order to get at the berries. Deducting our tithe, we sampled the red fruit until we felt sick, bursting with laughter and joy as if we were the same age. We picked, while the cook, meanwhile, brought great copper basins of the fruit to a boil, then filled the scalded jars lined up on a clean dishtowel with the steaming, unctuous puree. All summer long the house was filled with the fragrance of strawberries, cherries, raspberries, apricots, plums, and blackberries, and finally apples . . .

I'd never expected we'd be so lighthearted and gay.

As the days went by, Grandmother's friends and cousins came from Orgeval or Bazemont to pay neighborly visits. Then it was our grandmother's turn to ask that the carriage be hitched so we could go as a family to return the compliment. Sainte-Colombe rejuvenated her and she ruled supreme, even more than in Paris.

Given the profusion of blooms, I started an album of pressed flowers to carry the colors of the meadows and garden back with me to my room in Paris. Eugénie too began to dry leaves and flowers in the large books in Grandmother's library. Seeing Eugénie take pleasure in creating her own collection made my pleasure all the greater. She was finally taking pains to achieve something concrete. As I became deeply absorbed in contemplating each flower, I enjoyed again a sense of wonder very like the feeling I'd had long ago examining the illuminations. Ten years later I still have my albums with their notes on a shelf in the studio, but the colors have faded with time. All I have to do is to reinvent them in my paintings. As if I were dipping my brushes in skies, gardens, flowerbeds, and distant landscapes, their colors softened by an invisible mist, the seasons returning all at once.

Eugénie was part of everything I did that summer, and it plunged me back into my oldest habits of always sharing things with an accomplice: first my brother and then with blonde Alice, with whom I'd long corresponded. From birth I've only been whole when there were two of us.

Until William came at the end of July we moved around inside our exclusively feminine world, the only representative of the stronger sex being little François, if you didn't count the caretaker, who was also the gardener, the driver, and the cook's husband.

When we were around the infant, under the watchful eyes of our mother and grandmother, my sister and I were very careful to keep things quiet. Throughout his first months I felt once again the fascination I'd had for Eugénie, and was surprised to see that, unlike my little sister, who had a completely round head barely covered with reddish down, and a chubby-cheeked face pale as bisque porcelain, this baby had a skull shaped like an egg set on an angle, and his features were almost triangular, like Grandmother's. The arch of his eyebrows was clearly marked and there was something indefinable about his cheekbones and his dark eyes that was enough to indicate that, even sound asleep, this baby was no little girl. I didn't understand why, but visitors always commented on this. His tanned skin next to the white sheets made one think he'd been exposed to the sun ever since he was born. What did he have in common with those of us whose skin was light?

When his carriage was put in the shade of the big linden tree, he'd suddenly launch into happy, high-pitched babbling; maybe it was the movement of the mosquito netting or how a branch waved in the breeze that set it off—or maybe just seeing his hands flying above him like birds was enough, not knowing they belonged to him. My sister and I would come running as soon as he was awake and our interpretations of how he used his mouth, his little noises as he stretched his tiny hands out to us, sent us into gales of laughter. I watched how his face changed from one day to the next, and listened with delight to the little crablike chirps that came out of his mouth along with the clear dribble drawn out by his fist, which he liked to chew on. His almond-shaped eyes stared at us so intensely that the mysteries deep down in their fathomless depths, of life and death and who knows what else, made me dizzy. In a fraction of a second his gaze could change from solemnity to amusement. You'd have thought he was trying to begin some intelligent conversation with us, so it always seemed surprising to me that he still couldn't talk. Sometimes his face would briefly resemble that of a toothless old man. I kept having thoughts like this, ones I'd never had when I looked in Eugénie's cradle. I even thought I might have caught a glimpse of God in the depths of his pupils. But then it occurred to me that Bluebeard, Attila, and Jack the Ripper had all been babies too, in the arms of a mother or a nurse, and they had made the same little enchanted sounds to welcome the life that they were just beginning to experience. It came to me that such a sweet, vulnerable being could become either the best or the worst, and I felt a sort of animal fear rising inside, fear of this infant, this stranger. To get rid of this feeling I lifted my eyes to look at the landscape with all its copses, its wheat fields and prairies dotted with poppies and cornflowers, the peaceful villages on the hill across the river. I calmed down right away, left only with surprise that I'd ever had any such thoughts. But I could never completely erase them. Like the memory of some mortal shock.

I'd never dared dream of having our mother and her two little ones all to myself, so I took full advantage. I considered Grandmother a person to be obeyed, but not one with whom I could share things; she was in charge of running the household, that's all. Our getting along so well brought an air of celebration to our lives. We probably had M. Versoix to thank for our happiness, because he must have gone, as he often did, to his preserve in Divonne-les-Bains. For two generations now, the family lands and forests, looking down on the spa resort that was becoming increasingly developed, had been growing more and more valuable. He used to go there regularly, but of course I had no idea what he did or how much the two branches of the Versoix family were involved with the expanding town and the company that ran the spa. Really, the only benefit of it that I could see, that I could enjoy, was that this second husband had given my mother back the lifestyle to which she had been accustomed—her panache and her happiness, as I've mentioned. After the exhibit at Willon I'd started calling him "Godfather," as Eugénie did, and in return, his attitude toward me had softened somewhat—his smile, anyway: the way he looked at me.

Our mother often rested in the shade on a chaise longue with baby François beside her and a book in her hand. Then I'd take out my drawing box, my pencils and pad, and Eugénie did the same. But I didn't *sketch* my mother—I devoured her with the point of my pencil, whole or in bits and pieces: the curve of her neck with the little strands of hair escaping from her hat, the way her stole draped over her shoulder, her ringed fingers preparing to turn the page of a book, doing minutely detailed openwork on a piece of delicate lawn; or even, when there were visitors to serve as bridge partners, plucking a card from her hand, which was fanned out before her, organized by suits. She'd glance at me from time to time, laughter in her face, as if to say, "I know what you're doing. I have eyes in the back of my head!" I could tell she was flattered. I wanted to see every detail of my mother so I could catch her every expression and gesture. I felt an almost physical pleasure in possessing her that way. And the fact that I could share the experience with Eugénie greatly increased my pleasure, because my little sister was positively jolly when she was with me. Sometimes she would even suggest posing for me herself, so long as she didn't have to spend too much time in front of my easel. I discovered how beautiful a fine ankle and a curving foot could be as I made studies of this charming model. I could never do enough sketches of my little sister, even when she was in her little nightgown, washing, her feet in the tub. The various parts of her began to take on their own existence in my eyes, like a vase or a lamp. Soon enough, I'd begin again drawing from a different angle, if she hadn't gotten bored. But she never liked doing the same thing for long.

Less and less did we hear scales floating from the open parlor window. But I liked hearing the piano, even when the notes were just repetitions, when Eugénie was practicing. There was something about that sound which was like the voice of a child stumbling over her reading every day. Behind all the blunders, the breaks in the rhythm, there was a will: concentrating on loosening her fingers and her mind through daily work, applying itself to growing up. I sent her encouraging thoughts for her efforts while I worked hard at my own practice, perfecting a still life or a landscape on paper or canvas.

But Eugénie was giving up on the piano.

Drawing at my side became more and more important for her. With each pencil she put to her pad she was sharing not only the reassuring comfort of our feminine clan, but also the impression that she *possessed* the land around us, simply because we were imprisoning stretches of the panorama in our notebooks. "The part from here to the mill belongs to me, what about you?" one of us would say and the other would reply, "The whole island, the village and the forest across the way . . ." The next day we'd trade our properties in a serious tone of voice, as we thought businessmen must do. But really, if I felt that anything really belonged to me, it was the ephemeral colors of the landscape, impossible to count because they multiplied so rapidly, merging, one shade running into another or standing out distinctly, depending on where the sun was in the sky—and the reflections in the water beneath that changeable sky, which wasn't even faithful to itself. I could never have invented the variations of color constantly at play in the light, so that, though every day I was seeing the island, the mill, the village on the other bank, it was never the same river, the same hill, the same little village, the same island. As I sought to discover what was truly before me, it seeped into my flesh before flowing with great difficulty onto my canvas. Our game, however, made it more fun, and all the time we spent together bridged the gap between us. Both of us needed this, one as much as the other. And yet, there was a sort of devotion in the way she looked up at me that was a crushing burden despite being so flattering. It was the same way I looked at my mother. I knew the powerful, silent expectancy that lay behind her eyes and sometimes it frightened me; I didn't feel I had it in me to give her whatever it was she wanted. She was making me responsible for some essential thing that was beyond my means. I didn't know how to give Eugénie a portion of the treasure that I felt entrusted with, nostalgic for: the wealth stored up before her birth.

M. Jacquier had encouraged me to give landscapes the colors I saw, not the colors that might, objectively, be there for everyone. That wasn't easy. What I got from it, however, was the pride of discovery. "Work, work, work!" M. Jacquier kept repeating. M. Thorins hadn't told me anything different. Still, he'd suggested—yes!—that I speak to my mother to get her permission to take lessons from him to supplement the things I'd learned from M. Jacquier. I hadn't yet asked her, afraid perhaps of breaking the spell of our days in the country. I thought about it constantly, but still kept it to myself. Because, ever since the exhibit at Willon Gallery, I'd felt proud simply because of the flattering manner in which Frédéric had introduced me to that journalist. And I still felt shaky when I remembered the way the men had looked at me. I was sorry that I'd only been back to see Frédéric twice in the intervening time, always with Mme Chesneau, if for no other reason than to see his eyes again and find in them the same depth and brilliance that had so shaken me, the strange play of emotion on his face when it lit up in a smile. I went over and over it all in my memory, those fleeting moments that had made me conscious of a new way of feeling.

When Eugénie and I were at our easels, Grandmother would sometimes come to see what we were up to. She couldn't resist a need to make observations, judgments based on the academism of her youth. That day the problem was my tree. And not just any tree—the willow I was so fond of. It was not gray-blue with glaring green specks the way I'd painted it, she exclaimed indignantly, and it didn't lean so far over the flow of the Seine, which, moreover, was not really so yellow either. Holding tight to M. Jacquier's advice, I didn't change anything. Having watched that willow for years, seeing it lean far enough to dip its leaves into the sandy water at the tip of the island, I thought, each time I saw it, that I might be seeing it just at the moment it would finally fall. After each winter, when we arrived, the first thing I'd do was go to see if it was still standing. My stubborn insistence on painting it in such unlikely colors was shocking to Grandmother, who thought this was just about equivalent to a child's scribbling. She walked off grumbling, "Well, after all, if you're having fun . . ." in a condescending tone of voice, the way you'd dismiss someone engaged in something trivial. I knew she didn't take my desire to live for painting seriously. Eugénie, in a burst of solidarity with me, offhandedly called after her, "You're not the one taking lessons, she knows what she's doing!" I was shocked at my sister's boldness but Grandmother didn't bother to turn around, she just lifted her cane as if to say, "I really don't care!" I never got used to the fact that Eugénie was so willing to speak to our grandmother so informally, as though she were a friend on the street, whereas William and I always addressed her solemnly as "Grandmother." And the tone of voice she'd used took my breath away. Deep inside, however, I envied the freedom shared by my grandmother and her granddaughter.

Eugénie used to go and get a book of the tales of the Comtesse de Ségur in order to have her mother all to herself, asking her to interrupt whatever she was doing to read more of the story they'd started the evening before. Sometimes our mother would balk and say, "You know how to read for yourself now! Just sit here quietly next to me . . ." But my little sister would insist until she got what she wanted. Then mother and daughter, their blonde and red hair mingling, would bend together over the printed pages. One ran her index finger along the lines as she read, the other followed with her eyes, lulled by the adored voice. It gave me pleasure to sketch this scene. But it wasn't a pure pleasure. Great waves of jealousy had me glued to this almost unbearable image of the little one resting her cheek on the beautiful bosom I no longer even dared brush against, leaning there the way I'd done once upon a time. (Between then and now, in the convent, I'd been made to see evil in all sorts of places I'd never suspected of harboring it.) Fixing the two of them on a sheet of paper was the only way I had to possess them, master them, and anesthetize the pangs piercing my heart. I'd been an affectionate child, but I'd had to learn to restrain my impulses. A month away from my seventeenth birthday it still hurt me to see that beautiful scene. I'd have liked to smother my mother in my loving arms and I was ashamed to be looking at them like a jealous little girl. Then, all of a sudden, Jeanne Versoix would proclaim to all present, "It's time to take a walk!" And she'd lead us off on a grand tour that inevitably ended on the towpath.

The air in the tall meadow grass smelled like summer, like freedom.

11

William arrived at the end of July on the same train as our cousin Dilys Lewly—a cousin whom, for that matter, we called "aunt," because she was ten years older than our mother.

I was immensely surprised when I saw that young man with shiny curls the color of ripe chestnuts falling around his laughing face step down from the train, as if it had been years since we'd seen each other. How had I been able to do without my brother? How could there have been any flavor to existence in his absence? All the greetings, all the happy, welcoming jokes suddenly emerged in English among the four of us. At the train stop in Villennes, which wasn't yet a station, and then in the carriage, our euphoria was like some secret between us, an indulgence in our kinship from across the Channel.

Today I think that Grandmother had only invited Dilys out of sheer politeness. It was a way of thanking her for the lessons in English conversation that she gave me every week, ever since I'd noticed, to my great despair, that I was losing my ability to speak the language, since I was no longer using it regularly. My mother had gone to see the mother superior, who'd set the condition that I had to have a lady from the convent go with me to Passy every Thursday afternoon, if I wanted these lessons so badly. As the years went by, I became wildly attached to Aunt Dilys, whose life seemed colorful to me, full of mystery. In time I learned she'd met many of the people that she associated with through her friendship with the Natanson brothers, the creators and directors of the *Revue Blanche*. Their pages were open to both known and unknown artists, writers, poets, and journalists; they promoted exhibits and had sided with Captain Dreyfus, whose name was not to be mentioned in Grandmother's house. Aunt Dilys used to meet with people of a sort we'd never seen, and she even dined with them, something I found very exciting. I found out, just by chance, that it was at one of her parties in Passy our mother had met M. Versoix.

In the carriage taking the four of us to Sainte-Colombe, you'd have thought that even our laughter had an English accent. A cool shower after a long walk in the noonday sun couldn't have made me feel any better. Ah! If only the horse weren't trotting so fast!

William's voice was done changing. I saw him less and less as my twin; instead, he seemed a big brother who was waiting without much anxiety for the results of his baccalaureate exams. I was as impressed by this as if he'd digested the entire encyclopedia. I was above all impressed by how, just by being his assertive self, he stood out in any group. His presence exuded an inner strength that was enviable, a quiet confidence in himself and in existence. He didn't speak too loudly and never said things just to be saying them. Now that his arms no longer looked too long for his body and his head didn't resemble a peony perched on a yielding stalk, his body had a natural balance that gave him a remarkable presence. He looked at people when they were speaking, listened attentively, and always gave the impression that he thought that person was very important.

August was beginning under the best of auspices.

And yet, once we were through the gate and around the turn in the driveway, I knew even before the horse stopped moving that things wouldn't be that simple. Grandmother was waiting there on the doorstep with our little sister hidden in the folds of her gown. I knew my sister well enough to know that this was a sign not of some discreetly hidden happiness on her part but of her great anxiety. I had no trouble sensing when a situation had wound her up. I was burdened by this, but I couldn't pretend to be insensible to her feelings; I could read them too easily for that.

How could I have expected that, just because we'd been close for one summer month, our relationship had really changed? She'd grown up being treated like a little queen by her mother and grandmother, and this continued when her mother became Mme Versoix and she moved with her to the rue du Four. She'd always regarded William and my natural rapport with something more than suspicion. She would never get over the pain this had caused her, and I knew it. Even when my brother and I weren't actually talking to each other, she would watch us closely and try to interfere. But then, speaking English when we were not with the rest of the family was for us something more than a necessity—how could she deprive us of that? You could tell by the way she acted that she'd have liked to make us repudiate our first nine years and see us become amnesiacs; I couldn't help but recognize Grandmother's influence in all this. When she was very little, our sister would sneak after us to the study that served as my bedroom at the house on rue Moncey. Usually, William and I would hide out there to talk in the language we'd shared since birth. Because she didn't understand us, anything—whether we were building with blocks or playing games, or just talking or reading—was an opportunity to blame us for abandoning her.

Those precious moments prolonged a life in which she hadn't had a part. Worse, they were proof of a history that was still so real for us, and still had such power, that she could only imagine our enthusiasm coming from some Eden on the banks of the Thames. How many times did she stammer out something of this nature through uncontrollable sobs? As if we were depriving her of something just for the pleasure of making her sad. She was fighting an imaginary war against ghosts. But, basically, she wasn't wrong; it was our paradise, and she would never have access to it. It was no use telling her again and again that she couldn't fill the gap of the nine years that separated us. She ended up by setting herself up as our enemy and trying to pick fights using her tears and threats, which was terribly exasperating. I'd sometimes look at her and think that even having her mouth awry and her hair sticky with tears and mucus wasn't enough to make her look ugly. I'd be charmed and yet still want to give her a good slap so she'd leave us in peace. As long as we were alone together, our grandmother respected the powerful need that William and I had to go back to our roots together by immersing ourselves in the language of our childhood, but as soon as there was a witness . . .

When Eugénie had learned to read and count, we'd taught her our games, but it wasn't enough; you could see she was waiting for something else. I considered her a spoiled child who didn't deserve to spend so much time with her mother. She was a tattletale about everything, anything at all. Nonetheless, she wept on Sunday night when she saw us going back to our boarding schools. Her misty, imploring eyes unnerved me, made me feel guilty in spite of myself. I wanted to protect myself from her nameless grief, as if it somehow might increase my own.

As Eugénie clung to our grandmother on the front steps, she was brooding over the torment she felt just seeing how happy we were as we came back from the train stop. William was the first out of the carriage so he could help Aunt Dilys and our mother step down. After having kissed our grandmother, he took Eugénie's hand sweetly and said, "Take me to our little brother's cradle, I've barely even met him . . ." Without raising her eyes she led him like a blind man over to the shady terrace by the linden tree. Together they murmured endearments to the baby who babbled back at them, and after this private conversation Eugénie's good spirits returned. The three of us walked all over the meadows and along the edges of the woods; we ran up and down the towpath and when we played ducks and drakes on the water, William claimed to be strong enough to make a pebble skip all the way to the island. Speechless, Eugénie stared at him with admiration. The three Lewly children played happily together, enjoying those carefree moments in the warm summer afternoon.

It wasn't until we came across a skiff tied to a moss-swollen post in the grass along the riverbank that this harmony was suddenly threatened. If any one element has always united William and me, it's a river. How could we ever forget the games we played along the banks of the Thames? Our house was so near to it. We reacted instinctively the instant we saw the boat. Not stopping to think, William jumped into the skiff and took on the role of the ferryman, fat Mr. Champion, who used to be in charge of shuttling people back and forth between Twickenham and Richmond aboard a barge bearing a sign with his name on it. We'd always considered him an old seadog because we'd never seen him set foot on land. My brother remembered the way he'd row us out to the barge. William put the oars in the oarlocks, all the while discussing the movement of the clouds, the strength of the current (real or else invented for the occasion just so he could talk about it) in perfect imitation of the ferryman we'd known. We were always daydreaming about rounding that island in the Thames, overrun with vegetation, which we could see from shore; so much so that our parents would often offer to take us on the trip across that river, swollen twice a day by the tides, for no more reason than pleasing us. Just going over and back, never even setting foot in Richmond, was enough to allow us to imagine we were off on a great adventure. Our father conjured up exaggerated risks with words like "storms" and "pirates," and invented for us a tribe of savages who lived on the island and only came out of the forest at night. And as soon as the barge stopped rocking he'd memorialize our happiness in photographs. We often used to see him organizing his snapshots by the light of a table lamp and putting them into large albums with marbleized cardboard covers and leather spines the color of polished wood that he'd had made to measure.

One thing followed another on the banks of the Seine that day; we never intended it to happen, but there was no way we could restrain ourselves. I couldn't resist the pleasure of talking the way our father did when he spoke to Mr. Champion, and William was a natural in the role of the ferryman. So Eugénie, of course, began to cry. William and I both turned around and said in the same weary tone to our little sister, "Eugénie, please, don't you get started again!" Our almost perfect simultaneity made us burst out laughing. Seeing how desperate she looked, William invited her to get into the little boat, but she was already pouting, her arms across her chest as if to challenge us, her feet and the hem of her dress hidden in the wild grass. How will she manage to ruin things this time? I wondered. She knew every blackmailing trick in the book and I decided, for once, that I wouldn't let her win: "If you don't get in I'm going to untie the rope!" I shouted. Her eyes set defiantly, her lips sullen, she didn't budge. And, as she watched us row off toward the island, that Fury shouted after us the worst threat she knew: "I'm going to tell Grandmother!"

All the grace of July had just vanished.

I caught myself being envious of William because he'd been able to find some equilibrium for himself outside the influence of our family. I too had been kept at a distance for almost six years, but I still depended on them completely. My brother seemed beyond their influence. I couldn't imagine the power of the friendships that, for him, had already replaced our private circle. The gap between the two of us had long ago begun to deepen. As a comfort to Grandmother, I hadn't pursued my studies—it was as if they had asked me to stop growing up. "You'll get married," they told me again and again; that was my sole consolation. They thought I'd learned enough good manners to enter into society, and that was certainly sufficient for a young girl. My painting and drawing lessons with M. Jacquier were only intended to occupy me until I'd become established in society through marriage.

We were returning from our escapade on the island at least an hour later when, halfway up the slope, as we walked in our renewed togetherness, William put his hand on my arm and stood perfectly still, his head inclined toward the house. "Listen!" he whispered. Floating from the open windows of the parlor there came a sonata we'd last heard on the day of our eighth birthday, a few weeks before Eugénie was born. Was it possible that our mother had started to play the piano again? We looked at each other for a fraction of a second and, with the same burst of joy, rushed toward the house before her fingers could strike the final notes of the piece. If she was playing the piano again it meant that happiness, real happiness might just reenter our lives.

In my elation I had the courage to ask her before I went to bed if I could take lessons with M. Thorins when we were back in town. "If he's willing to take Eugénie along with you, it would be fine. . ." she replied.

I stood there speechless. How strange it was that she'd done everything possible to separate the two of us ever since our return to Paris, and now was rushing to make one of us guardian of the other.

12

But M. Thorins didn't want to "give lessons" to both the little girl and her big sister, so my mother decided that neither one of us would have them. In her opinion, M. Jacquier's lessons were quite enough. Without realizing it, by depriving me, she reawakened my boarding school self, the impassioned pupil who was so experienced in repressing that very passion. After her refusal, an underground Mathilde began stirring. Vague dreams of seduction that had been on the prowl at unexpected moments during the summer began to become obsessions once we were back on rue Moncey. Knowing that M. Thorins's studio was so close by meant I was already breathing the air he breathed, perhaps walking in his footsteps on the sidewalk along rue Blanche. I needed to see him as soon as possible.

In less than a month I'd made two tentative visits to the rue Chaptal under the watchful eye of my chaperone. How to keep my breath measured and even and reveal nothing save the fact that I was decently curious about the furnishings of his studio. What I really wanted, of course, was to know things about him, the master of the house, things that were unseen. How could I control my voice—so likely to become shaky, the words pouring out, rashly, more and more words to cover up all the things I was feeling?

I was now thinking about Frédéric Thorins day and night, about his straightforward, kindly gaze that seemed to sooth my otherwise constant anxiety. I'd been warned about the artistic milieu. How they were all fickle, all unstable, and often ill-mannered . . . Despite knowing nothing about his life, I recognized none of these flaws in him. Yet I wouldn't have been able to tell you the color of his eyes—though they moved me so deeply the instant they turned toward me and plumbed my soul. I never lowered my own eyes, but I had no sense that either of us was being brazen; instead I felt that I drew strength from such encounters.

I had to hear his voice again, had to meet his eyes. I was drawn by the life I could see plainly in that young artist's studio, and then the other that I only suspected was there. The desire to be part of that life was becoming irresistible. I felt I was my grandmother's prisoner, in danger of suffocating. Because he'd mentioned exhibits at the Puel Gallery, I talked Mme Chesneau into going there, one day, rather than to the Louvre. It was hard for me to apply a curious, attentive, and critical mind to his pictures in the way he would have wanted, a critical way, making it possible for me to understand the changes taking place in art as a whole. Occasionally, yes, I'd manage to do so, almost by accident, struck by the power of this or that canvas, and then I'd study the painting carefully: the choice of colors, the brush-strokes, the light effects. This made me feel that the artist was speaking quietly to me, directly to me, teaching me his methodology. This lifted my spirits and gave me something to think about: a distraction. Until, emerging from these technical thoughts, I'd have a relapse and return to my amorous obsession, once again indifferent to the paintings. Moreover, Mme Chesneau came as my companion and I never thought once about her comfort while we were there. Today I can see the extent of my youthful egotism. She was one of those indispensable creatures whose importance in one's life can only be appreciated after they're gone. I didn't know if I loved Mme Chesneau, because she was neither an aunt nor a cousin, and I thought that one was only truly fond of one's relations. How could I guess in those days that I'd miss this plump, reassuring woman at the most crucial moment? I didn't realize that she'd already guessed what I was feeling—probably before I myself understood what was happening to me.

I repeated my earlier solo flight one day when Mme Chesneau wasn't available. I went out into the streets alone and took the risk of knocking on the door to M. Thorins's studio without first sending word. The sofa there had inspired what I would at the time have considered "unmentionable" thoughts in me, so I think I must have been hoping to interrupt the scene I so shamefully and repeatedly imagined in my bedroom most nights: a woman posing there, wearing practically nothing, or even—heavens—naked. What would I have done had I gotten my wish? What would I have felt? But, in fact, I found the artist conversing quite decently with one of his friends, Lucien Morel, who, though he preferred painting, had chosen, at the insistence of his father, to study engineering at the Ecole des ponts et chaussées rather than a bohemian lifestyle. He was still in contact with the artists he'd met with his friend, Frédéric Thorins;

he took part in their gatherings and stood by them during those delicate moments when they were preparing for an exhibit, but he didn't dare give free rein to his desire to paint.

When I arrived, the engineer was listening to the artist's comments about his most recent canvas. He was smoking a pipe as he looked at the still unfinished work, with his hand in his pocket as if he were waiting for a train in the lobby of the gare Saint-Lazare. Uncomfortable, I shook both men's hands but then stammered that I'd just been walking past his porch and had stopped in for only a moment, and turned toward the door. But Frédéric Thorins was at the threshold ahead of me, to block my exit: "Shouldn't you show me a few of your paintings?" he asked. I promised I would. But I'd have to come in the company of my chaperone, and that was beyond me. I hoped I could think up some other way of seeing him alone.

Who, in Grandmother's household, could guess that when I began to draw various perspectives of the rue Blanche in my sketchbooks, as I looked out the parlor window, it wasn't to study the lines created by the rows of windows, balconies, and rooflines receding to the point where the two sidewalks met at the boulevard de Clichy? The mineral nature of this treeless city street that I'd thought so cold before had, for some time now, become a piece of the city that was full of poetry—just because my heart beat faster every time I slid my eyes beyond rue La Bruyère. Farther up, rue Chaptal emerged, and I was hoping to see the tall, slender silhouette of the artist go by, either as he left or as he came home. I trembled at the thought that there might, any day now, be a woman with him.

13

I guessed from the way William closed the door behind him, when he showed up unexpectedly at Grandmother's that day, that he was more than a little anxious. He barely took the time to give his grandmother a kiss, and without removing his overcoat, he told her straight out: "I'm going to snatch my sister away for the afternoon!" He didn't ask her permission, he simply informed her. It took me less than five minutes for me to get ready.

"I have to talk to you," he said, slipping his hand under my arm the minute we were out the door. His voice was simultaneously curt and full of emotion.

I took us, without thinking about it, toward the end of rue Blanche, then onto rue Ballu, like a rat terrier sniffing out a trail in one direction while its master is whistling it in the other. In my obsession I was dying to find the Café Prosper, where M. Thorins and his friends got together on the corner of place Clichy and the boulevard des Batignolles. I'd feel more self-confident going there with William. But he was walking in silence, completely absorbed by his thoughts, and I finally asked him if it was something serious. Deep down I guessed that it was indeed serious, and I was afraid.

"At the end of the summer Mother gave me a crate from Twickenham. It had remained in one of the outbuildings at Sainte-Colombe, and she hadn't touched it since we moved. She probably thought she was just giving me some photography equipment. The old camera was in there, as well as the one Dad had just bought and had never had time to use. But that wasn't all that was in there: I found a bundle of letters in with the photo albums. Mum must have put everything that he cared most about into the same crate. I definitely had the impression that the letters had been hidden. The envelopes had no addresses, just the name 'Jeanne' or else 'Darling.' Can you imagine that I didn't even know what Dad's handwriting looked like! It's a very strange feeling . . ."

I didn't know what his writing was like either, and was amazed that I hadn't realized this sooner. My brother went on:

"Suddenly the words became so alive that I thought I saw his silhouette bent over his desk with the lamp behind him and heard the scratching sound of the pen as his hand moved it across the paper . . . Then, when I returned to reality, I felt his absence more than ever. I began reading one letter, then another, though I felt ashamed for committing such a grave indiscretion. There were little love notes that he used to leave before going off for a day of hunting, or Lord knows what escapade, without her. And then there were real letters. When I read the fourth one I understood why he wanted so much to convince her of his love. Then I read a fifth, and a sixth. But I couldn't go on . . ."

"Why?"

"Too painful. Especially concerning Eugénie . . . I've been hesitating to talk to you about it . . . I've had these love letters among my possessions for more than a month now . . . Still, they cleared up so many questions for me that in the end I made up my mind to tell you."

We emerged onto Clichy, and on the other side I caught sight of Café Prosper's red awning. William's words had already too much, and yet nothing of substance; if they hadn't already alarmed me, perhaps I'd have left him and hurried over as if to some urgent rendezvous. But I was too troubled by both his voice and his silences, as disturbed by them as by the fact that he was clearly on the verge of sharing some confidence.

Together we turned our backs on place Clichy and that was enough to pull me out of my reverie. Willliam remained inscrutable, or maybe he was still just hesitant; he let himself be led through the streets of the neighborhood. Seeing that I had to draw him out, I reminded him of how we used to share everything when we lived on the other side of the Channel. Then he took my hand, and as if reciting the plot of a nightmare at the very moment of his dreaming it, he said:

"His death wasn't an accident."

Yes, the accident. They had told us about it so many times. So many times that I dreaded now even the prospect of William's revising the story I knew so well. I forcefully reminded him of the fact that it had been, as we were informed, very foggy on the Thames that day. I'd accepted that once and for all, you see. But William muttered that the reason for their repeating it again and again was to convince the people around them of this, and to leave vague the facts of what had really happened. Because, really, nobody ever went out on the river at night and in the middle of the winter. The grownups had insisted so firmly, in those days, that we not talk about anything connected with our "former" life, that we both, William as well as I, had forbidden ourselves to wonder whether or not what they'd said about the catastrophe made any sense.

"Do you mean he was pushed?" I ventured only half aloud, as if afraid of the sound my own voice would make in uttering such horrible things.

William spoke fast and hard, straight to the point: "Rather, that he jumped into the frigid water to get it over with."

I could have been punched in the solar plexus and felt it a less violent blow. We both walked a bit farther without saying a word. My throat was on fire; I hadn't realized how dry it was. Terrifying pictures scrolled through my mind; I began to feel my legs trembling and grabbed hold of my brother. And then I heard my voice whisper softly, without my intending it: "Did the letters say all that?" I didn't get an immediate response; the body I had thought so solid, that I needed to lean on, was shaken by a sob. We walked a little more, and then we stopped, unable even to look at each other. No doubt we looked like two drunks stumbling along. I'd asked a question and didn't want the answer, but he stifled a sigh as if he were exhausted and then let it slip from his lips. "Not explicitly, perhaps. There was no suicide note. But it was all hinted at, yes. He was overwhelmed with gambling debts . . ."

I was in shock. All those cherished, cheerful images that heretofore had haunted my Parisian life popped again into my mind to contradict this hypothesis. And yet my brother's grip was crushing my fingers, and at the same time my general anxiety and confusion sharpened to become a specific pain digging horribly into my chest, telling me that what he said was true.

If he hadn't have had the letters with him, I would have begun right away convincing myself that this was indeed some nightmare from which we might soon awake. But no, they were right there in his pocket, in one large envelope that he brandished then as he looked around for some comfortable café where we could sit down away from prying eyes. We contented ourselves with the brasserie on the corner of rue Duperré and place Pigalle. He handed me the thick envelope after we sat down. First I pulled out two sheets of paper covered with beautiful writing, its shadowy strokes and thick loops all slanting in the same direction, every single letter perfect. The upstrokes reminded me of the elegance and cheerful charm that I remembered of the poor man. Before I read them, I looked at the pages as objects, studying them the way I'd contemplate a delicate, harmonious painting. Is there anything more physical than writing, or a work of art that remains after the artist's death? Perhaps a piece of clothing that's kept an elbow's bend, or that of the knees . . . Or, then again, a tool handled throughout a lifetime and worn down in one place by a hand's repeated action.

There's no use my trying to describe what I felt as I read the letters.

I knew that Frank Lewly had been capricious, extravagant, something that guaranteed him a circle of admirers and inventive partners in crime; it was the extravagance of a spoiled child who didn't understand the value of money—an inveterate gambler. He and our mother would often go away and I didn't know where they went or why he was frequently away by himself. The one thing about which I had no doubt at all was Grandmother's opinion of her son-in-law. After we returned from England, she'd often reminded her daughter that he'd brought his family to ruin, and she ought to stop being so sad that he was gone. Our presence in the room never kept her from speaking plainly. It was one of the reasons I've always been on the defensive with her. There are some things girls figure out quite quickly, though they may not know how to express them, and I knew that my mother had married for love when she was twenty and that she'd been profoundly happy. She'd learned how to laugh after the austere years of her youth, spent like mine, in a convent—how to have fun at the great picnics to which we were invited in Kent or Cornwall; she even enjoyed the times when it was just us four. She used to turn our problems into a game, taking advantage of a power outage, for example, to make up fantastic stories in the dark parlor and make us shiver and shake until our good giant took us into his arms to reassure us with a fatherly hug. Our father also liked to knock on the front door after dark, disguising his voice and face behind a beard that seemed to go on forever, and thick bushy eyebrows. Wearing a clown's costume, or else ridiculously decrepit rags, he'd ask us to tell him how to get to the island inhabited by "savages." He'd do almost anything to have a good laugh with his twins! He enjoyed life and made us share in all his interests—except one. Gambling.

It wasn't hard to imagine our mother as a young fiancée at nineteen, fascinated by this charmer with his melodious accent. He was always well-dressed and, when in Paris, always stayed with his friends in the stylish Plaine-Monceau quarter. He took young Jeanne Nolès out to the opera, to the best restaurants, and, with his cousin and a Belgian friend visiting Paris, to enjoy the other pleasures of high society. What a wonderful revenge for the privation she'd endured at Sacré-Coeur!

Could William and I ever have imagined that this brilliant couple had been weathering a terrible crisis ever since our mother told her husband that there was a third child soon to come? Could we ever possibly have imagined that he'd seen this birth as a catastrophe?

This father, who'd grown up living a life of ease, had left his wife ignorant of the fact that, after ten years of marriage, his love of gambling and lavish expenditures were plunging the family into ruin. Wrapping his wife in the loving words of his letters, he was covering her with the last jewels in his possession before he delivered the staggering blow. But one page especially froze me: he confessed that he could not face up to the collapse that lay in wait for them, or to the disenchantment that his recklessness had caused, the bitter resentment that would go on and on. He couldn't bear the thought of seeing contempt and shame in eyes that had been so adoring; he wouldn't be able to face the grief that he'd caused. His wife and twins were the dearest parts of his life, yet he would leave them destitute. A few words here and there gave voice to his insurmountable remorse but, at the same time, demonstrated just how irresistibly he was drawn to gambling. He'd never imagined that the source of his wealth would dry up. Again and again he'd go back to the gambling table in the hope that his luck would return. He'd never again get to play the magician who knew how to spark peals of sweet, loving laughter from his little ones, and to this overgrown child it seemed a fate worse than death. One never overcomes a dishonor of this sort, he wrote. I think he must have wept as he did so, and my throat was choked with tears as I imagined this. There wasn't a single word about the baby my mother was expecting, as if it didn't exist, or as if he'd already decided never to see it grow up—which seemed quite in keeping with the desperate tone of his letters.

That's what our mother had to face at the age of thirty, when she sold Swann House. It did seem that he'd made some little effort to stay alive after the baby was born, but got carried away nonetheless, a few months later, in the fog of the Thames, on the darkest of nights, shortly after the first of the year 1895.

William and I sat there with our drinks before us. Our hands were clasped so tightly together that it hurt. With our cold cups of chocolate before us, we wept in silence. In facing this second wave of mourning for our father, we had only this corner of the brasserie to serve as a refuge. But here at least we were free to express our emotions, hidden among these anonymous customers.

Soon, driven by a need to wander through the city, always hand in hand, we walked as far as the place Vendôme, then to the quays along the Seine, always without speaking. We had to learn to accept the unacceptable.

14

That week I woke up one morning calling for Eugénie. I saw images of her childhood, the tears welling up in her eyes always full of expectation, as she gazed steadily into mine, where they met only pity and fear. I'd always turned my eyes away from this silent appeal. That green gaze so often became imperceptibly accusing, and her pouting face took on expressions in which, for a brief second, a bit of naked malice might surface. Even today I have trouble not dwelling on that horrid flicker—something about it continues to make me very uneasy. But during that crisis, in the days after reading my father's letters, it was something else that disturbed me about my sister's accusing stare.

The memory of the English magician so in love with his French wife and his little twins was something no one could take away from us—not till time erased all our names. All we were dealing with, really—though no small thing—was that, at the age of seventeen, we now had to acknowledge a difficult thing: that *that* wasn't the only person he had been.

But Eugénie? Eugénie had no father; she only had his name, which seemed ridiculous on her, as she had no idea what was so special about it. She grew up solidly positioned on the maternal side of a family that hid its paternity behind a thick veil. Besides which, even if he had conceived and acknowledged the child, I wondered whether a man who didn't *want* that child could ever be considered, morally speaking, its father? And then, what about the mother? What about all the mothers who don't want to give birth but whose bellies distended over the months in their despite? When he climbed into the skiff, Frank Lewly wasn't held back by any thought of his children; indeed, any such thoughts might well have driven him to the fatal act, if shame had so clouded his mind at the time. Anything is possible; we'll never know.

It occurred to me that our mother had carried that baby with a profound feeling of solitude, alongside a husband who was trying to resist the call of the void. As for us, the two big children, at the age of eight we hadn't yet noticed anything alarming, merely a slight hesitancy between our parents . . . During the last months he was alive, Frank Lewly often used to take William away for a whole day of riding. Was he doing this to leave his son with happy memories of their special relationship? Their repeated flights into the frozen countryside were certainly delightful to my brother, but perhaps they were good for our father too, perhaps they helped him live one more day—or several. Exhausted when they returned, he'd feign happiness over a day well spent before once again going to try his luck at gambling. Because, as soon as he was back and had changed his clothes, he was off again—trying at that point to fill the financial abyss that he'd dug beneath our house . . . Yes, I was now searching through my memories, interpreting them according to the new information in those letters. The Lewly couple's downward spiral was becoming clear to me, gradually, but always in a manner that was incomplete, indeed distorted by my own grief. I once again became aware of my mother's languor, the little light deep in her eyes that I'd seen go out, but I couldn't remember if that had happened before or after Eugénie was born. So I'd noticed one change, yet hadn't taken note of my mother's gowns growing larger as the months went by. What use is memory?

Would we be able to talk to her about all of this now, in order to find out more—now that she was happy once again? No, unthinkable. Besides which, very much against my will, I had begun to feel some liking for M. Versoix, who had given her back a taste for life. But did that mean that she'd forgotten or erased her first love? All these questions crowding into my heart and mind were enough to choke me.

Only one thing was certain: I no longer had the right to "abandon" the baby, my little sister, the way I sometimes guiltily desired. A voice inside said in no uncertain terms that I had to stand by her, no matter what the cost, and pass on to her whatever I could of our former happiness. There was something in all this that was beyond me, something appalling to me in this commitment, but I felt a duty to that voice which had emerged from the depths of my conscience. I'd often wished, for the sake of my own freedom, that the Versoix couple would move to Divonne-les-bains permanently and take Eugénie and little François with them. But now, my feeling that my father had let go of his baby's hand compelled me to hold it tight, as if I could no longer even count on our mother.

I felt that, in her newfound happiness, she was paying less attention to Eugénie. Hadn't she shoved her off in my direction as often as possible during the past two summers at Sainte-Colombe? And she'd insisted that I share my drawing lessons with her, though the child had never, up to that point, demonstrated any attraction to my discipline, but seemed to prefer playing the piano. So M. Thorins had refused to take on two pupils. Fine! But why then would my mother deprive *me* of his knowledge? It was simply another way of tying me to my little sister, making me a sort of second mother by delegating her powers to me when it suited her: "Go see what the baby's doing, darling, I can't hear her anymore . . ." she'd say, not even looking up from her book; or else: "Go tell her to practice the piano seriously and stop that obnoxious banging! It's getting on everyone's nerves!" I was my mother's spokesperson; I watched her child for her and I ended up with the sense of being the only one invested with the authority to keep the peace—and for me, ever since she'd become so grief-stricken, my mother's peace of mind was essential. Consequently, Eugénie had to obey me, but when my baby sister used to come and bother me and I'd try to make her go away, I'd be called back and put once more into the role of the guardian: "Come now! You know the oldest has to be the one to give in!" With that same sentence our mother would disavow the authority she'd earlier given me. I was again impatient with my sister.

I thought, as I woke up that morning, that she was now my permanent responsibility, and I swore to take the time to teach her how to draw or paint or share in life's little pleasures. I let the love I'd had for her as a baby flood back, back from the time when she belonged only to her nurse and to me. At the time I hadn't understood the extent to which she was really an orphan, even before our father's "accident." Eugénie would forever remain my baby sister, and I'd be responsible for her forever. It was an overwhelming realization, but one not to be ignored—just at the time when I wanted to set off on my own life. It didn't occur to me that someday she'd be an adult as well.

15

The hardest thing was being face to face with Grandmother every day; I'd been living with her now for three years.

Teatime seemed interminable to me; she'd sit there erect in her armchair and never once lean back. From time to time, embroidery in her hands, she'd stare at me, her fingers suddenly motionless talons resting on her skinny knees. Feeling the weight of her eyes, I'd pretend not to notice, and tried to persevere with my reading or sewing, but I no longer understood the words my eyes skimmed across, or else I'd mess up my stitches. As soon as she looked away, I'd steal a glance at her delicate face, prettily wrinkled: her small mouth narrowed by a thousand little folds, and her lower lip looking like it was gently sucking on the upper, as if it were a candy. Above all, I could tell how full her silences were of thoughts and judgments concerning the tight little family circle around her. I'd heard her cursing her daughter when she married M. Versoix, who, being a divorced man, was scarcely better than the gambler she'd first married: "What on earth are you thinking?" Her daughter and granddaughters had been dependent on her at first and she took pleasure in her power. Eugénie, the baby, knew how to get past her and have anything she wanted. I was struck now by the fact that I hadn't seen Grandmother grow old. To me she'd been very old forever. Her memories of her youth went back past any era that I could picture in my mind, because it was unthinkable to imagine us eating rats, as Grandmother claimed they had once done in Paris. She described how the city had been so famished that first it ate the domesticated animals and then hunted the streets for rats. It struck me that the fatigue I saw in her, how long it was now taking her to stand up, combined with her increasingly obvious misgivings about so much as crossing Paris in a fiacre to visit the Versoix on the Left Bank, was something more than temporary.

I didn't know what to make of my rebellion against this woman who'd forced us never to mention the memories of our earliest childhood in her presence. Living together there on rue Moncey, I felt a dizzying abyss opening up between the apparently obedient attitude with which I did what was expected and the murderous thoughts spinning around inside me. No insults, no insolence ever emerged—but I had visions of my hand holding a knife and stabbing her in her sleep. She'd have no time to suffer, no time to see death coming. I was obsessed with this, as with so much else. Even if I didn't do it—still, she had to die. A death without suffering. Like fainting.

As the weeks went by my resolve grew stronger not to let her give orders to me or forbid me to do things I wanted to do. It wasn't easy. I was afraid of her. It would be a silent war. I was like an animal tugging on its tether. I'd have liked to feel as free as William, but it had been many years since we'd had the same upbringing. My mother escaped Grandmother when she crossed the Channel on the arm of the wealthy heir to a fortune. And I? Would I, in turn, find some way of imposing a similar distance?

I'd learned to be afraid of the unknown; I'd buried my curiosity about life, which used to be like my brother's. Every morning I'd say to myself once again that I'd change something and every evening I reproached myself for being so spineless. I was running away from myself and I'd lost my appetite. Especially at the Versoix's home on Sundays after Mass. My mother and her husband's home was in a newly painted apartment with new furniture. My little sister had her room there and the baby and his nurse did too. As for me, when I went to my mother's house, I was a visitor, just like when I came "home" from boarding school. Did we ever once talk about anything that was intimate, important? Never.

Whenever I'd touch something in that apartment or sit down in a chair, Eugénie would make some disparaging comment, as if I'd helped myself to something that was hers. She used to do it back when I was making my monthly visits, and still seemed to take pleasure in the fact that I was just passing through, and, as if she were the lady of the manor, receiving the poor, seemed indeed to relish my uneasiness.

I'd sworn to take care of her, but it was an enormous effort to manage this. I was committed, but wanted nothing more than to be free of my commitments. I needed to become someone else—but who? And how?

Sometimes, when they can't control themselves, even timid people exceed and overstep the proprieties they respect, and one day at the end of that year I simply walked out of the apartment with no one to accompany me. Grandmother was determined to take me to the seamstress to try on my gown for *réveillon,* but I really didn't care what I'd be wearing on that particular occasion. I put on my warmest clothes and a fur toque and just said I'd be back that evening, nothing more, no details, not even responding to the hoarse voice calling orders down to me from the spiral staircase. An invisible thread tightened in my chest, as if, by pulling away from my grandmother, I might be cutting some cord deep inside, even tearing something out of myself. I had to break loose from this mooring and yet keep myself safe from the possibility of drifting toward a situation even worse than what I'd left.

I didn't go to Café Prosper on that cold day in December, but rather walked very quickly straight to M. Thorins's studio.

16

He was at his easel finishing a portrait of the model standing before him. You could see at a glance that she was a lady of high society. After he'd introduced us, the rebellion that had driven my footsteps there was quickly neutralized by a feeling of admiration for the elegance and inner strength emanating from this woman. I couldn't help wondering what it was in her that Frédéric touched with his brush, what the texture of her skin awakened in him, what it felt like to know her personality, exploring it deeply and revealing it on his canvas as he added his final touches. I thought about the almost carnal relationship connecting me to my mother and my sister when I caressed them with my brushes or charcoal on paper or canvas.

It was unseemly for me to be there, or at least I thought it was. I'd wanted to turn right around but M. Thorins simply called out rather tersely: "Sit there in the armchair and have some tea!" The stove, eating up tons of charcoal, was heating the room nicely. Something about this wealthy lady reminded me of when our parents used to entertain at Swann House—the comfortable way she wore her fine clothes, perhaps. I was curious and fascinated and began to think my life at No. 1 rue Moncey was dusty, old-fashioned. About the most exciting thing I ever did there was, if I was lucky, to go along on Sundays with my grandmother to Mass at eglise Saint-Augustin because we liked what they sang there better than the hymns at eglise de la Trinité. However, I didn't even know how to pray anymore, and made do with thinking of it as entertainment.

Once the elegant lady had departed, all wrapped up in her furs, I could breathe the air of freedom wafting through the studio; the passion that had driven me to flee my grandmother rose silently inside and, as it did, I wanted more and more to possess this freedom. Ever since I'd met with William and read our father's letters, several weeks earlier, I'd been haunted by a pain that left me no peace.

While the artist cleaned his brushes and set them in little bunches in terra-cotta pots, I curled up on the sofa and watched him silently, filled with immense respect for his ritual. He seemed to have forgotten I was there.

After a long silence, however, and without a glance in my direction, he pulled me out of my pleasant sense of well-being with a short question: "Heartache, maybe?"

I sat up straight, simply stunned by this provocative tone and exquisite audacity of his words.

"Did I have to have an invitation?" I asked, feeling compromised, perhaps because I was justifying myself.

Nothing could have disturbed me more than his confrontational tone, since it was so hard for me to hide my feelings about him. It occurred to me that I could just jump on the bus right then and there and go take my English lesson with Aunt Dilys—despite the fact that she wasn't expecting me. After all, there were many questions about my father that were still tormenting me and his cousin might have the answers. The last time I'd seen her she'd talked about him a bit and shown me some photos of him posing between her and my mother the day of their wedding, as well as some others in which, riding his horse and surrounded by other men on horseback, wearing their hunting jackets, he was waving good-bye with a gloved hand.

I felt my cheeks growing red from the insult and quickly grabbed my coat. Was it his words or the curtness with which he was suddenly addressing me that hurt the most? I thought I'd detected some contempt in his voice.

"Weren't you strolling hand in hand with a young man a short time ago? The two of you looked like you were dragging along with your hearts in shreds. You didn't even see me as I went by."

But if I'd indignantly exclaimed that it was my twin brother he'd seen me with, this would have meant I felt I needed some justification, that I too saw myself in the degrading image he was reflecting back at me.

"If you had any idea of why we were so overcome, you wouldn't talk to me like that."

At which point I grabbed my hat and purse as well as my coat and fled as if the studio were on fire. On my way to Passy.

17

Aunt Dilys intrigued me.

I was maybe thirteen or fourteen years old when I heard her whisper to my mother, in English, "Did you know, cousin dear, that it's possible to love the way one did at twenty well past the day you turn forty? You should be encouraged by my example, since you're not even thirty-five . . ." I myself thought that being in love was something reserved for youth, yet I'd just caught these two adults, whom I considered ageless, and certainly unlikely to harbor any intimate secrets, speaking of precisely that. I found this troubling, really disturbing, and it began a new train of thought, one reflection leading to another. It was quite a while before I realized that Aunt Dilys, when I caught them talking in Passy, was no doubt in the process of beating down my mother's last resistance to the courtship of M. Versoix.

But what was Aunt Dilys doing alone in a house in Passy when her family lived in Richmond? She was the niece of my strict grandfather, but never talked about her family or even about her country of birth, though she had a photograph in her parlor of the estate where my grandfather, his brother, and their sister were born. We used to go there as children to celebrate Christmas with them as well as the rest of the extended family, which included some little cousins. I had no memory of having seen Aunt Dilys there, and one day, worried that I'd just forgotten, I'd asked her about it. "I was travelling, dear, at the time . . ." she answered, her soft hand caressing my cheek, looking me right in the eye, smiling vaguely, an odd smile that gave me the impression that I had brushed up against some new mystery. Was that intense look a warning that I shouldn't continue my questioning? And yet! How much I'd have liked to understand why she was so silent about our family. Where had her travels taken her?

And then, I was intrigued by the photograph of a little boy on her mantelpiece, the same little boy whose portrait in oils hung in the entrance hall as if to welcome visitors. I couldn't say how I knew that it was her son, surmising that his father had died before he was born. Children pick up information, they feel it, sniff it out just by watching and listening, supplemented, where necessary, by a little research. Later, the memory of their curiosity fades, and doubt takes its place. Did they dream the things they thought they knew? Sometimes their reluctance to fault adults whom they love makes them erase any damning secrets from their consciousness. I still had many questions waiting to be asked, because Aunt Dilys had never once spoken about that child in my presence. Yet, how then did I know that his name was Thomas and that he'd been sent off to boarding school at the age of ten? As far as I could remember the name of Aunt Dilys had never been uttered in the presence of the Lewlys of Richmond. But at Swann House it was. In the big living-room there were photographs of my father's cousin with a strongly built man who was staring at her solemnly, and another one in which she was looking down a road by the sea and holding a little three-year-old dressed as a sailor by the hand.

I remember that my mother had gotten in touch with this cousin in Passy as soon as we arrived in France. Their embrace when they met was quite touching. Our father had only died a few months before, so my brother and I had thought that the strength of their mourning was what bound them so tightly together in that moment, and probably we were not wholly wrong. Aunt Dilys and our father were the same age and had grown up together in Richmond. They had never once lost track of one another till the day of the fatal accident.

This cousin of mine wasn't burdened with sadness, however; far from it, despite the fact that her husband was gone and she was separated from her son. She saw a lot of people, went to the theater and art openings, and was always throwing parties. And soon, accompanied by Madame Marcelline, I was entitled to leave boarding school on Thursdays for lessons in English conversation with Aunt Dilys. She used to talk to me about life in Paris, describing evenings at the theater and promising to take me there when I was older, which she did in fact do after I began living with my grandmother. But on those Thursdays, despite the strict surveillance of my guardian from the convent, we were nonetheless free because she didn't understand the language we spoke. My chaperone mended linens she'd brought with her while we were talking to each other.

Everything I knew about the outside world I learned from Aunt Dilys. She'd told me about how unjustly Captain Dreyfus had been treated by our officers. Now a convict on the Caribbean island of Cayenne, he was doomed to solitude and despair. One day she opened a copy of *Aurore*, the newspaper, to show me how the novelist Zola had courageously challenged the president of the Republic in large headlines, accusing the highest ranking officers in the army of fabricating evidence to condemn an innocent man. And then, at the beginning of 1898, it was the writer in turn who found himself facing the judges, who sentenced him to a year in prison. He had just barely enough time to escape to England. Aunt Dilys felt passionately about these incredible events in which the destinies of two men who'd never met were forever linked in history. She signed a petition with other supporters of the novelist, whose accusations proved not to have been in vain; the judgment was reviewed and Dreyfus was brought back in June 1899 to be tried again before the war council in Rennes. Zola was able to return to France. It had never occurred to me before that a woman could support a political act. That was men's business, according to Grandmother, who had forbidden even the mention of the name of Captain Dreyfus in her house. Without Aunt Dilys I'd never have known that France, for several years, was seriously divided on the issue: there were those who supported the convict from Devil's Island and others, more numerous, who considered him a traitor. Probably I'd even have remained unaware of the name Dreyfus. Not that this motivated me to get involved, but at least, thanks to the attitude of my English cousin, I knew that there were huge things happening right at our doorstep and that I knew nothing about them. No longer could I tell myself that the world worked the way it should: that there were right-minded people and then there were others who were getting well-deserved punishment. As a result, I took advantage of the time I spent with her to leaf through newspapers that reported the various ideas then brewing. Awaking to all this was no simple thing after having believed that the entire world obeyed the rules of social etiquette that my grandmother endeavored to pass on to us.

The only living evidence I ever saw concerning Aunt Dilys's past came in the person of a man who turned up at her house from time to time, a Belgian with a big gray mustache by the name of Puck Chaudoy. "A friend of the family," she told me in introduction. I didn't recognize him as the same man posing with her in the photographs in our living room at Swann House; the years had bleached his mustache and stripped his hairline bare. In the years since, William and I had found other pictures of him in our father's albums. I was told that when M. Chaudoy was in Paris on business, the guest room was always available for him in Passy. Clearly, both he and Aunt Dilys were completely at ease with his living there in that nice little house. He came and went and the servants addressed him as if they were used to having him around, or else as if—and I was to learn that this wasn't far from the truth—he was the master of the house. He expected to be waited on, as if it were perfectly natural, and he took part in our discussions freely. He was always traveling a great deal. Spinning a globe with one hand, he'd describe rivers and mountains, mud huts, palm huts, people with extraordinary customs, pointing out routes he'd taken on distant continents such as India, and even farther away. The reason Aunt Dilys had travelled a lot was that she'd accompanied her lover, apparently. I didn't know this when I was taking lessons from her and simply believed whatever people told me about her. When they finally got married, a year after Chaudoy's wife died, I learned that the child in the pictures had never lost his father and now spent most of his time in the Arabian desert because of his great passion for archeology.

I felt comfortable with them. It was easy. Aunt Dilys had a knack for comfort. I felt that the Thursdays I spent in her house let me breathe the air I needed to maintain my equilibrium, and not just because she spoke the language of my forefathers.

18

Could I ever have imagined that my argument with M. Thorins would topple us into marriage?

I'd been working so hard to stifle my feelings about him—because I thought they were foolish and probably sinful—that, consequently, I hadn't seen through his behavior during my last visit, hadn't seen them as simply an expression of his jealousy. No, I was convinced that I'd been banished from his studio.

However, not three days later, I got a letter. He was in despair over the thought of having made me angry and asked if he could meet me, talk to me; if I would just give him a chance to explain himself, even make some plans, that is if I had even the slightest feeling for him. He suggested that he wait for me early in the afternoon on some day that suited me in the New Year. We were just about to reach the last moments of 1903, which lay at the end of a dark tunnel—the *réveillon* at the home of the Versoix family. An obligation that I submitted to willingly, knowing someone would be waiting for me on the other side of the celebration.

Two families, strangers to each other, celebrated upon the stroke of midnight. Completely correct and proper, each family standing on an opposite side of the living-room on Rue du Four, champagne glasses in hand, we smiled our empty smiles. Even Eugénie, despite her skill in oozing herself into the good graces of strangers, stayed in the background when faced with the parents of our "Godfather." They and their grandson, Alain, little François's other half-brother, stood next to the piano, while Grandmother remained beside the fireplace with my sister hanging on to her. And what was William doing as he pensively studied the assembled gathering? I'd rarely seen him so introverted and couldn't rid my mind of the conversation we'd had as we read our father's words written in blue-black ink on sky-blue paper. Was he still in shock? Our mother and her husband were endeavoring to bring the two clans together, shuttling endlessly back and forth, flattering one person's clothing, another one's jewels. They even made cheerful conversation about the snow covering the mountainsides in the Jura, that grand balcony overlooking Lac Léman, the fiefdom of the Versoix family, hoping to stir up some enthusiasm in them. But mountain folk aren't given to talking, so their son didn't insist. No one dared cross the invisible frontier.

Frédéric's letter was right next to my heart, inside my dress; it made me giddy. I felt a sudden need to shake this gloomy crowd up; I danced a few quick steps across the room with my arms outstretched, letting my chiffon sleeves flutter around me. First I kissed one person and then another, right down to the last, convinced that I loved them all, feeling fantastically alive. I could have gone down to the crossroads at rue Cherche-midi and clinked glasses with strangers as we all sang the New Year in together—I felt just as new myself. Somewhere else in the city, under some other mistletoe, someone was thinking of me; the very idea had me bursting with joy. My excitement broke the ice that was holding everyone in place. Grandmother began to exchange a few words with the parents of her second son-in-law. When he offered her his good wishes for the New Year, she embraced him as if welcoming at last into our midst.

I found myself at the center of the celebration, laughing as I hugged my mother, who was in the arms of her husband, embracing the latter enthusiastically, dipping my finger into a glass of champagne and touching it to the lips of baby François, telling Grandmother how much I hoped she'd be with us as long as possible, and wrapping Eugénie in my arms, after calling out to William, "Happy New Year!"—it all seemed easy and even perfectly natural. My happiness spread all around me. I felt so intimately part of this gathering that I'd forgotten all about my torment of the day before, when I'd wanted desperately to escape it. As if, by allowing myself to radiate outward, I'd finally found my place. I needed to share my secret and would have willingly announced to all present at the top of my lungs that I was going to sneak off to pay a visit to a man who had declared his feelings to me. William was watching; he seemed distant, though still courteous, wearing a smile that seemed a little forced. He just couldn't help but bring me back to the last time we'd spoken. All that misery came back to me as if from another life.

Then he just couldn't resist any longer; he pulled me into the dressing room where we'd piled our coats, furs, toques, and hats.

"You," he said in English. "You're hiding something from us!" And I told him the whole story. The words flowed rapidly from my lips like a torrential spring that had long been blocked. I felt, for the first time in years, that I was alive. He listened incredulously, no doubt feeling a little hurt, for, in a low, reproachful voice, he cut off my flood of words as though it were some outrageous heresy. "So that's your reaction to my revelation about our father's death?"

Seeing a person you feel so close to missing the point of something that touches you so deeply is a strange experience. It was because he was happy in his boarding school that the despair I'd felt when I was with the nuns hadn't felt real to him, but now that I was finding a way to escape the walls around me, he couldn't see that I'd probably reached the limit of my capacity for sorrow. This curse just had to end now that, thanks to the letters I'd read, I knew what it truly consisted of. I needed to be with men and women who would sweep me off into places where everything was still to be discovered, everything to be built. A strength I didn't know I had swept over me and I defied my brother openly: "And what do you know about it, living the good life hidden away at your lycée?"

He raised his hand like a preacher trying to quiet his parishioners. He too had something to tell, something connected to the contents of our father's trunk: ever since he laid hands on the photographic equipment, he'd no longer wanted to continue his studies. In the trunk he'd found the old camera that still bore Frank Lewly's fingerprints from when he'd last used it, as well as the one our father had purchased so soon before his death, and so had never been used at all. Something about them moved him deeply, fascinated him, as if, with them, our father had somehow intended to start his son on this track. William had decided to make photography his profession. He was signing up for the photographic studio at the lycée in preparation. This way he'd be able to satisfy his never-ending hunger for action, for new experiences, his desire to enter into different milieus. He'd learn to wrestle with the world, to be at the right place at the right time, and then he'd sell his photos to newspapers.

"I won't be a dilettante." Then he paused a second, like a hunter sure of catching his prey, and put his index finger under his nose to add, "I can just smell it . . . I'll have the advantage of speaking two languages fluently and being able to get by in German too . . . yes, I'll have a good chance."

"You've had a dour look on your face all evening long . . . if all this is true, why bother reproaching me for being lighthearted?"

"I didn't recognize you . . . I suddenly felt I couldn't tell you what I was planning . . . seeing you participate in this party . . . it's like asphyxiation, not a celebration at all . . ."

"Let's go back and this time when we stand under the mistletoe we'll each know what the other is wishing for."

I'd barely finished my sentence when Eugénie stuck her head through the half-open door. "Are you two up to something again?"

"Can't get rid of you, can we? Okay, come on, we'll all three go and make a wish for 1904. What will yours be?"

"To learn how to paint with Mathilde . . ."

She said it in her wheedling voice, her green eyes beseeching. I looked away as I took the child's warm hand, hoping not to betray my frustration. Our mother was in the parlor playing a Christmas carol on the piano—and not just any old Christmas carol. No one there had any idea how much it recalled our happy, English days. Not even Eugénie. William and I applauded with more enthusiasm than all the others and, as Mother struck the final chords, she gave us a knowing wink.

19

At certain moments you live with such intensity that you never again forget them. Moments when you feel the dream of loving become a reality. Something happens, completely beyond your willpower to control, something driving you inexorably toward the other, no matter what the cost. Frédéric's hands removed my hat, my gloves, methodically, respectfully; his face was lit with a smile that was triumphant but at the same time vulnerable, generous, and disarming. It seems easy to describe what happened now, ten years later. Almost trite. All lovers experience this exquisite, dizzying sense . . . they say one goes weak in the knees . . . and that's what happened the instant I entered the studio. I'd read his letter over and over again, and now was full of the joy of return. Of course, it wasn't much: a beginning that came after other beginnings, other beginnings stretching back without end, infinitely preceding it. How many beginnings does a love story have, anyway? Well, after I'd received his note, my daydreams alone had made me feel faint; the mere thought of the next time we would meet made me tremble all over. I imagined and revised the scene endlessly in the moments before I went to sleep each night. When he thought he'd lost me, he'd become aware that the affection he felt for me was fatal, and, gripped by both terrible anguish and passionate hope, he'd written me.

The instant we met again I felt I'd been granted the power to divide seconds into thousandths, the power to be everywhere at once, to float above us and register the slightest agitation fluttering from one body to the other, without knowing that I was etching all the details permanently into my memory. We both had the same impulse to approach one another as though we were made of crystal; short of breath, we touched each other so lightly, our hands trembling. The fear that speaking even the least word or making too bold an advance might break the crystal held us quivering exquisitely in this silence. Oh, and I've left out how his smock was spattered with more or less fresh paint. An embrace, not yet a kiss.

Shivering together in the certainty that we were setting out on a long journey together, there was nothing much to say. I'd read the silent commitment in his eyes and guessed he was reading the commitment in mine as well. Certainly, since that moment, squalls and high waves have almost overturned our boat a hundred times—but they never sank it. That day we knew each other without knowing each other, but, in the way we looked at one another and in the way we spoke, there was a certain quality of silence and curiosity concerning the works we had each created, images that already revealed things propriety had censored . . .

Emboldened by the letter that I always carried with me, I'd made my getaway, escaping Grandmother's supervision as soon as I heard her sending Mme Chesneau off on an errand. The man who sold me supplies on rue Amsterdam was once again my alibi. And even if there'd been no man selling supplies, I'd have taken off anyhow, one way or the other.

Blissfully letting our hair down, so to speak, we went through all the feelings we'd had about the too few times we'd met since the days when he'd watched me sketching, accompanied by my chaperone, on the pont de l'Europe, up to when he'd passed me and William on the boulevard de Clichy.

He liked the stubbornness with which I worked. And I could see, for my part, that I'd be able to live my life alongside him because he encouraged me to paint. We had a good laugh when I confessed that, on the pont de l'Europe, I'd thought he was old. Laughter followed, which, as I look back on it, was really our worries coming unwound. Now I didn't see his face in the same way, and, even better, I saw in them the flowering of a youth that I had never allowed myself. His energy, the way he saw everything anew, his playful nature, always quick with a joke, how sensitively his fingers grasped his canvases, these were things that echoed inside me, making me feel close to him.

We were forgetting that the hands of the clock were turning and that night came early at this time of year . . . In the half-dark his voice was now preparing the ground for our future. If we were to marry, we'd no longer be supervised, we could play in the paint together, come and go in Paris, meet his friends at Café Prosper, each make the other stronger, and simply love each other. Meeting from now on would be too difficult if we had to hide our feelings.

By the time I rushed out into the dark, we'd agreed: he'd go speak to my mother and ask for my hand just as soon as we'd gotten used to our plan ourselves. Today I no longer remember which of us was able to muster that much good sense.

20

Frédéric's parents lived in Burgundy, where they sold their wine and hadn't intervened for years in the choices their son made. They had hoped that, as the eldest son should, Frédéric would take over the vineyard and make a successful business of it, but Frédéric had left that privilege to his brother. During his first years in Paris he'd lived in the Batignolles quarter and his parents had sent him a regular allowance. When he was twenty-five, a wealthy woman of society had commissioned a fresco from him to decorate the entrance hall of her house, which had big windows looking out on parc Monceau. That gave him a leg up with a certain group of customers. Since then, he'd had other commissions, allowing him to buy the sheds in the back of a courtyard on rue Chaptal and fix them up as a studio along with some friends. His parents then bought the apartment on the first floor of the same building for him. According to them it was better to invest one's money in stone than to put it in a bank, and this was a chance to do so.

Frédéric and his father got along wonderfully well. About once every three months the son would take the express train out to visit his family, and if he couldn't, for some reason, the father would come to Paris, using his time there to meet with important clients.

The first time that I saw them with each other, I felt there was nothing and nobody who could come between them. They had a complicity one rarely sees, as if they were in telepathic communication. A word, or even less, some simple onomatopoeia on the part of one, was enough to bring out a conniving look, a laughing reaction, or a frown in the other. A relentlessly approving father.

I counted myself lucky, then, to have a place not between them, but close to them. M. Thorins was clearly proud of his son's life and perhaps even envied him for it, but apparently without a shred of bitterness. He'd accepted Frédéric's artistic leanings and, as often as possible, used to come in from the provinces to attend any exhibition in which Frédéric was showing a few paintings—or even just a single one. This man from Burgundy had probably never questioned his own fate when his parents had passed the estate and its vineyard on to him as a young man. He had always assumed he'd be his father's successor, just as the eldest had always succeeded his father from generation to generation. The Thorins family had vineyards in their blood. The hillsides with their perfect stripes of vines, taking on each season's particular coloration, had been their horizon, their earthly and spiritual nourishment, the expression of their talent, the very essence of their existence.

What had happened to Frédéric?

He told me about it when we were in the process of completely reorganizing his studio in preparation for my arrival, and as he spoke he remembered, it was all still fresh for him, the powerful reaction he'd had when he felt the first impact of art. When he was seventeen, he'd gone with his father to Paris and, as he waited for him to finish his business in the bank, Frédéric had wandered down rue Lafitte. Rather absentmindedly, he'd looked at a number of canvases on display in the windows there, and suddenly stopped in front of one of them, surprised but also dazzled by the singular nature of the colors that were juxtaposed on one of the canvases hung there. As he looked at this landscape overrun by light and made more emphatic by blue and red shadows, he felt nailed to the spot, fascinated, as though witness to some scene of violence. But what violence? Was it his or the painter's? He was so astonished at feeling this turmoil that he ended up going into the gallery. The dealer showed him a still life by the same artist: fruits brightly lit by multicolored patches of sunshine that only suggested their shape, a bottle and a carafe arranged without symmetry, a wrinkled tablecloth on which the contrasting colors of the objects splattered against his retina as if they were the representation of pure chaos. And yet he'd been overcome by the serenity emanating from the work, the same serenity as he'd once found in the kitchens of his ancestors, in the provinces, with everything done in its proper time, season to season, from time immemorial. How strange it was to be struck so deeply by an entirely new way of thinking, conveyed in so provocative, almost indecipherable, a style which seemed moreover to be addressing Frédéric specifically. He'd never looked at pictures so attentively, never been powerfully wounded by the intention of an artist about whom he knew nothing—though he tried in vain to puzzle out or intuit precisely what that intention was.

His attention had been caught by brushstrokes that seemed to be conveying a particular message, as if they were a code to be cracked.

Yes, he was in a daze as he left the gallery and stopped to take a last look at the landscape there in the window, shading his eyes with his hand to block out the reflections in the glass, and then he walked on, deep in thought, to meet his father in a brasserie on the Grands Boulevards, as planned. Filled with a new sense of anticipation, he looked out at the streets of Paris without seeing them, or perhaps projecting his dreams onto them. In the train going home he told his father that he would like to take classes in drawing and painting in Dijon. His father agreed, thinking little of it, satisfying his agreeable eldest son's latest whim.

When he was twenty, in 1897, Frédéric had wanted to experience life in Paris, and, convinced that his destiny awaited him there, enrolled in an academy at the École des Beaux Arts. This proposed vocation caused some strain in the relationship between his parents; his mother fiercely opposed it. She'd never been able to form the wonderful complicity with her offspring that her husband shared with their son. She couldn't help being jealous and barely even tried to hide it. The conflict between them put off Frédéric's departure for the capital by a year, but his father had stood by him. Frédéric had told me that, well after he'd moved to Rue Chaptal, on the day the dear man was buried three years ago, he'd learned how much his decision had cost his father who, though pushing Frédéric to fulfill himself, had always secretly hoped he'd still return to their estates. That hope had been put to rest when Frédéric bought the shed in the rear of the courtyard, but still the father had encouraged his son in his plans by purchasing the first-floor apartment.

Ever since Frédéric completed the large fresco for the socialite's residence in parc Monceau, there'd been an art dealer, M. Willon, who had bought paintings from him on a regular basis. He displayed them in his window and exhibited them at shows and soon he'd begun to sell them, mostly in England and Belgium.

When I came into the life of this painter, I set out on something like a great journey into a world in which everyone, all of Frédéric's artist friends, seemed to have one object in mind: the freedom to express themselves, to tear accepted standards apart, to throw every established way of thinking out the window. It made me feel that, joining them, I was embarking with Jules Verne from the earth to the moon, the home of dreams and poetry—or else, knowing deep inside that one might never reach that point in the heavens, deciding, nevertheless to spend, one's whole life on this quest.

21

We had to wait until the following June before Frédéric and my brother had a chance to meet. As soon as we'd set the date for this meeting, all three of us became impatient and on edge. My happiness was marred by an odd sense of apprehension about seeing the two men I loved come face to face. What if they didn't like each other? Or what if they got along so well that they'd forget I was around? Or if Frédéric paled in comparison with William's charm? Or if one looked down on the other? The closer we got to rue Chaptal, the faster my heart was beating. I felt an unusual silence deep inside myself as I prepared for this momentous encounter; it didn't keep me from speaking, but my voice sounded to me like a sound echoing over a still lake high in the mountains. Words I spoke too quickly in tones that sounded alien even to me skimmed over my sheet of silence. They echoed back to me, making me all the more nervous.

William's questions about Frédéric had begun to rain down almost immediately, once I made my announcement. Under such a barrage, it wasn't at all easy to confess how I'd been feeling; I didn't know how to put any of it into words, didn't know how to explain.

My mother hadn't consented to the marriage until after a long discussion about the financial situation of Frédéric's parents. Reading between the lines I'd understood that she was saying her daughter could marry anybody, really, as long as it wasn't some happy-go-lucky gambler. At bottom she was hoping that Frédéric might indeed return to Burgundy and take his place in the family business, and this prospect reassured her. Why not let us live off our paintings as long as that lasted? Our vocation as artists didn't seem important to her; she barely even mentioned it. If anything really concerned her, it was the environment I was about to enter. She'd had to have a long conversation with Aunt Dilys before she could agree to my choice, and then, faced with Grandmother, defend it.

I was hurt by how angry Grandmother was when she learned of what she referred to as her daughter's inability to stand up to me. "She encouraged you in this idiocy, did she? So it wasn't enough for her to have barely escaped being destitute herself! You're too old for coloring books, my dear, you have to set your mind on marrying a man who has a real position in society! I've given your mother a piece of my mind on *that* score, never fear . . ." Her words made me fall to pieces. How I hated the fact that her opinion still mattered to me. Spoken with such conviction, it all sounded true—I couldn't have been more shaken if I'd actually seen my own future penury in a magic mirror. I felt that no matter what I set out to do in life, I'd be reduced to this: an accomplice in my family's perpetual malice and confusion, as if it were some congenital weakness I'd inherited from them.

How could I fight the feeling that, if I didn't obey Grandmother, I would be headed off a cliff, right into the abyss? She pressed her point: it was obvious to her that neither her daughter nor her granddaughter intended to give her the satisfaction of seeing them well married. Would she have enough time left to see Eugénie do better? Why exactly did I find it so difficult to contradict my grandmother, what compelled me to fear her so? If I were to have a life of my own, I had to have the courage to stand by my own decisions.

It was possible, I knew, to be born wealthy, in a sumptuous house not a hundred yards from the Thames, surrounded by a family leading a most comfortable life in Richmond, and in a few weeks lose this paradise; that I knew. So what little happiness I'd now found myself could surely be lost more easily still. It's not that there wasn't a certain temptation in what Grandmother was proposing. I'd always felt as though my nerves had been peeled, that my senses were exposed directly to the air, and the pain of it made me acutely aware of how intensely I experienced things from moment to moment; this pain told me I was still alive. I'd often dreamed of leading a conventional existence in order to escape that painful intensity—but in the end there was no way I could imagine living and dying in a world like Grandmother's, where one risked sleeping all the way to the grave without feeling much of anything . . .

For years I'd been moving into the future like a sleepwalker, a brush in one hand and a pencil in the other, just to keep my balance. But on the far side of the void I'd been crossing for so long, William and Frédéric were waiting for me on solid rock.

They shook hands as if they'd known each other forever and all my worries vanished. The moment we were inside the studio, my brother began to look around at everything like a child in a toymaker's shop, his imagination stirred by seeing the inner life of an artist. He understood the value of tools, that a studio can be organized in a way that looks disorderly but which is perfectly comprehensible to its owner, because he'd spent a lot of time in such places when he was in the lycée. The two men had this in common to start them off on good terms, and already they were speaking to each other as equals.

Frédéric asked William what he wanted to do in life. He was delighted by William's reply and exclaimed impulsively: "Photography! And you want to focus on motor sports? That's the wave of the future! There'll be more and more automobile races and rallies, new airplanes will be put into production . . . I'll introduce you to my friend Alfred Molinier, a journalist who'll give you the dates of the big expositions coming up . . . He'll be a big help in getting you started."

Frédéric turned to look at me as he finished talking, his arms outspread as though he was telling us something perfectly obvious, his eyes sparkling. He poured three glasses of wine in celebration of our meeting and suggested we stop off at Café Prosper while the sun was still out.

"You never know who'll be there . . . It's always a surprise!"

We found ourselves among the café's regulars as we followed in Frédéric's footsteps, into the future. My brother and I entered into a new world together, and at the same time: a second birth, likewise shared. Never mind Grandmother's consent. When she saw that her grandson too was taking off, along with me, she gave up her arguing, albeit not without muttering a few words about how our generation was going to hell in a handbasket.

22

The three of us often went together to Café Prosper, that spot favored by the artists who lived in the Batignolles and Clichy, when they weren't off slumming in Butte Montmartre or at the Moulin Rouge.

Everything I saw there was new to me and made me shiver with a sense of transgression. I wanted to find some way of entering into the freedom that the place emanated, and while at first I was happier if I had my husband or my brother with me, I soon was able to venture there alone. There was no fixed time for the group's regulars to meet, save on exceptional occasions, but a tacit ritual had been established according to the hours each one of them kept.

Despite the place's name, the boss wasn't named Prosper. He was known simply as "Friend Jean." There was something monstrous about his barrel-shaped body, barely contained by the belt of his huge pants and topped with a head like a big marble that bristled with short hair not unlike porcupine quills. And that marble's mouth, surmounted by its two kind if mischievous eyes, and despite pressing its lips together to hold an eternally extinguished cigarette in their right-hand corner, was constantly yelling orders to the people in the kitchen or working at the bar. What would the Café Prosper be without the ever-vigilant Jean, whose father had opened the place? He needed to have everybody feel at home. And, in fact, one of the regulars, Ernest Ponsal, a painter, did indeed spend almost all his time there; it's where he got his mail, and he'd set up his easel on the terrace when the weather was nice, bringing it inside if it rained, so his pictures were mostly of the crossroads outside or of the interior of the café. Sometimes the local prostitutes would pose for him if he could afford to buy them a drink. But generally he could only scrape together enough for his daily cup of black coffee, sitting there in his special spot, where he spent most of his days, being served plates of food—by order of the boss—with no more ado than it would have been delivered to customers who actually settled their bills. From time to time he'd clear up this debt by giving Friend Jean a canvas. This son of a fisherman on the Riviera also used to be regularly invited to dine by some of his affluent friends. Ernest Ponsal still had the strong accent of the fishing town where he'd been born; he played it, as well as his habit of always wearing a navy-blue captain's cap pulled down tight on his head, for laughs. Dark strands of hair could be seen sneaking out from under that cap to curl around his ears and tangle around his neck. He was a respected artist who sold his paintings to Willon the dealer, but not frequently enough to make a good living.

And then there were the others.

Every day, after he'd put in his hours at his printing press, plus the time reserved for visiting clients, Loulou Chevrier loved to make a detour through this neighborhood, about a mile and a half from his place of business, which was situated out past the Batignolles cemetery. When he was at Café Prosper he forgot about his responsibilities. Once relieved of the pressure of his work, he apparently knew how to do only one other thing in life: make everyone around him laugh. And his tool? The piano. He improvised words and tunes, satirizing political events in his powerful voice, or making fun of the regular crowd's everyday life, especially their torments in love and their poor decisions. Some of the men standing around, leaning on the black piano, would add their own couplets, singing back to Chevrier about his own not-inconsiderable flaws: he stuttered, he had a slight squint, he waddled like a duck, and his opinions were as fickle as the weather. The only authoritative assertions Loulou Chevrier ever made, in fact, were ones he'd heard the majority of the group state repeatedly. He truly had no point of view of his own, and didn't dare confess what he was really thinking. In conversation, he'd interrupt people only to mouth, in his thundering voice, precisely what the person had been saying. He did it with such self-assurance that you could almost believe they were his own convictions. The game among the patrons was to trick him into saying the opposite of what he'd just stated so dogmatically. When he wasn't there, they all went at him, criticizing his lack of character, but no one would have wanted to do without his presence, because when he was there he made the evenings so much fun. Molinier the journalist, who was of a more introverted nature, must have been slightly jealous of the pianist's success; he was the one who most often denounced Loulou's shortcomings in song. Loulou would then pick up the refrain and, accompanying himself expertly, would go ahead and sing along in that loud voice of his, all the way to the end of the mocking couplets, as if he didn't realize they were at his own expense. He didn't really seem to give a damn. And it was the best way to get the others laughing even harder—his just sitting there, solemnly striking the keys with his long, nail-bitten fingers, bellowing the refrain alongside his enemy.

His friend, the poet and writer Gaston Maloux, was the one who first introduced him to the group. Gaston had spent almost ten years working as a pen pusher for some lawyer. There he'd discovered just how low humanity could sink, and had become fascinated by the case files—the more obscene, the better. The details of the most reprehensible affairs—things you'd never have thought such respectable clients would be capable of—had served as inspiration for the dark, pessimistic novels that had assured Maloux's notoriety. Concealing his insatiable curiosity behind the yellow, inexpressive mask of a misanthrope, borne above a long, reed-thin body wrapped in a voluminous cloak, he still—despite having left the law office—was ready to pounce on any sordid conflict in his vicinity. He collected gossip all day long and at night wrote down whatever he'd gleaned. He hung around all sorts of places in search of family secrets, brilliant crimes, underworld vengeance, bastard children. His gray silhouette in its clerk's cloak slipped quietly along the quays to stand like a shadow watching the barges being unloaded and the women there, who, despite their youth, had already been worn down by their labor in the washhouses along the river at Grenelle . . . He used to go to the park along the Champs-Elysées to study the behavior of the "petits Jésus" with their languid eyes and heart-shaped mouths as they seduced passersby into giving them a few pennies, and then he'd roam around the high-class places by Saint-Germain-des-Prés. Sometimes, as if nothing was going on, he'd chat with a friend, there was always some contact nearby, walking the streets; but you never know, really, whether he was in fact staking out who knows what at the gate of a nearby mansion. It fed his imagination; it was how he vivisected the Parisian life that the sordid case files of the lawyer's office had taught him to relish. At the bistro he'd pull out his notebook from time to time and write down a few short phrases, just a word here or there, the way a painter draws a few lines on a sketch-pad, a scene or portrait that he'll complete later in the studio. Then, later, Gaston Maloux would have a drink at Café Prosper, where he'd join in the singing as if he'd shed the disturbing character he'd so recently played, walking the shadowy streets.

Before I arrived, there was only one woman among these painters and scribblers. A zealous, amateur actress named Caroline Mabain, the wife of the playwright, Emile Brochard. She went by her maiden name as an artist, as did I. Her dark, brilliant eyes, her laughing mouth, her abundant, witchlike black hair gave her a provocative beauty. Her lips seemed permanently on the verge of smiling, which made her seem strangely ironic, or else simply ferocious. Later there was another woman, Louise Foucher—she joined the group when she became inseparable from Gaston Maloux, the novelist.

Entering Café Prosper, each of us would glance quickly around to greet the staff and Friend Jean, and then head off to the corner hidden by a panel of frosted glass, our haunt, a sort of private parlor with a U-shaped bench around a big table. There were endless comings and goings in the café. Lucien Morel, Frédéric's closest friend, whom I'd met in his studio on my first impromptu visit there, was one of the regulars, despite the fact that his obligations as an architect made him frequently absent.

All this gaiety hid grief, failure, and loneliness. I learned this as time went by. Ruined love affairs, financial difficulties, illnesses, betrayals—everyone went through moments that were more or less painful and which, depending on the sufferer's character, he or she would confide between two glasses of wine, or else stash away in silence. One day Alfred Molinier told me, referring to Friend Jean, whom he singled out with a glance, that our crowd was now his only close family. Jean had lost both his wife and his only son in a train accident, which explained why he opened the café as soon as he was up in the early morning and closed only when the last drinker deigned to leave. Then, no doubt terrified by the loneliness awaiting him, his eyes would follow the silhouette of that man into the darkness as if he were committing it to memory, or else simply accompanying it as long as possible, for the company.

Part Two

23

Whenever a disaster occurs, one develops the irresistible urge to revisit the events preceding it to see whether there were any signs of the storm to come. Ever since that day in June 1912 when Eugénie and I almost came to blows, I've wracked my brains constantly, looking for early signs of what had set us on that path. Eugénie and I had an unexpected quarrel in the Luxembourg Gardens, you see—a quarrel different from any of the others that had divided us up to that point. It felt grim, dire, irreversible.

We were side by side at our easels in the shade of the paulownia trees, facing the light beating down on the pool where our little brother was sailing his toy sailboat, his governess within earshot. There'd been a long silence between the two of us, during which I was completely involved in mixing my colors; Eugénie broke the silence with loud, provocative comments about a certain couple who were leaning on the semicircular balustrade above the lower level of the garden with its round central pool, always crowded with children, in front of the Palais des Medicis. The couple's two rear ends seemed enormous in the foreground and we hadn't been able to resist giggling nervously like little girls, though I was going to be twenty-six at the end of August, and my sister eighteen in mid-November. I was conscious of our acting like fools, but couldn't seem to stop myself.

We'd been together for almost an hour, during which the flattering remarks we shot back and forth at one another had become more and more nauseatingly trite. This almost always happened at the beginning of our meetings; it was our way of neutralizing the apprehension we each felt, knowing that our work would be subjected by the other to a very critical eye and, often enough, some nasty digs. We spouted polite compliments about what each of us was wearing and how well she looked, encouraging words about everything and nothing. In our attempts to win each other over, we hoped to break the tension that almost always threatened to set us off. One little misstep, one little word, whether openly hostile or simply too knowing, one simple act would betray all our suppressed impatience and awaken old grudges.

I would, for example, let slip a comment to my sister about her fickleness, so she'd reproach me for how harshly I saw the world as soon as I got down to sketching it, and soon we'd be fighting, saying the most hurtful things imaginable. And this was happening more and more often.

That time we were hiccupping from our giggling and still sneaking glances at the two offending backsides, and I began to feel our levity gradually turn into something a bit ugly. I tried to pull myself together, and her as well, and began talking about our watercolors in a voice that was meant to be measured and kind. I even stepped back a bit so I could get a better look at my picture as a whole and said, "Have you ever noticed how you can be dissatisfied with your work for a long time, without really knowing why, and then all it takes is to add some little touch, a simple stroke of the brush, to make the subject powerful again, to give it back the spirit you'd hoped to capture . . ."

Before I'd even finished my sentence, a sort of arrow flew past my nose, slashing the foreground shadows that I'd just finished painting with yellow. At the same time, a great burst of laughter pierced my eardrums to resonate terribly through my entire body, leaving me stunned, dumb with rage.

Is there any name for the wave that sets your blood rushing through you at such moments, burning till you find yourself imagining a rock in your hands smashing downward with murderous rage? That monstrous wave that lifts you up and makes your voice so loud—ringing with every curse under the sun—until it's capable of booming across the entire city? Where does it come from, this sudden wave that makes you imagine, as though it were quite a simple thing, drowning your little sister? How, standing under the pure sky in the majesty and serenity of the Medici garden, is it possible to be assailed by such monstrous thoughts? Why doesn't the beauty of things have any influence on one's temper? For a long time now, I'd been wishing I could be magnanimous enough to overcome such fits of murderous rage; I never felt like that when I was with Frédéric and his friends. But, honoring my promise, I continued to devote one day a week to Eugénie, and in her presence I frequently felt myself being sucked back into our all too familiar, stagnant pattern.

I didn't scream, but stifled the sound inside me the moment I saw that yellow streak, like a gash, while my sister shook with laughter, staring wide-eyed at the harm she'd done, her hand covering her mouth. For God's sake, I begged *in petto* to God or the devil, make her stop trespassing on my life, even on my painting! Make her go away once and for all! There was no longer any question of upbraiding her as one would a child. I'd only ever slapped her once, the day she insulted a peasant on the path in Sainte-Colombe because he was drunk and staggering and talking unintelligibly . . .

Overwhelmed by this flood of violence that I was endeavoring to contain, I was torn between two reactions: either I could go back home immediately, even if it meant an open battle with my mother who'd asked me to give my sister these weekly sessions, or else I could keep on with my work as if there was nothing the matter, in order to minimize what that fiendish child had done. She was a burden, as ever, but she was still, in my eyes, "the child." At this point I no longer knew which one of us presented the greater danger to the other. When I'd been let out of the convent to come for my monthly visits to rue Moncey, my mere presence had made her take offence, but they told me that as soon as I was gone she always wanted me back. Later, the choice I'd made not to live within the strict limits imposed by Grandmother was considered to be a bad example for her. And yet still, still she'd been forced upon me.

I wanted to knock her to the ground and tell her how much I hated her. I made do with staring daggers at her pretty head.

"So?" she simpered. "Why not have a little fun? After all, somebody exhibited a canvas that a donkey's tail had splattered every color in the world at the Salon des Indépendants, and signed it Boronali! Remember? Two years ago. Everybody said it was genius and it got written up in the papers as *Sunset over the Adriatic* . . . See? A little random stroke of yellow and everything's changed for the better. That's what you just said yourself! Just now!"

She'd ruined my picture, and there she was: derisive, triumphant.

Because I'd continued persevering after my marriage in doing the one thing that had always kept me going, pencil or brush in hand, it ended up by winning me some respect. I'd realized, as a result, that I'd become disproportionately important in the eyes of "the child." Whenever people spoke about me, or about Frédéric's projects, or William's photographic reports in her presence, she'd fly into a stunning rage, repeating how nobody thought she counted at all, over and over. Yet she'd always been Grandmother's favorite. But then, when she was twelve or thirteen, Grandmother died. Was there anything we could do to appease her? Should we hide everything we did, our projects, our lives? Or, on the contrary, involve her in whatever we were doing? But if we did the latter, we'd be running the risk of sucking our own friends into these ridiculous family conflicts. She'd invent every means possible to keep us from devoting ourselves to the work we'd chosen. Since we couldn't trust her, William and I simply avoided her as much as possible.

Frédéric would sometimes sketch Eugénie quickly in pencil or charcoal when we'd visit the Versoix family together. He could do it when she wasn't paying attention to him, but he'd given up on having her sit as a proper model for him, because she was always interrupting her pose. She was terribly pleased to know she was being admired and examined by an artist, with her hands on the keyboard of the piano, so she'd wriggle around and make up endless puns, giggling uncontrollably and, in short, making it impossible for Frédéric to concentrate.

Why hadn't they encouraged Eugénie to go on studying music rather than making her follow so systematically in my footsteps? I looked at my watercolor that day in the Gardens and all I could see was her yellow streak. My heart was beating so hard that I could feel my pulse in my temples, making an ear-splitting buzz, like bumblebees helter-skelter. What I was feeling frightened me: perhaps I couldn't kill her, but why not hit her, really send her home bloody? She'd done something that couldn't be undone, yes, but there was more to it than that. Despite wanting to remain calm, I realized that she'd moved then just as though she was striking with a knife . . . and I was the one she had stabbed.

If I responded to her, I'd be playing her game, but I couldn't keep from saying, "Well, you'll never be as famous as that donkey, that's for sure."

She already knew what I thought of her work. And I knew that my words had been more vicious than the imagined slap that was still vibrating in the palm of my hand.

"Who gives you the right to judge? Just because Willon chose to exhibit three or four of your paintings doesn't mean they're any good! You're always trying to belittle me! William and you are always plotting something in English. And what was it you were saying about me to Mother?"

By the time she'd finished her tirade, she was in tears. There would be no end to this war. It had been exhilarating for a moment, but now the old, familiar guilt was back. Yes, my real life had begun; I was free of the family circle, by and large; and yet, there was no restraining the thought that then popped into my mind, a new weapon, something that would really hurt, be a decisive blow, lay her flat once and for all.

"Sometimes it's better for us to speak English, otherwise you'd be even more upset than you already are . . ." I said, just a bit under my breath, to lead her on.

"What are you hiding?" she cried out, as if she'd been expecting the worst for a while now.

"Oh, things from before you were born. But since you've forbidden us to discuss them, that's all I'm going to say . . ."

She was livid: "What on earth were you talking about?"

"I remember that Mum used to cry a lot that summer. We were sent off to stay with our grandparents in Richmond . . ."

"So? That's all ancient history!"

"I found out afterward that it was because she was expecting a baby, and that our father didn't want another child."

Well, it was unforgivable—but irresistible. I felt nothing much, staring her down, almost satisfied at seeing her suddenly get so quiet, so pale. It was like the two or three times when she was a baby that they'd put an end to her tantrums by setting her down in a tub and splashing cold water on her. It had a startling effect. First she'd choke and splutter, then be sweet for the rest of the evening. My revelation about her birth had silenced her, and I took advantage of that to add, without inflection, "I have to go to the studio and finish a painting for the autumn exhibition now, so I'll leave you with your picture. I won't be coming back next week or any other."

At which point I folded up my easel, put away my paint and brushes, and, without even telling François good-bye, down by the pool, I went to take the bus for place Clichy that stopped at Odéon.

It was almost summer. I knew that the Versoix family would spend part of the season at Divonne-les-Bains, then at Sainte-Colombe, which my mother had inherited. They'd be gone, then, and I was relieved to be spared the sight of them anytime soon. Frédéric and I had been invited to visit some people on the shores of Lac Léman, so that was that. We'd be traveling back through Burgundy, where I'd fallen in love with the vineyard landscapes. Storms of leafy greenery there broke over the curving vines that lay in well-defined, ever-so-disciplined levels in manmade billows. At every instant the daylight worked to create deep thick shadows between the rolling waves of shifting green streaming down the hills. And in Switzerland I was breathless with wonder over the magnificent lake dominated by the Alps veiled in a thousand folds of white.

I forgot my sister and her jealous fits, my mother and her weakness as she played at being a noble lady, and also perhaps what might have seemed my own cowardly nature—if I'd bothered to examine it—because I had proven myself unable to halt the process that made each of us a prisoner of the others.

24

Eugénie had guessed right, I'd spoken to our mother in private a few days earlier, which was a rare thing. Our memories of all those times our parents kept us waiting expectantly for their attention when we were children are so strong, so lasting, that even now, as an adult, I thought the note she'd sent me that morning meant she just wanted the pleasure of having a special bit of time with me alone. So I was more than happy to go to the rue du Four, during the time that Eugénie, François, and the governess were taking their walk, as we'd agreed. But the minute we sat down before the tray with its ritual tea and fruitcake, I understood that I was there so she could tell me about how much trouble she was having with my sister, and ask me to help her.

All the same, she did begin with compliments: I was a devoted, stubborn worker and she admired the faith that kept me going. There was something austere, stern about me that surprised her, but also made her respect me. For years now I hadn't deviated from the road I was taking, always moving toward my goal. She found the path I'd chosen frightening, but I went into things with great seriousness and that, in the end, was something good. She'd have liked so much for the child (because we always called Eugénie "the child" when we were talking to each other) to see me as a role model. The child still didn't know how to spend time alone, still never finished what she started . . . Just as an example of how unacceptably irresponsible Eugénie could be, she'd once dared give Mother a silk stole made out of a remnant bought at Bon Marché, and then had the nerve as she gave her the present to say casually, "You'll just need to do the other hem yourself!"

It was hard to figure out whether it was disappointment, disdain, or pure sadness that had the upper hand in my mother's emotions.

So that's why I'm here, I thought. She wants me to put Eugénie on the right track. Was she perhaps beginning to understand why I'd always been so impatient with the child? After that description of my sister's effrontery I was tempted to make Mother really indignant by telling her that all the finish-work on the tea napkins that

Eugénie had given her while Grandmother was alive had been done by the old lady's skillful fingers, but she'd probably guessed it by now anyhow. I don't know why I bothered, but I did once try to get my sister to understand that there was little value in giving a gift under false pretenses, claiming she'd made it herself. My only reward was an exceptionally dirty look.

My mother expected something from me, but I really didn't know how to interpret her sighs, her gestures and looks, all the little signals we're able to perceive in people with whom we are intimate. I couldn't read her now—I hardly knew her anymore. She only *looked like* Jeanne Lewly. Inside, she was a stranger. And even on the outside! Her face had new expressions. Was it age? Her second marriage? My heart told me that the real Jeanne was the one she'd been during her first marriage, but I'd never know for certain. Anyway, as for myself, I'd changed the way I saw things. I was now part of a couple. I was now named Mathilde Thorins—I belonged to Frédéric's little world in Clichy, even if I signed my pictures "Lewly" (just that, because I liked the two vertical lines framing the little waves made by the *W* and followed by a diagonal emphasizing the whole . . .). Stealing a quick glance at my mother, it seemed to me that even Grandmother's expressions would have been easier to read than hers. I could never have imagined the day when this would be true! The relief I'd felt when I learned of my grandmother's death was almost euphoric, but as time went by I sometimes noticed that she was still with me in little things I did, still had an unexpected influence on my thoughts. I began to regret that it had never occurred to me to find out anything more about what she'd aspired to in her youth. After her death, I tried to imagine her having been young and wanted to know about the little girl she'd been, and then what kind of young woman she was, what kind of wife, what kind of mother. And did I ask her daughter? No, the nuns had taught me too well: I didn't ask questions.

My mother had chosen to confide in me about the child just at the moment when I was pulling myself together to take my first flight: I would be making my debut, with my first paintings in the upcoming autumn exhibition at Willon's gallery. It was no small matter for me to get ready for it. But here was Mother putting me back into my old role as the pawn they moved around at will, depending on what the family needed from me, with no thought for my own ambitions. I couldn't believe it. It made me sad, even bitter. I just sat there and listened.

"I often use you as an example, hoping that will encourage her. She admires you so much!" Mother sighed. I replied that this was, rather, the best way to set her against me. I'd come to think that my years in boarding school, which had been so hard to endure, had driven me to resourcefulness, had forced me find a way to invent my own existence and so saved me from a certain emptiness—the empty life in which I now saw Eugénie losing her spark. Other than the affectations she put on whenever there were people around, what kind of life did she have, a young girl barely done with childhood? Why not have encouraged her to keep on playing the piano? My mother had only one answer, utterly appalling: "She told me that when I went back to the piano again she lost all hope of playing as well as I did. So I too stopped playing in the end."

I didn't hide my indignation, but, in order to get a grip on myself, I kept my response soft, firm, but to the point: "Did you do her a favor by depriving yourself? She never goes into anything with any depth and then she makes us all feel guilty about our accomplishments! If I'd stopped painting to keep her from being jealous, what would I be doing with my life today? Would it have given her the tenacity she lacks? You always let her do as she pleased and today you find her fickleness unconscionable. But what can I do about it?"

I said what I thought unemotionally and with a determination that surprised me. I imagine that, in a courtroom, the sentence is pronounced in just such an uninflected voice. It was only when I saw my mother's bewildered look that I was able to assess the force, maybe even the violence of what I'd said.

With every passing minute a new question arose in my mind: Who was my mother? Why was she consulting me now? What could I hope to change? My feelings for Mother had always been pure and passionate. This very morning I'd felt them all over again, reawakened simply by seeing her handwriting on the note, and I'd run to meet her with all the hopefulness of a child, again prepared to start all over with her from the beginning . . . but the longer we sat there together, the stronger my accumulated resentments grew. What's more, the further we went in our conversation, the more I felt my love drain away. It was hard to believe, but I no longer felt much for my mother. It seemed to me that she had let go of my hand when we'd come from England to France, and that from then on had kept the best of herself for the baby, now "the child." To my great astonishment, I found I wasn't sorry that she had. If I'd stayed with her, I'd perhaps have met the same fate as my sister. Eugénie was always bored and always had been, whereas I never was. I just didn't want the child to eat me alive in order to fill her own emptiness.

A soft crumb of fruitcake was dissolving in my mouth with its delicious taste of the past, and I remembered the last time I'd felt a hint of kindness for Eugénie. Men were lowering Grandmother's coffin into the earth, and the rhythm of the child's sobs was disrupting that of the *Dies irae* being chanted by the priest and the choirboy. Unexpected tenderness made me move closer to her as I remembered how much she'd loved her grandmother, the old woman who'd utterly pampered her in return. At that moment I probably experienced once again the pure, sweet feeling I'd had for the child when she was an infant. Sensing the loneliness awaiting Eugénie, a solitude for which she was unprepared, I took on the role of a protective sister quite naturally. With all the power of love in my heart, I went and stood behind her and crossed my hands over her breast. I could feel the spasms of her weeping and the wild beating of her heart. I hugged the thirteen-year-old child tightly against me as if I could warm the innermost depths of her soul despite the gusty winds of November blowing down upon us. Her hands burrowed into mine like two kittens curling up in their mother's warmth. But before nightfall I would be going back with my husband to the neighborhood where Eugénie had spent all her earliest childhood. She'd left it behind when she went to live on the Left Bank with her mother, when she remarried. Once again I had the sense that I was abandoning her to the vagaries of life.

There, as I sat in the parlor of the apartment where Jeanne Versoix, her husband, my sister, and little François lived, I went back over that sweet moment in my mind. It led to a staggering realization: I didn't trust Mme Versoix, my mother. Not at all. Did it date back to the birth of my little sister? Or to when we found ourselves so strangely transported from paradise to Paris? Or had my mistrust, perhaps, developed when she'd left me shut up in boarding school? Or maybe later, when she'd taken me out only so I could keep her own mother company? Grandmother had become so sad after her daughter remarried that she'd lost all her pleasure in life. For her mother, yes, Jeanne Versoix would take action, but she had never been there for her children, never given them any guidance.

What would have become of William and me if we'd stayed in Twickenham with wealthy but frivolous parents who'd have brought us up in comfortable circumstances, where we were doomed to live among people just like them? Would we ever have developed the self-sufficiency we now enjoyed? Would we ever have felt a passionate desire to express ourselves, develop a talent? We remembered a childhood bathed in sunlight, but were these idyllic memories not perhaps the result of having been brutally uprooted at a time when we were too young to tell reality from fantasy?

Unconsciously crumbling a bit of uneaten fruitcake between my fingers, I blessed the day my friend Alice had taken me to see the illuminations, thus outmaneuvering my ever-present despair. Would I have been able to love the radiance of colors so much if the light inside me hadn't gone out, making me have to crane my neck in search of a different source? And how would I have discovered and appreciated those marvelous things if I hadn't been shut up in that eighteenth-century mansion, which had been a luxurious private home before being turned into a boarding school for the girls of fine families? It had been stripped of its gilding, its carved woodwork, all the frescoes and medallions that stood as testimony to how the property had been passed down from generation to generation until 1820, the year when it was turned over to the Society of the Sacred Heart of Jesus. The duchess of Maine died within its walls. Through an incredible coincidence, she had been also the owner of the chateau de Sceaux and its grounds, which one could see from the windows along the front of the lycée Lakanal. It was as if my brother and I were under the protection of this same soul, reaching out from the other side of time.

Back when I'd first learned all the history of those places and the people who haunted them, I even came to enjoy them a little. I liked sleeping in the cold dormitory where Marie d'Agoult had shivered; I liked having yearned for affection in the shadow of the garden where she too had dreamed so sadly. And my mother as well had strolled along the same paths and wept there, once upon a time . . .

Even today, I get no small satisfaction from the law imposing the separation of church and state in 1905, which served to take back that property from the nuns. It was a lovely revenge: artists moved in almost immediately.

And yet, in a sense, for all the pain it caused me, that drafty old building is where I was really born, or, anyway, where I first became aware of my existence, where I first came awake, sunk so deep in grief that I found ecstasy. Encouraged by sacred texts and the example of the martyrs, we practiced the formidable art of suffering. I'd taken refuge in my admiration of the illuminations and the stained-glass windows, to the point that I even forgot what it was that caused me so much suffering. They'd even encouraged these reveries of mine—they thought I was being pious. How lucky I was!

Now, sitting across from Mme Versoix, my mind was all confusion. I imagined her escaping that same austere existence at the age of twenty, her hand in the hand of a seductive thirty-year-old gentlemen, who promptly whisked her across the Channel. I was fascinated by their romance, but that letter from my father—written when his back was up against the wall, when he was refusing his coming child—haunted me still, like so much else. I remembered having seen my mother in tears from time to time, back then, mistaking this for simple grief, but now I understood, now I could guess how, at thirty, she had been torn to shreds by him, by her husband's confession. The letters had been addressed to her, after all. She'd read them so many years before I did. The temptation to talk about all that now was almost overwhelming! I curved the palm of my hand around her fingers to help distract myself from the terrible words I wanted to say; her fingers were still those of a pianist, and they closed around mine mechanically, in need of help. My voice shook as it all spilled out: "Now that there's no danger of Grandmother getting in the way to change the subject or let us know her feelings on the subject, please tell me, how did my father die?"

Mother pulled her hand back and put it on her forehead; then she put her elbows on the table, leaning heavily forward. She'd hidden the top of her face; all I could see was that her chin was trembling. A bit horrified at myself for my lack of self control, broaching a subject that had forever been shrouded in sacred silence, I waited for her answer.

"You know I've never been able to talk about that, Mathilde. Don't bring your father into the conversation . . ."

"He died scarcely three months after Eugénie was born. What was he doing in the winter fog on the Thames at nightfall? I have to say, it looks less and less to me as though it was an accident . . ."

It was as though she'd been singed: "Whatever would make you say something like that?" she exclaimed.

"His letters" was on the tip of my tongue: everything would have cleared up between us had she told me the truth, had I been able to ask her for it as shamelessly as I imagined. Except that now, because I could see how desperate she was to maintain her pretenses, nothing more came out of my mouth. What I'd been tempted to do bordered on sacrilege, and I'd now managed to get myself under control. Still, the sense that I'd always regret doing so now had me paralyzed.

"You have a little sister, you know. Don't insist. Don't torture me. Think of our responsibility to her. Besides, they'll soon be back from their walk."

But just because I'd turned back from the great leap I'd hoped to take, it didn't mean that I couldn't still poke at our wounds. "So, in the end, it wasn't Grandmother who was forbidding us to bring up our days in England?"

"I had to keep my feet on firm ground, for your sake. And now I owe the same to my new family. Don't go digging . . ."

"Don't go digging! As though I had any choice. William and I have already found . . ." I swayed, dizzy, on the threshold from which I found I had not stepped back soon enough. "I'd hoped I'd set us both free by bringing up this subject, but I can see that I was wrong . . ."

Today I regret not having been more straightforward in taking vengeance.

"What are you saying? What did you find?"

"You just told me not to ask you, so don't you ask *me*. If you want to protect Eugénie from herself, by all means do so. As for me, despite what you think, there's nothing more I can do to help."

And three days later my sister would stab me with the tip of a brush dripping with yellow and I would turn on her with a weapon that had a different sharpness to it, and plunge it into her with all my heart. Not that I could ever have foreseen that then.

Just as Mme Versoix was about to reply, we'd heard the front door slam and the voices of children calling out to her. My mother and I had the same impulse and hurried into her bedroom, giving her just enough time to pull herself together, dust on a bit of powder; we both needed a few moments to get our pulses under control. Our conversation was over: its time had passed.

I left quietly as soon as the young ones had gone off to the kitchen with their governess. My mother and I, both more upset than I'd have thought, had scarcely time to say good-bye.

I rode back to place Clichy on the top deck of the bus; there was some little relief in that I found I was no longer so upset about my father's letters—no, I was upset by the fact that I had dared to speak to my mother about them, and *that* distress outweighed all others, at least for the time being. I realized that I had just finished what amounted to the closest thing to a heart-to-heart talk I'd ever shared with my mother, never mind the first addressing our family tragedy directly. I was torn between wanting to take back my words and wanting to say more, because we hadn't said everything. Once the truth begins to surface, you have to go wherever it takes you—follow it through to the end, I thought. But what does it mean to come to the end of a truth? It seems a vast expanse of possibilities was spreading out before me, new ways of thinking, as new worlds always seem to lie beyond the horizon, beyond the world you now traverse, and I felt very small indeed in the face of that infinity: the end of a truth. I hadn't yet learned that the truth is something you can never really possess.

Soon the Versoix family would go off to its mountainside. I wasn't to see Mother again until my autumn exhibition. Though I still had two or three drawing lessons to give Eugénie.

And yes, three days later, the fight. I went home from the Luxembourg Gardens carrying the watercolor "the child" had slashed. I renounced giving her the promised lessons. Was this at least something approaching a decisive step toward freedom?

25

It was a lovely day in fall of 1912 when Frédéric and I walked over to Willon's gallery with our paintings. Frédéric was showing two very large canvases and I had two in the show that were medium-sized and then two smaller watercolors.

We'd been jumpy with anticipation for days. He was better at controlling his excitement than I. Previously it had been above all for *his* works that we'd gone various places. Now, over the past year or two, people had also become interested in my own.

I was trembling as we made our way to the gallery, never for a moment thinking that Frédéric might be as nervous, as fragile as I, despite his greater experience. He did his best to conceal his hopes as well as his fears of how he might be judged by this or that jealous or malicious critic. And it didn't matter to him, in the end, whether this viciousness was directed against me or against him; all ferocious criticism was equally painful to him. I felt just the same, though he knew better than I the harm caused by such harsh judgments, and he also knew that there were some critics who weren't worthy of the name to begin with, egotists who only wanted a column because they could talk about themselves in it—never mind the artist—and who were encouraged in this by their sensationalist papers, far more interested in power and personality than painting. No matter how many artist friends I'd accompanied to the Autumn Exhibition or to shows at dealers, no matter how well acquainted I was with their vulnerability when faced with criticism, I still hadn't *really* felt—with every fiber of my being, as they say—the anxiety of facing the firing squad myself . . . nor, for that matter, had I experienced the thrill of being in the spotlight. Indifference, they all told me, was the worst fate of all—or else, they supposed, having your work hung in some dismal little corner with bad lighting, where nobody would even see it.

There was no rivalry in our little horde—our styles were so different. Frédéric had never stopped practicing his bold, new type of painting. Despite having done academic portraits and landscapes, he preferred to exploit a different side of his art and, carrying on with the avant-gardists, he was exhibiting paintings of subjects that had been dissected—more and more over time—into geometric figures. I had come to understand what he was after, what he was thinking, in the days since I was first shocked by this approach, seeing his canvases in his studio. A line, an angle created by a brush or palette knife revealed just how powerfully he'd mastered his art. There was living thought in it. It was searching for something. I felt, finally, studying his canvases for so long and so closely, that my mind might almost pass through them into Frédéric's body, feeling that body exhaust itself like an animal as it devoured his subject. People who haven't made art their calling have no idea how much physical stamina is required. What a pleasant moment it is when you and your friends agree to take some time off and relax after that awful mêlée . . .

When we arrived at the exhibit Willon had mounted, we naturally went to see where ours had been hung before even glancing at the other work on display. The gallery had been divided according to style—the modern in one room, the figurative in another. Had ours been hung too high up, or in a corner that was poorly lit? Or worse, somewhere people hardly went? Or too close to other paintings that were so large and bright that they might make ours look dull? Such anxieties are very hard on the nerves, besides which, being so prey to one's emotions makes for poor judgment. Ernest Ponsal, wearing his usual captain's cap, was waiting for us. He'd already located where our work had been put up and led us there before even showing us where his own paintings were hanging. I began to keep an eye on the other visitors, paying careful attention to what they were looking at, waiting to see if the faces looking up at our creations showed curiosity or delight, and naturally dreading the sight of any silent scowling, any too-brief appraisals of a canvas leading to summary dismissal. What, I wondered, did the silences of the silent ones really mean? It took me a while before I went to see anyone else's work, and then I chose to look for my friends' pictures first.

I ended up going around the two large rooms with Louise Foucher and Ernest Ponsal, whom I soon found again in the crowd. They too were exhibiting. Louise looked distraught and couldn't even force a smile; her paintings had been hung far too high for anyone to appreciate them. I was deeply sympathetic, yet, at the same time, considering the placement of my own pictures, pretty pleased with my own good luck.

We finally rejoined Frédéric, who was surrounded by a group that included Alfred Molinier, the writer Gaston Maloux—who was looking around for Louise—the playwright Emile Brochard, and his wife Caroline Mabain. There were also some aggressive visitors who were up in arms about the insanity of modern painters who disfigured their subjects with large angular strokes of the brush and yet still claimed to be artists. Others weren't speaking directly to Frédéric but were scoffing at his geometric style and his use of colors in voices loud enough for him to hear. You could tell how much they wanted to hurt him, their utter delight in cutting the artist to the quick. Molinier was trying to explain the painter's thought process to the grumblers, he was expounding upon how his thought followed the path the eyes take in processing the way the world is constructed. You could see he badly wanted to rescue his friend. Frédéric knew that only a minute fraction of the onlookers would ever care for his style, but one never gets used to being lambasted, even though we keep telling ourselves—as I know so well—that words shouldn't hurt so badly. Luckily, there were a few visitors who spent a great deal, in the end, to buy his canvases, and others too who made appointments to come by his studio. That encouraged him—as well it might.

M. Willon and another man walked over to where I was standing. He introduced us. M. Oostreling, with his well-groomed beard and proud moustache, was a Belgian critic, and he wanted to meet the mysterious artist who'd signed the painting of a wild, untended garden behind a worm-eaten fence.

That garden, surrounded by old houses, no longer existed. A few years earlier it had been across from Aunt Dilys's house, until a stone apartment building had been built in its place. The demolition process had dragged on for a long while, and every time I saw the ruins of the house that had stood for several centuries behind this garden, I was haunted by the fact that this home to several generations of unknown people had been obliterated. The only traces remaining were some of the roof-beams, and then two adjacent walls still covered with the remains of yellowed wallpaper on which you could see bright spots in the shapes of picture frames and crucifixes. Looking at that disemboweled home, abandoned to wind and rain, I wondered about the souls that might still be roaming through it. What, for example, had guided their choice of décor, color, woodwork? Who had given birth or died where the crucifix once hung? Did she love the husband who, in the life they shared, had made love to her so many times, so many nights? What troubles, what remorse had eaten away at the old man sitting in a daze before the fire that his servants kept alight for him? Vestiges of lives that had run their course were now there for all to see . . . Their indignant ghosts shivered in my imagination.

I'd wanted to contrast that desolation with the undiscriminating generosity of nature in the first fine days of spring. I was haunted, you see, by the thought that Swann House had perhaps been torn down after our departure, and that passersby could now have portions of its walls, built in the first quarter of the eighteenth century, exposed to their scrutiny. When I was at Aunt Dilys's house, I went upstairs and sketched the remnants remaining from the family that had now gone, recording too the glorious spectacle of their wild lawn studded with thousands of jonquils. No one would ever have known of the now purposeless splendor, down there on the ground, if I hadn't gone up to look at it from the balcony. The fence protected it from the eyes of people walking by. And now a stone building has crushed all that abundance, all that history.

In the spring, when I was a little girl, and the days had begun to be sunny, I used to squat down on the edge of the lawn at Marble Hill Park to watch how the yellow of the daffodils became even more intense against the carpet of blinding green. My eyes were just barely above the golden wave moving softly in the breeze. Had I been able, I would have drunk it. This is what I'd attempted to render with the tip of my brush. In the wasteland of a house that was being demolished, behind its worm-eaten fence, I had erected in my devotion something better than an altar of a thousand thousand jonquils as I turned my thoughts back to a different, lost home. No one was likely to guess that this apotheosis of color was the expression of my mourning.

It all intrigued the Belgian critic, so he'd wanted to take me aside to get to know me, to chat a bit and learn this and that. In all that hubbub, how could words translate my obsession with color into words he might hope to understand, and in only a few minutes? I long ago learned that those who create have nothing to say about what they've created—it's enough for them to have done it. They've put their blood, their nerves, their willpower, their passion, their most intimate confusion, their very life into whatever it is they've made. It's up to other people to think whatever they want about it. Ah, but this man wanted to know *when* and *how* I'd begun to want to paint, and he wanted to know other things as well . . . I had to answer him then and there but without betraying anything I might later regret, without letting out any of the tension inside me that was the source of my art. As usual, I was too overcome to be good with words under such circumstances. Some of his questions touched on things I didn't want examined, spots where I'd been burned; then I wasn't able to speak at all, or else I'd find myself forced to blurt out X or Y as though they were absolute truths, whereas I really wasn't sure of anything. Then he pointed out a sofa under the window where we could continue our conversation.

Just at that moment, a bouquet of flowers whipped me across my face—about as far from a caress as possible—slapped me there good and hard. Eugénie had snuck up behind me. I hadn't seen her—didn't see her even now—and yet I knew it was her, I knew this attack to be one of her provocative, teasing gestures. I spun around and we glared at one another from under the shadows of our wide-brimmed hats. At some strange depth in her eyes I found something hard as ice. I like to think she was cut by the sharp blades of my stare in turn.

"Congratulations to the artist!" she exclaimed, raising the volume of her voice—a stage trick designed to take over a space or an event. She paid no attention whatever to the man with whom I was speaking.

I had no other choice, with the bouquet in my arms—asters, which I really don't like anyway, come to think of it, because they predict that winter is coming, and cemeteries are always full of them—than to look as though I was grateful, whereas I could see the whole scene had been staged just to put me on the spot, or perhaps to outright humiliate me. We hadn't seen each other since she'd ruined my watercolor. That had been four months ago. I'd really welcomed the separation, even more than I'd thought I would. The reason my sister was reappearing with her fake, vicious flattery at the very moment that I was fulfilling my oldest dream was that she was trying to finish me off, in her way, while at the same time keep up appearances—just in case there might be something left to take for herself. What other people looking on would have seen as a gift was not one, not at all, and I alone knew it. As soon as she'd made her spectacular entrance, she'd put me in an untenable position. She would have been brilliant had she ever gone into the theater. But no—there too she'd have had to work.

Frédéric and our friends were the only people that I wanted to share the evening with, and yet, no mistake, there she was—triumphant as a jay decked out in peacock feathers. She had the advantage now and looked me up and down with pride; I asked loudly if she'd come without a chaperone, just to emphasize how young she was.

It was still up to me to consent to her intrusion. The violence of our last exchange had put a definitive end to our weekly meetings. Too bad for our mother, who was in no hurry to come see me, or my pictures either. A kind of barrier had now come up between us. Had Eugénie, shocked and hurt, talked about what I'd revealed about our father? That seemed likely to me. She'd come to announce her retaliation with a bouquet of flowers. Being the guilty one, I had no proper defense.

I expected that, if she spent any time where my pictures were on exhibit, my sister would eventually overhear comments that either put me in a good light or, on the contrary, cast me down into the mud; I knew she would somehow manage, however, to turn everything she heard into one uniform, negative judgment, that she would manage to take away all the magic of my success, or else, from her vantage point, transform it into defeat. The innocence of this baptism of mine, this debut as a real artist, had been extinguished not by the child in herself, but by the blast of hatred she drew out of me. Lifting the edge of her hat, she gave me a kiss. I hated myself for letting her bring her pale, youthful face, her forehead with its fringe of red hair, so close to my cheek. She did it just for show, for people to see. I wanted so badly to grab her by the shoulders and throw her out into the street that, to disguise my anger, I once again went for flattery and, hugging her around the waist, complimented her on what she was wearing. I was overcome by shame at being so weak, but I had to save face; this was no place for a quarrel. The combined voices of my mother and grandmother telling me I had to give in to her rose up inside. Eugénie clearly understood those voices; they were the driving force behind her tyranny. For a split second I saw the diabolical chains binding us. At that moment, once more, I felt capable of murder.

"I have to continue my conversation with Monsieur Oostreling. I'm going to leave the flowers with you and come back later," I said, happy to get away before my mother, her husband, and their son all reached us—because now I saw they'd come too, wonder of wonders, the whole clan was approaching us slowly, looking up at the works on display as they came.

A sweet look rippled across Eugénie's face, the way it does in children who stop being angry as soon as they've gotten what they want: now she wouldn't have to look at me for a while. I was so exasperated when I turned back to the Belgian that it really made me want to ask him to take me away to his country immediately. Belgium or even hell would be far preferable.

Just as I was about to follow him I saw Frédéric and his friend Lucien Morel coming toward us through the crowd. Lucien, the engineer, had taken William to see the spectacular damage caused by the floods of 1910 to the railroad bridge at Lurey-Conflans near Romilly-sur-Seine. Both piers and superstructure had been carried off in the raging waters, and all that remained, hanging above the muddy tumult, were the rails and a few crossbeams. William had taken some impressive photographs, and they'd already begun appearing in the papers.

Once again I made the journalist wait. He went back to my paintings and was again studying them carefully.

"Is this your sister?" Lucien Morel asked, apparently touched by having caught sight at a distance of the two of us in our fake demonstrations of affection.

"My little Eugénie," I replied in dulcet tones, putting my arm around her shoulders—she'd wafted nearby—to make it clear that the child was only a child.

My sister did a pirouette to escape my hand. Her way of letting him know that she was not "big Mathilde's little Eugénie."

"And do you paint as well, Mademoiselle?" Frédéric's friend asked.

"Of course! Also I play the piano!" she replied with a wheedling smile before fixing me with a steely gaze to keep me quiet.

"She's particularly good at acting, too!" I tossed off as I went to pull the Belgium back into our conversation.

Frédéric, at least, appreciated my fillip. He knew all about what he called "your little sister's soap bubbles." He considered her current enthusiasm for painting a fad, just a pastime, and saw no personal vision in her daubing—just poor imitations of real painters. "Did you ever notice that she's always trying to follow in your footsteps?" he'd once remarked when we were coming home from having dinner with the Versoix family. Yet he let himself be fooled by that bouquet of flowers, saying that very evening how nice and unexpected it had been that she'd brought me that thoughtful gift. And, what's more, while I was talking to the Belgian journalist, Frédéric had invited her to come visit us at the studio! I almost choked on my own breath. How could I make him see that her only desire had been to destroy me, and that he had unwittingly become part of her game? How could I confess that I felt the day coming when Eugénie and I would wage open warfare? Oh yes—it was coming.

Alone again with M. Oostreling, I was talking and talking, but I hardly recognized my own voice. I remember mentioning my passion for illuminations when I was nine. That, he said, was probably the source of my vocation . . . I didn't react. It seems to me, rather, that a person is born a painter, because art is a way of seeing the world and also a way of approaching one's own self.

Fifteen newspapers covered the exhibit, and most of them mentioned my name as one of the revelations of the evening. Both Frédéric and I had sold our paintings. We were euphoric. We had an open house at the studio for any of our friends who wanted to celebrate the occasion. William, just back from covering a story, came along too. There were journalists, dealers, and collectors who came as much to see what Frédéric was doing as to see my pictures, including my sketches and all the copies that had piled up since my arrival there. I sold a great many of them. And in the papers there were photos showing me surrounded by a few of my works, along with columns discussing them, but—despite the fact that I was bursting with happiness—I didn't know how to take this unexpected fame. It was unexpected and overwhelming.

26

After two weeks of silence, my mother, who'd barely given me a kiss on the day of the opening, but just gone her way, sweeping François in her wake through the crowd, as if he were a buoy in the current, asked me to meet her at Chez Angélina. Eugénie and I used to go there often to drink hot chocolate after we'd visited the Louvre or taken a walk along the quays. My favorite table was the one right next to the big window. From there you could see the chestnut and beech trees in the Tuileries Garden framed by the arcades along the Rue de Rivoli. Sometimes the foliage with its unpredictable greens beneath the changing skies of Paris provided me with a sense of absolute bliss. I had the same experience watching the reflections in the Seine from any of its bridges as Frédéric and I strolled along it when the weather was stormy, amusing ourselves by letting our eyes get lost in that indescribable mixture of colors, like torrents squeezed from huge tubes of paint by some gigantic hand, right into the middle of the river—which did a poor job of diluting them. The colors rippled through the nonchalant current there to separate around the bridges' piers, which transformed them into flat, round cakes of light that the barges pushed off to the banks, where they became absorbed completely in the reflections of the thick plane trees and the thin poplars. I felt as if I were rediscovering all the same dominant colors I so often mixed on my palette, finding them dumped in a raw state right into the Seine, a thousand reflections fallen from the rainbow, creating transient images instantly clouded by its sandy, muddy waters.

At Angélina's that day, my mother was in no mood to share my enthusiasm for the wild reds of the trees. In a voice that was unfamiliar to me, because so harsh—as hard, indeed, as the look on her face—she stared me down accusingly, which was, to say the least, unusual. She'd been right to choose a public place; it helped her keep in control. How strange, for that matter, to see her daring to confront me, when she'd never once been able to stand up to Eugénie.

It all began with an accusation. Never, she said, would she have expected that the result of my painting lessons would have been the shock I had inflicted upon her at the Willon Gallery.

This, I assumed, was something to do with a particular painting I'd exhibited, since Mother was no doubt willfully ignorant of my simmering hostilities with the child: perhaps, the portrait of Grandmother, completed a few weeks before she died. But what, if this was the matter at hand, was so offensive about that? "It's not really about her!" I said, hoping to calm Mother down.

"Don't make fun of me, Mathilde. She's wearing precisely the same clothes she always wore, and her chair is the same as the one she always sat in, and any idiot would recognize those curtains on the double windows in the background! And, to make matters worse, it just so happens that it was that very picture that caught the critics' attention . . . And then there were the photos of you posing next to it, as if you were going out of your way to provoke me! I was so ashamed! Such an attack on the sacred memory of the departed!"

"If you were paying such close attention, then certainly you must have noticed that I titled it *Old Age*, not *Mme Nolès*. It could be anyone. I'll look that way myself, one day, if I live as long . . ."

My grandmother, despite her ill health, had still been the mistress of her domain, of herself, of the people around her, right up until the months preceding her rapid decline. I'd immortalized her in her chair with her cane beside her; there too was her sewing box overflowing with tangled skeins of color. She was holding an unfinished placemat on her lap, just like always, a placemat with a design she never completed because she couldn't see well enough anymore, and because her fingers had become slightly crooked, her movements unsure. I'd taken it from among her things after her death, to keep it just as I would have kept an unfinished letter written by someone I was about to lose—precisely on account of its shaky, awkward handwriting. The irregular stitches that Grandmother had left behind moved me more than all the perfect embroidery she'd ever finished. I saw in that placemat her will to live. As long as she could make one more stitch, she was still among the living. The countless napkins, tablecloths, placemats, and pillowcases that had passed through her hands were like the pages in her book of days. Even when her fingers had lost their suppleness, she'd known how to fool you into thinking they worked perfectly well, and doing the things she'd always done probably made it easier for her to hold her proud head up high when we were in her presence. With the thimble on her middle finger, she used to plunge her hands into her box full of spools and skeins as if preparing to thread her needle with another length of color, and she'd handle the fabric same as ever—all sorts of little gestures recalling the days when she embroidered so skillfully. Such were the habits that kept her going. But it became clear to me that she was no longer really sewing. Yes, that square of cloth with its uneven stitches moved me more than any of the others, because it showed me her strength of character, the power in her that made her determined to maintain her state of alertness as long as possible. It was only before she died that I began to appreciate certain facets of my grandmother's personality.

And so, if I'd reproduced the blue veins running through her temples, what was the matter with my doing justice to her wrinkled forehead? Her scarce white hairs, no longer buoyant, were held back by a comb that was too large and too heavy. Her face was like that of an emaciated cat, and perhaps I'd emphasized the way her lower lids seemed to collapse beneath the weight of her eyes, the way the tears rose periodically in them as if she were staring into a blizzard all day long; and then, too, her wrinkled lips beneath her terribly bony nose. But, in my defense, I hadn't stressed the way the complicated network of blood vessels stood out against the knots and creases of her thin hands, tempted though I was. The picture was, quite simply, true to life: nothing more or less. The vulnerability of this woman who had controlled all the people around her with a look or a word right up to the spring before she died had shaken me profoundly. With the tip of my brush I had touched her as if were holding her hand, looking inside her, making her my own, but without ever saying so, because I'd learned not to be too demonstrative. The weaker Grandmother became, the more compassion I felt for her. She was searching the eyes of others for approval of some sort, which made her more pleasant, but also more pitiful, and I was struggling, precisely, *not* to feel pity. Old age frightened me even more than death. We all have our own way of dealing with these inevitabilities.

"Who, besides other members of the family," I said, "could ever guess that she's the subject?"

"Whether or not you intended it to be my mother, that's who it is, and you've served her up in all her weakness, exposed her to the public, Mathilde! The very basis of your fame is your humiliating her! Why, I don't even think it's an especially good likeness . . ."

"So you acknowledge it! It's not a good likeness—precisely. Anyone who never met her would hardly make the connection. So what difference does it make? Don't tell me that, when you've gone to exhibitions with Aunt Dilys, you cared about who was sitting for what picture!"

Momentarily stymied on that front, she changed her line of attack: "They're hardly the best sort of people—those artists you and Frédéric run around with . . . I can see quite clearly that the effect they're having on you is hardly salutary."

"That's the real issue here, isn't it. And the lessons I took from M. Jacquier on Aunt Dilys's recommendation, you only let me have them because you didn't think they'd lead to anything. Just a nice way for a nice girl to waste her time till a nice man came along. Maybe it's not Grandmother's death that's changed your opinion, but rather the fact that Aunt Dilys has gone away to Brussels."

I spoke these words with such restraint that they crossed the table like cherry pits flicked silently from between my thumb and forefinger. Little projectiles fired with no great fuss, yet my mother was taken aback when they hit. I went on to defend the people "we ran around with." Our friends had, and still have, what it was I had been looking for and never found either in the apartment on rue Moncey or at Sainte-Colombe. They were wonderfully alive, madly inventive. They'd opened the doors and windows in my life. Even if I still wasn't always comfortable in my new milieu. Comfort wasn't the only thing in life. The time I spent with them was important, and the way they shook me up was good for me, all told; it was my great good fortune to share with them the freedom to paint for our living.

William frequently came back to spend time with us. He, in turn, used to take us along into his universe, wide as the sky, plentiful as all the roads in Europe or perhaps in the world. My mother didn't take *him* to task for his new life. I reminded her that she'd even gone proudly, when he'd asked her, to see the first aeronautical exposition under the glass dome of the Grand Palais. That was one month before the Paris floods. She cut me short in the middle of my tirade:

"Well, naturally, dear—that's different. He's a man . . ." As if, after all the trouble I'd taken merely to exist, she was telling me that, after all, I'd been brought up to be the dull stooge of some dull stooge of a husband, that I should now become gray as a stone wall. Only, even were I willing to play along with this idiocy, there was no way that I could strip away the years that I'd shared with Frédéric, that I'd spent working. The colors and shapes that I sold were permeated with my self, or should I say my selves, both physical and moral. I wanted to make my living doing this. We no longer, in fact, belonged to the same world at all, Mother and I. When she took little François to the Grand Palais to show him first the dirigibles and the famous Blériot XI that had crossed the Channel the year before, and then Santos-Dumont's *Demoiselle*, as well as numerous other giant birds with wooden wings covered in cloth that men had made so they could see the earth from above—well, she did it because he was a boy. I remembered Mother pointing out to her son all the extraordinary inventions at the exhibition, encouraging her little man to be fearless. As though the injustice done to me wasn't already so flagrantly obvious.

"Well, naturally," I said, "just because François will grow hair and have a gruff voice when he gets older makes it quite all right for you to encourage him to go out and break his neck. I was supposed to do embroidery when I got married, or perhaps paint pictures of little flowers to sell at charity events? A Sunday painter. Maybe I'd have a little time to doodle or do a little crocheting while my children were napping or when their nurse took them out for a walk. And meanwhile Eugénie would continue to flutter around while she waited to make the right match! So that's the ideal life you had in mind for your daughters?"

"Listen to you, Mathilde! I no longer know who you are."

"I'm speaking to you as someone unable to take another breath in the narrow-minded existence staked out for her. The existence you fled on the arm of Frank Lewly, who took you across the Channel. Yes, my husband comes from a family that had to work for a living—and that makes me very happy."

She hadn't touched the two little madeleines gleaming with orange marmalade in their saucer, and I no longer had any desire to sneak little looks at the trees in the Tuileries. I was surprised in spite of myself that Mother had nothing to say about my other pictures, all the ones hanging near the portrait of Grandmother—nothing about the originality of my subjects or the personality of my brush-strokes. She'd been a lot more articulate at exhibits when Aunt Dilys was with her.

"No, I don't recognize you either—it's been a long time since I did . . ." I murmured under my breath, but clearly enough for her to hear it.

What a good influence, in retrospect, father's cousin had had on my mother. I remember her much-talked-about entrance at Willon's Gallery barely ten years ago. How sure she seemed of herself with both her second husband and her cousin there! She'd spoken like someone who knew something about art! As I thought back, I wondered if she hadn't simply echoed the tastes of Dilys Lewly, if she hadn't just sprinkled opinions around simply to announce she was back in the fray, reentering society thanks to her remarriage and the recent birth of her son, which gave her a secure redoubt in the Versoix family. I'd been astonished to see her acting like a connoisseur of art.

So what was it that made up the character of my mother? Without Grandmother, without her English cousin and her husband, was she just some overgrown, lost child, or was she just Frank Lewly's widow now reclaiming the education composed of dour certainties to which she'd been subjected? Did Madame Versoix want to be a credit to her in-laws, a family composed of landowners who had become businessmen then men of some importance in Divonne-les-Bains? Aunt Dilys, who no longer spent any time with journalists and writers, had also been responsible for my mother's agreeing to my marriage. My mother was impressed, and at the time, influenced by her culture, her seeming prestige. However, it had been two years now since our cousin moved to Brussels, where, triumphantly, at the age of fifty, she'd just married the man she'd once made me believe was "a childhood friend." It had never occurred to me before this that M. Puck Chaudoy was the father of her child. So, this Belgian industrialist had been providing for a second family in Passy, waiting for the day he became a widower. Now I understood the mysterious look in Aunt Dilys's eyes and the secret of her self-assurance despite her being alone.

Had the Belgian critic who wanted to meet me at the exhibit been sent by her? She'd always encouraged me to paint—was she still looking out for me? That was something to think about.

The elegant woman, soon to be fifty years old, still sitting across the table from me at Angélina's, seemed very much alone to me. I could feel her dragging my sister into the shallow life that she had intended for me, the life led by so many other women. Despite my distaste for the child, it caused me no small anxiety. A hell of tedium. My mother couldn't have done more to convince me that all the images I had of her from our early days were false, had been a pretense, but here I was I was still trying to believe that I was wrong about her. But no—Jeanne Nolès, a Lewly by her first marriage, Madame Versoix by her second, was drifting along on the current of the established rules of the society that had produced her. She was taking up her own mother's role, now, in rebuking me. What sort of grandmother would she make? We'll see about that when her other three children provide her with descendants, I thought, because I didn't want to become a mother. I'd known for a long time that I didn't want to pass on the blood running in my veins. There was something unwholesome about it. And then, I was aware that children ate their mothers alive, leaving them scarcely any time for creative work. And, truly, being a mother scared me. Luckily, my body has naturally accorded with my decision. Or vice versa.

Mme Versoix was still beautiful, I saw. She was still charming, in her way. And yet the thing that I'd been most afraid of for the past few years was that I might one day resemble her. A fear of mirrors had come over me, of late. This despite the fact that I could still remember the days when my only ambition had been to be as much like her as possible.

27

The direction my life would take had been established for me one evening in Grandmother's house when I couldn't get to sleep. I'd formulated it clearly: when it comes time, I'll choose to *be* someone rather than *looking* like someone—existence over appearance. After the exhibition at Willon's I felt I was really alive at last. What I'd wanted was "to be someone" and now I *was* someone, and people knew it. Of course, it wasn't all about existence; I was flattered by all the talk going on about me; in spite of myself, I might even have become a little conceited.

Reading and rereading compliments about my work, hearing people speak well of me—well, it went to my head. I'd abruptly left my ordinary reality; I felt there were two of me, now: the celebrity and the woman. Despite the fact that I'd been waiting for this moment for years, I hadn't really been prepared for it; fame was like a hurricane knocking me on my face; it changed the way I saw myself to such an extent that—more or less as my mother had predicted—I no longer knew who I was. The earlier Mathilde was a stranger to this new one—the one now pleased with appearances, happy to be invited with Frédéric to receptions in the homes of renowned collectors and art lovers. So many Belgians—Americans too. Their compliments and observations were more than flattery to the child inside me who'd latched on to colors and lines as an escape from convent life; no, the little shallow girl inside me found comfort and consolation in all this. Yes, I passed along the flattering words and the approval I saw in my admirers' eyes to the little person curled up deep inside me, refusing to grow up.

It wasn't long before I felt an irresistible need to be seen alongside my friends in the fine restaurants or on the café terraces, making a spectacle of myself, to the amusement of everyone at my table. If there was a piano our friend Lulu Chevrier pounded out an accompaniment as William and I bellowed out the old songs we used to sing in our native language, or sometimes more recent ones in French. Our group's mounting euphoria only encouraged me to think of new ways to act out. I was unrecognizable when I was like that. To myself as well. Or, rather, I was letting that little monster within me peep just a little out into the open air: rediscovering the feelings of the child who'd been so full of life when my brother and I were the blissful center of our little universe. All the lively pleasure of those days had been channeled directly into my paintings.

But now, here I was, opening up in public. And I was beginning to like it.

Frédéric and I were having a second honeymoon. Our physical relationship was something we'd only gotten better at as we came to know each other so well after seven years of marriage. And then, I had money in my purse for the first time. Not the money Grandmother had left me, not my housekeeping money—it was definitely mine, and I paid for everyone's drinks just to show off, and moreover show I was free of all the old prejudices. I discovered what a voluptuous pleasure it is to have money I'd earned myself and to spend it—it was almost sensual, in fact, to complete furnishing our apartment or the studio, but also to buy new clothes, to treat everyone to whatever they wanted, to arrange to spend some time on the Riviera with Frédéric.

This was a notion that had been making some headway ever since we'd gotten a letter from our friend, Ernest Ponsal, who'd been down there since the end of summer. For several days I'd hesitated between returning to London, which I figured would be a somewhat overwhelming experience, emotionally; or, instead, taking off for the south. It became clear to me that the trip across the Channel was one I should make with William and no one else. And so I chose the Côte d'Azur. That this was now accessible to us was enormously satisfying in itself. I was in a hurry to leave, to immerse myself in a new landscape at last. I told myself that when I was there I'd pick up my pencils and brushes again and get some new work done.

Ever since the exhibit, I hadn't been able to concentrate well enough to take up oil or charcoal or even pencil; the studio and walls of the city felt too enclosed. I had a great desire to get away, to open myself up to new horizons. But we couldn't leave for the village by the bay in Provence until mid-February. As I waited I took advantage of what was, no doubt, a superficial and worldly life; I "did the city," as my mother would say. But I always kept my sketchbook and pencil in my purse or my pocket, and occasionally I'd make quick sketches of street scenes or the people on the café terraces.

I was looking forward to getting away. It would be an adventure.

28

Frédéric had extended an invitation to Eugénie at the Willon exhibition; she said she'd come to visit us before the year was up. To my great astonishment, she tiptoed in, when she finally took us up on that unfortunate encouragement—as though she was the sort of person who didn't want to get in the way, as though she was content to remain in the background. She was wearing a dress with a thick, winter lining and a collar edged in broad white lace; over it there was a dark, obviously well-made cloak trimmed in fur hung from her shoulders. Our dear old Mme Chesneau followed behind her, tightly wrapped in the thick boiled-wool cape that gave her the shape of a Russian doll. (Our governess, who had come to Grandmother's from Normandy when she was very young, had been so much a part of our life that our mother had kept her on to be with Eugénie and François.)

The minute she came through the door, I was reminded of the place Mme Chesneau had in my life. She was a stable element, even-tempered, her calm, steady gaze ever on the lookout to make sure there was nothing one needed. I'd become very attached to her. When I was married, and since Frédéric and I had no servants, she was the one who taught me how to cook the dishes she'd learned to make in Normandy; she'd taught me the art of making preserves, especially the quince jelly which she dripped through a cloth, refining it until the color was crystal clear, a red that was just barely orange to be lined up in jars on the pantry shelves. I wanted very much to welcome her in a manner proper to a lady worthy of our respect. Luckily, she was younger than my grandmother and still had many years ahead of her.

It was her presence that made me smile, because I found Eugénie's new discretion troubling rather than reassuring. Considering the state of our relationship, just about anything she might do would seem suspect. I dreamed of the day when we'd be separated by a good many miles. It would let us forget the now tainted connection between us and give her the time and distance to construct a personality far from my presence. It's intolerable to be able to read someone so close to you as though she were, indeed, an open book. I didn't even want her to see where we lived. But there she was, poking around!

Eugénie had just turned eighteen at the end of November. I hadn't gone to the party, since my mother hadn't answered the note I'd sent her after our last, unpleasant encounter. It occurred to me that my sister was only visiting because she wanted a birthday present, or maybe an early gift for New Year's Day. I resented the fact that she'd gotten me so unsettled that I had to read petty, untrustworthy motives into her every action. Recently, some American dealers who sold paintings abroad had held a gala affair. She'd begged me to get her an invitation, staring into my eyes so tenderly, just like in the old days at Grandmother's when she expected her big sister to give her everything she wanted. Because I wanted to make her understand that there was something more to life than the emptiness of her daily existence, I gave in. And then, too, a small voice inside kept reminding me of how long she had seen me as a villain. I was incapable of untangling these contradictions. Anyway, I certainly didn't mind showing her that I had new acquaintances in a world that she knew nothing about.

My sister stood perfectly still in the center of the room, glancing quickly and amiably around at everything and looking at all the changes we'd made to the studio. I suggested that she sit down on the English parlor sofa that we'd recently acquired from an antique dealer. Neither she nor I was acting naturally. Were we perhaps being extra careful after the terrible things we'd said in the Luxembourg Gardens, followed by that hateful encounter at the gallery? Or were we just harmlessly curious to see each other again after the Americans' soirée, which had much impressed her?

Mme Chesneau took a seat in an armchair far more comfortable than the one she used to have to contend with there in our studio; the springs in that old chair poked out in odd places. I sat in it instead. Frédéric, who was nearest his sister-in-law, began to tease her, as he often did, because it amused him to see how quickly she got upset. There was plenty of heat coming from the stove, enough that the teapot was soon hissing with steam. I put on a brave face and brought out a tea tray with a bowl full of madeleines. I didn't like seeing "the child" sullying this place where we spent so much time, either just Frédéric and I alone, or together with friends. I had a very strong sense that, even just by looking around, she was still managing to steal something from me. But I had to be nice.

Then came a sudden outburst, as if she were just waking up: "So! This is your moment of glory?"

Her tone seemed rather forced.

"Let's just say that things are going well for us both, but what's important for us is that it has to last. There's nothing more fickle than people's tastes, you know. Or an artist's aspirations. What an artist is trying to do, wants to do . . ." I replied.

I was toning down my enthusiasm in hopes of mollifying her. She'd do anything she could to bother me. But still, I couldn't help but want to wave this newfound happiness in her face like a flaming banner.

"Still," she said. "Having your picture in the papers! Not everybody gets to have that . . ."

Frédéric broke in: "So, my sister-in-law would like to have her photo in the paper, would she? Remember that first you'll have to produce a piece of work that has some character!"

I panicked. That was more than enough to trigger a cataclysm.

"Really now!" Eugénie exclaimed. "You mean to say I don't have any character, just because you've managed to make a name for yourself?"

"As for having character, *you* do have some, no one would deny it, but you'd have to assert it in your watercolors and drawings, my dear! I'm going to repeat what I said to your sister when she was your age: you either have or don't have talent, and if you have it you have to work, work, work, work, and work some more. In your case, you're doing yourself no favors keeping up this pretense that you were born to paint. Why not focus on your actual assets? You used to play the piano so nicely when I met you, but that seems like a lifetime ago!"

"Besides," I added. "Fame isn't the issue at all. What's most important to me is to spend my days doing what I love to do with people I love."

My sister's expression showed not only how hurt her feelings were, but also the indefinable pain gnawing away inside her. On the sofa the smile she put on to show a brave face was dulled—to me, at least, this was all quite clear—by her torment.

Now she caught sight of the three volumes of my plant album and exclaimed in astonishment, "So you kept that up?" So she must have lost hers, or perhaps forgotten about it—what a surprise.

I couldn't resist making her admit it: "And how is yours going?"

She rolled her eyes, looked infuriated, and sighed. In the ensuing silence I served everyone another cup of tea. Frédéric went to look for his pipe and tobacco. Eugénie, lolling against the back of the sofa with her legs stretched out in front of her and a thoughtful air, was looking around once again at our home, while I began to chatter away with Mme Chesneau. She'd spent several days, the All-Saints holiday, with what remained of her family in Normandy, she said. She'd been to visit her departed family as well, first among them her husband, who'd been killed during the siege of Paris. They'd both been born in the same village and it was where he now lay. Believing that her life had been filled, fulfilled by ours, I hadn't realized how alone she must have felt. Members of the French branch of our family who had died were buried seven or eight miles away on the plateau above Sainte-Colombe, in the cemetery near Bazemont village, and Frédéric had never visited it. As for the cemetery at Twickenham, I no longer had any memory of it.

I could hear Eugénie murmuring now, talking to herself, as if she were dreaming, and we were brought back to rue Chaptal. "It's nice here, in your place . . ." This simple observation, spoken unaffectedly, astonished me for a moment; then I thought, perhaps too quickly, and perhaps wrongly, but nonetheless with conviction: "A cuckoo in our nest!" I hoped I had misinterpreted. After all, wasn't she simply dreaming of the life awaiting her as soon as she was married? I can still remember the both wistful and envious sound of her voice as she spoke. I'd done everything to keep her from setting foot in there again, since the day of her first visit. When Grandmother died and the apartment on nearby rue Moncey was sold, keeping our distance was easier. I preferred going over to the Left Bank to having her come here. Why did Frédéric have to encourage her to come when we saw her at the opening? How could he ignore the danger she posed to me? I had the feeling, now that all the madeleines were gone, that she still wanted some cake. A huge cake to herself—but not one she'd have to knead with her own hands. To hide my uneasiness, and even though I knew I'd be sorry, I stood up and gave her one of my big drawings, and told her that she could also pick out one of my gouaches for her birthday. It was my way of saying, "The things I give you are things you won't take." Of course, I didn't clarify this point, merely adding, "Make sure you have it framed right away, it's likely to get ruined otherwise!" My hands were icy. I don't remember if they were shaking. I was a fake. My mouth tasted like the silt left at the bottom of a glass of cheap wine.

Our two guests stayed for almost an hour and a half, and we filled the time with apparently vapid conversation in an atmosphere that was far too calm. I would have liked not to be able to see through that calm to the hidden turmoil beneath; it didn't bode well at all. Calm lakes in the mountains frighten me: there are dangerous undercurrents moving through them, down deep in their depths; sometimes there are gaps and trenches that can swallow you whole, sucking you down horrible whirlpools. When we were with each other, Eugénie and I could sense everything the other was thinking. She was so nice that day that it put me on the alert.

The chaperone and her charge were preparing to leave before the dark December night shut in, when they were held up by an unexpected visit from Lucien Morel. Frédéric's friend greeted Eugénie with great cries of joy. I had a clear memory of Lucien emerging from the crowd when we were at the opening and discovering to his great delight the insolent young lady with a wheedling look on her face who had just slapped me with her bouquet of asters. A few minutes later I closed the door behind Mme Chesneau and my sister and hoped it would be a long time before I saw "the child" again—a very long time. I immediately told Lucien about our planned excursion to the Riviera and Frédéric suggested that he join us there. Ernest Ponsal, who was there already, was working on finding us a little house to rent.

Lucien's energy and his endless disagreements with Frédéric (an engineer's logic versus an artist's lack thereof) took over the studio. It brought us back to being ourselves, to doing the things we always did. I quickly cleared away the remnants of our afternoon snack and brought glasses and bottles out. Lucien—collapsed in the armchair that Mme Chesneau had just vacated—stoked his pipe with black tobacco and lit it dreamily.

Emptying their glasses, the two friends talked on and on. I loved their brotherly relationship. Just being with them, the feelings of constriction and suffocation that I'd felt with my sister went out the door behind her and vanished into thin air.

29

In mid-February we took the evening express and by morning were spellbound by the colors of the clear sky and their contrast with the great rusty shape of the Estérel plateau. The sun was rising and the closer the train came to our destination the more weightless some of its curves began to seem—the jagged rocks, brick-colored, had spurs studded with scrub growth and it all seemed lightly poised on the delicate limbs of almond trees, thousands of them in bloom, along with flowering mimosa.

Ernest Ponsal greeted us at the station in Saint-Raphaël; he was wearing faded clothes, not blue, not white, and clogs without socks, and, like any good local, was shading his eyes from the brilliant sun with his usual captain's hat. There he was, more intimidated than we. In Paris he used to wear a sleeveless vest over his shirt with a threadbare frock coat hiding it all, the visor of his cap pulled down low over his forehead . . . the only thing reminding us of the character we were used to seeing in Paris was the short briar pipe he chewed on even when it was unlit.

He looked happy on the station platform, if just a bit embarrassed, as though afraid of how we Parisians in our city outfits and with our city minds might judge him. It only took a few seconds for us to see that he was actually almost ashamed. And I understood immediately how ludicrous we must look in the crumpled city clothes in which we'd spent the night. He made us climb up into an unpainted wooden cart that he'd borrowed from the baker, then took up the reins with the air of someone who'd learned to do it before he was even born. He proudly planted himself in the white dusting of flour on the planks in front of us, and took the mare along the coast road between the sea and the hills, which gave us a chance to go into raptures about the splendor that had surrounded him ever since childhood and was no doubt the reason for his excellent way with bright colors. The moment we left town and discovered the green of the fallow countryside above the red rocks and the incredibly transparent sea, I recognized his painting style, and I'd almost like to say his soul, in the landscape. Maritime pines, parasol pines, cork oaks, eucalyptus trees, so many trees I'd heard people talk about but that I'd never seen or smelled. Here they grew in the wild. The fragrance made me think we'd come to the other end of the world. Lavender, juniper, rosemary, thyme, arbutus, and scotch broom. It was one thing to know that this scrubland of Provence, this *garrigue*, grew here, but something quite different now to discover it out in the open, seeing it storm the mountainous terrain that we were winding through on the bumpy seaside road at a happy and lively trot. The cool morning breeze stroked our faces and invigorated our senses. Frédéric and I held our breaths and held each other's hands and squeezed each other's fingers as we took in each new sight.

A few lateen sails were heading out to sea in all that shameless blue.

Ernest let us off in front of a shack, hardly better set than a shed, "the little house" he'd reserved for us across the Bay of Agay from where he lived. When we saw it, the three of us went slightly crazy and threw our arms around each other. When you first see this countryside, it comes as a sort of physical shock. We embraced the panorama visually as the gentle mid-February sun caressed us in turn, the brush crunched underfoot and scratched our ankles, and little waves whispered to us below our promontory. Our eyes followed the jagged line of the head of a blood-colored rocky peak emerging from the chaotic reds and thickened in places by the *garrigue* as it descended to a sea of indigo.

When I saw our little house I felt everything in me begin to expand. Ernest looked soberly on at our wonderment with his calm, easygoing smile. You could tell how happy he was to have had this surprise in store for us, as if he were the one who'd arranged the scenery just for our arrival and was, accordingly, proud of it. The fragrances of earth and *garrigue* blended with the sweeter scent of mimosa.

We had a month to frolic in this palette where the strong, contrasting colors were enough to make you a little unhinged. That our home was extremely rustic didn't matter at all—on the contrary. If it had been well-organized or too comfortable we wouldn't have had as much immediate physical contact with all that splendor. "It's going to be great!" said Frédéric, emerging apparently from his long, silent contemplation. It was time to wash up a bit and change our clothes. On one side of the house the iron spout of a hand pump tilted over a washtub. A pitcher and a basin were there too, and a metal tub was leaning up against the wall to warm in the sun so we could bathe outside in a corner where the earth underfoot was encircled by scrub brush. We could look out from there onto the vast horizon, sparkling with bountiful sunlight. One more thing to be happy about! Ernest had been living in a shed adjoining the fisherman's house belonging to his father. It had been turned into a studio for him and stood between Agay's little river and the long beach. In short, we'd be right across from each other on the bay. We freshened up and changed so all we had to do then was go back to the port together. He'd thought ahead and gotten his father's boat ready so he could show us the view from the water.

Once he was in the boat, our friend no longer showed any sign of the embarrassment he'd radiated as he watched us get off the train.

Too much joy? Too much happiness with Frédéric? Some fear that I was reaching the perfection that is always a sure sign that something can't continue? Why was it that I didn't have the energy to paint the aforementioned splendor, despite having hoped to throw myself into my painting as soon as we were settled? Mostly I had a mad desire to go on long jaunts or to nap for hours in sweet torpor. I never tired of the landscape, nor of the wild fragrances—sometimes bitter, sometimes sweet—hanging in the breeze. Every day I watched the two friends working as they sat on their folding chairs or in the little sailboat rocking us at the entrance to a *calanque* or even beneath the viaduct that was around the point at Anthéor. I just couldn't get started. The other two each went on with their quests, their inquiry into shapes and colors. Frédéric saw amazing geometric forms everywhere in the geological folds emphasized by the sun, making striking, unpredictable contrasts as it accentuated the dark shadows or flattened the hilly landscape. From that time on I saw broken lines on everything. The two friends plunged their brushes or knives into the soft paint on their palettes while I sat there deep in thought or sometimes with my mind completely empty. The Paris-

Lyon-Mediterranean express snaked along the coast. Its steam hung for an instant in the shriveled bushes on the slopes of the Estérel. So we always knew what time it was—not that we cared.

When I look back on all our years together, that visit to Agay is the time that remains the happiest of my married life. The burden of my youth had dropped away; I was a recognized painter who was taking advantage of her complete freedom for the first time. And then, I experienced immense happiness in the arms of the man I loved. It had been just ten years since we'd met near the pont de l'Europe, the day that the baby, François, was born. The unforgettable sixth of March, 1903.

A dream month.

My two companions worked while I savored the richness of doing nothing. Ernest would grill a few fish caught that morning and toss them onto our plates, telling us to put some olive oil on them; we gobbled them down with potatoes cooked under the ashes. When we'd go to the market in Saint-Raphaël, my eyes were drenched by the colors in the stalls, and I listened in amusement to the musical roar of the crowd's particular accent, which sounded both angry and overflowing with joie de vivre. We already knew what the accent would sound like—Ernest hadn't toned his down much at all, despite his years in Paris—but isolated in Paris it had none of the liveliness we found in the local population.

The days were all alike. Living with two men who were bound by a friendship without pretense pleased me as much as if it were something I'd accomplished myself. I had an animal need to surround myself with love.

I know how much we loved each other. There is nothing that will ever take that knowledge away from me, and yet Frédéric never told me so. Not before and not during this blessed period. He told me one day that he didn't know the meaning of the little words "I love you." I was astonished. But one night, in the crook of my arm and under the thousands of stars, he murmured, "I'm so happy that you exist . . ." I think that's a far better compliment than any "I love you." Then, our arms and legs entangled in the restful moments after making love, he whispered, "Sometimes I wonder why, after all these years, you still haven't had a baby." The heavens seemed to flicker above us for a moment, and I almost expected that the usual voices full of reproach were going to rise up in the dark to echo his. I too was surprised that I hadn't gotten pregnant.

My mother, of course, had been abundantly fertile, marriage to marriage. But I, in my most secret prayers, had made a pact with the gods: "Please, I beg you, don't send me children!" I'd never dared confess how strongly, deep inside me, I refused to be a mother. Because he was nine years older than I, Frédéric would have been able to become a father long before we'd met. I often thought that I'd willingly raise his child, but would never subject myself to a pregnancy. Every month I'd welcome my period with a sense of relief. My tainted blood would stay put, wouldn't transmit its curse to another generation. Which is not to say that it wasn't a difficult transition, having cramps, hiding stains that now seemed humiliating to me, living alongside the man I loved. I had a deep disgust for myself and it made me afraid he'd find me repulsive. Though gradually I adapted to the intimacy of being in the same bed, I was never able to see my blood without a sense of panic. Even so, until it came, I was desperate to see it each month, because it was a confirmation that my body too had once more refused to give birth. "Don't forget that I'm almost forty," Frédéric added. He sounded resigned.

"Life will make the decision, my love . . . I'm still young."

As I murmured those words, I was saying to myself at the same time. "Let's hope it never happens . . . I was born to bring other things than babies into the world." All I had to do was keep my opinion to myself, on this score, and we could continue living the way we always lived, and now take advantage of the dazzling springtime on the Riviera . . .

But a change did come to the harmony of the informal arrangement in which we'd found places for ourselves, maybe roles to play, when Ernest got a telegram from Lucien announcing his arrival. He'd decided to come after he read our postcard telling him that we were going to stay longer, until the beginning of April. I'd forgotten that Frédéric had suggested he join us.

30

The two friends in their country clothes, clogs on their feet, and I, wearing a cotton dress, my bare feet in sandals, greeted Lucien at the station, with the odd sense that we were now on different wavelengths. The same feeling, probably, that Ernest had had when we arrived. Something in Lucien's eyes, his laughter and the way he moved, something too about his clothes, seemed exaggerated—too much. Frédéric and I realized that we'd put aside our city customs and that Lucien, even in the manner of his greeting, wasn't *with* us anymore; somehow, he was off. Actually, none of us had dared express our vague annoyance at the thought of Lucien's citified intrusion, but, honestly—he wasn't even a painter! Some slight uneasiness had been hovering over us since the day his message had arrived. Our friendship toward Lucien wasn't in question, of course, but perhaps we were apprehensive about how our peaceful lives would change, how we would have to adapt to a fourth presence in our Eden.

The Parisian tapped his old friend, Frédéric, on the shoulder, as if trying to bring him around, but it didn't elicit the reaction he expected. Frédéric just asked him calmly if he'd had a nice trip, then Ernest and I shook his hand in a friendly manner. We weren't hostile, we were just "different," and we couldn't say exactly how. We led him over to the baker's cart: "Come on! Forget everything else and jump in!" Frédéric told him. Lucien laughed heartily. But his laugh too seemed too much. Clearly he was more and more troubled by our reserve, by how insistently we were treating him like a stranger, despite how well we knew one another.

"So how are you, the three of you? Are you enjoying yourselves here?" he said, to break the tension.

"Open your eyes and tell us whether or not you'd be enjoying yourself here!" Frédéric replied, waving his hand before us to lead him to an appreciation of the Estérel's peaks and the thick vegetation plunging straight down to the Méditerranean. "All this is ours! And you've come just in time to see the fruit trees blooming . . ."

We were puzzled about where he should sleep. With us, since he was Frédéric's friend, or with Ernest, because we were a couple?

Ernest suggested, as if it were the most natural thing in the world, that he could set up a second pallet in his shack, which was composed of one room with one window and one door, the top of the latter with glass panes in it. Both looked out on the bay and both were almost always open. Fresh water came from the iron pump a short distance away, under the parasol pines along the pebble road leading to where Agay's little stream emptied into the bay. After they had unloaded their boats or mended their nets, a few local fishermen would gather there before they went up to the bar in town to drink their evening pastis. "Living like this is great! You'll see!" Frédéric insisted to forestall any disappointment on Lucien's part. Ernest sat down on the bench next to the door, leaving room for Lucien, then offered him some tobacco. Frédéric and I sat facing them on the tin buckets that turned the space outside into a living room. We looked at first one and then the other of the two men now smoking their pipes peacefully. Ernest's craggy face was roughened by living out of doors for six months, while Lucien's was gray and unshaven after the night spent on the train and, of course, months and years in the polluted air of Paris. Just at nightfall, an old man who looked as if he were carved from a twisted piece of cork oak limped by, carrying a basket. He was obviously very busy and determined to get what he had to do done, greeting us with only "good evening" as he vanished behind the beaded curtain of the house next door—Ernest's father. Some evenings he'd come over and we'd have a drink, but seeing the four of us together, he simply greeted us and looked busy so we wouldn't invite him to join in.

Early the next morning, our two friends came to meet us on the promontory where we lived. We had coffee together and shared a loaf of bread and some fruit. Then Lucien asked, "What are we going to do today?" We'd never given any thought to such questions. The day after we'd arrived, we were been irresistibly drawn to the hills and usually climbed them once a day, with our painting materials tucked under our arms. Or else, when Ernest could get hold of his father's boat we'd explore the inlets, likewise armed with the materials of our art—never knowing, as far as my own work went, that there would be no real use for them.

Frédéric stepped in to avoid an argument and suggested that he and Lucien climb "up there," pointing to Cap Roux. As soon as they were gone, I looked questioningly at Ernest. He had his hands full of his painting things, so I went to get mine.

"How about the viaduct at Anthéor?" I suggested, thinking how peculiar it was that Frédéric and Lucien's defection seemed to disturb us so.

Oddly, this was the day on which I took up my crayons and pastels again.

Ernest had promised to bring a selection of oils and watercolors back to his dealer, who was going off in June to sell them in the United States. Our arrival had stimulated him after his having been alone for months. I had no way of knowing in advance, but it seemed I'd been waiting for our trio to break up, as if I only knew how to paint with one other person around. I wanted and needed to change my style. I too had been struck by the shadows that were like clean breaks marked on the rocks, depending on the time of day, and I liked playing with the ochres and reds of the earth here. I didn't approach colors and shapes the same way anymore. I worked at giving the impression that the rock, the viaduct, and the boats, broken by imaginary lines, were just about to fall into the abyss of their shadow; I was trying to show them losing their balance between the light and the dark shadows splitting them in two.

Apart from a few excursions that the four of us made together, the group split in two every morning: there were the walkers and there were the artists. And it was fine like that. Our little group would get back together when it was time for an evening aperitif. Afterward, we'd put something together on the grill and throw a splash of the local wine on it. While we were eating, the two walkers talked about where they'd been, the fragrances and the overwhelming solitude in the middle of the mountains. Once, early in the morning, they'd even met up with some herds of wild boars. In three days Lucien had lost the "too muchness" that had bothered us when he got off the train. Glasses in hand, we greeted the dusk as the blazing light of the sun's last blessing fell on the Estérel. Then as soon as the sun vanished in the west the cool of the evening would send us indoors. At nightfall, under the starry sky, Frédéric and I would walk "back home" with our arms around each other, down along the beach where a few boats dozed, dark masses like large marine mammals asleep under the parasol pines.

One night he asked, in what seemed to me an odd tone of voice, "Do you know that your sister is painting quite a lot and hopes to exhibit her work at Lamain's gallery?"

"This obviously comes from Lucien . . ."

"I can't think of who it was that told me. But, yes, Lucien is encouraging her in that direction and acting as the middleman with the dealer. I don't even know if he realizes how trite and ordinary she is when she draws. In my opinion, he's crazy about her and will just do anything to please her . . ."

Ever since our exhibit I'd been expecting something like this, though I'd tried to repress the thought. If she ever managed to get her hands on Lucien, she'd become part of the crowd at Prosper and once again invade my life . . .

My reaction to the mere prospect of this was so violent that I nearly couldn't contain myself—something had happened at last, a line had finally been drawn. Though I would have considered it monstrous before to form the thought, it now became explicit in my mind: "My sister has become my enemy . . ." Well, it had been true for a good long while already, I still had never acknowledged it, even to myself, so explicitly.

"You don't have anything to say?" Frédéric asked.

"What do you want me to say? Or do, for that matter? She keeps on trying to eat away at my territory, just the way she always has. I'd hoped that sooner or later my marriage would put some distance between us, but now it seems likely that the opposite will happen."

"Do you think she loves him?"

"I think he loves her and she'll turn this to her advantage. He represents a door leading to a way for her to get back in with William and me, and at the same time Lucien will ensure that she has some real standing in our world. I'd rather she love Lucien for himself, but I doubt she does."

"Don't exaggerate. She hasn't invaded our lives as much as you say."

"Not *ours*. Mine."

The sparkling sea was surrounded by darkness, and beyond it I could make out a shadow descending on our corner of Clichy. And since I wasn't going to kill my sister, tempting though this solution was, I had to avoid who knows what catastrophe by trying to make her welcome in our midst. Once again, the big girl had to give in to the baby! At twenty-seven, I was being made to feel twenty again—and all because that little, empty-headed egotist was herself turning into a woman.

The final days of our vacation had been ruined for me. I couldn't relax with Lucien there. He'd already tried several times to make me talk about my family, about the days when we lived in England, as if he too wanted to intrude on my memories. And he took every opportunity to go into raptures about sister's impetuosity, her "unique" laughter. One day I cut short his enthusiasm by reminding him that I was there to forget Paris and Parisians. But I was probably a little too curt. Maybe even mean. My tone must have conveyed my bile, to some extent, because my three companions stared at me in astonishment thick with disapproval. Even Frédéric.

From then on, whenever I went with Ernest to set up my easel in one of the *calanques* or even just in front of his shack to sketch the men busy tending their nets or working on the hulls of their boats—caulking or repainting them—I felt I was in danger. But who could I tell?

April came. We were going back. The anger inside me was no less incredible, but still unmentionable.

31

For a month and a half we'd been soaking up the gentle Mediterranean climate where everything was in full bloom already, so the still shriveled foliage around Paris gave the impression that we were going backward in time. I'd have liked it if that had been true, if we could have returned to the days before Lucien had joined us in our paradise.

It didn't take long to find out how much trouble he'd gone to in order to get Lamain to accept Eugénie's participation in the exhibit he was planning for the end of September. Some people said that he'd paid to have one of her gouaches and one of her watercolors shown, which confirmed the reputation of this new dealer, a man who'd owned a junk shop up until just a few months ago and had not yet earned much respect in the art world. Real, long-established dealers wouldn't have let themselves be bought like that. Eugénie would have liked to show at least four canvases but there wasn't enough space in the one-room gallery.

I learned all that from Frédéric as the days went by. He seemed amused and joked about it the way an older brother might, seeing his little sister make a silly mistake. He never dwelled on it, but would come out with a remark here and there, when it occurred to him. One day he told me that Eugénie was signing her works simply with a first name—*Eugène*—so as not to be the second of the Lewlys. Besides which, using a man's name probably made her think that she would be able to buy herself some credibility by pretending to have the same temperament as a George Sand or a Daniel Stern. I knew she was capable of asserting a will strong as any on earth, but it had always and only been to shoot me down. Beyond that, did she have any real interests? I couldn't think of a single one. My mother had been in despair on the subject when we were at Angélina's. "Do you have any idea the extent to which you overshadow her?" Frédéric asked me one evening as I sat on the sofa while he was cleaning his brushes. Here was cause for alarm. He'd spoken to me as if he were gently reproaching someone for her bad treatment of someone who was, perhaps, just a bit simple. All the compassion he seemed capable of feeling was in his voice and mustered on Eugénie's account rather than my own. It left me terribly anxious.

I was appalled by how much this clash with my sister was weighing me down. And, since I'd never managed to fulfill my mission of passing on to her some of the happiness we'd gotten from our father, my conscience was still troubled, especially since I'd told her that she'd been unwanted, as far as he was concerned. Eugénie had a mother already—why had I taken on that role? How was it possible that the pure happiness I'd felt during the first months of my sister's life could turn into such intense hatred? I was continually baffled by it, as I'd been, it seemed, for most of my life; one word in particular kept running through my mind, more and more often now, though it was still hard for me to say it: *hatred*. If I'd been able to get it out of me, put it on the table, I don't think I would have been able to look at it. I was afraid of its shape and texture; I was afraid that, if it had eyes, they would be accusing—forcing me to lower mine.

In the studio, something had changed in our life.

Lucien, who used to drop by frequently to have a drink and smoke his pipe, now only paid brief visits to take Frédéric off with him. The two of them spent longer and longer away. Not even at Prosper's Café. I was excluded from their secrets and sensed that Eugénie's influence was behind it; not satisfied with infiltrating my world, she was trying to chase me out of it. What had she said to Lucien that made him seem so distant toward me now? I went back over the scene in the Luxembourg Gardens and saw myself telling my sister that her father hadn't wanted her. I was ashamed and furious at myself. However, all I had to do was remember her monstrous attack on my watercolor; the mere thought made me want to tell her the truth all over again, or else, as they'd have said in the port of Agay, just beat the tar out of her.

Eugénie used Lucien because he loved her. When you knew her as well as I did, it was hard not to assume that. And he was unaware of it precisely because he loved her. One day, when Frédéric was away, I'd welcomed him into the studio and suggested he wait a while on the sofa and have something to drink, maybe a cup of coffee, but he'd seemed so at a loss, so uncomfortable and hesitant to say anything that I let him go without insisting. I thought: He can't face me anymore! So he fled, as it were, turning around to thank me far too profusely, with gestures that were frankly ridiculous, his eyes begging me not to have any hard feelings, before disappearing behind the privet. I was sad, very sad to find myself alone there where the memory of our laughter and wonderful conversations seemed to echo still, but now in a strange void.

I had a premonition that our crowd in Clichy was coming apart. Though there had been crises between one clique or another, they'd never made a dent in our overall understanding. Some of our heretics went across the Seine to join the artists in Montparnasse, but without causing any real imbalance in our existence. We'd see them every now and then, run into them when we'd be walking around that part of Paris. Montmartre was a cosmopolitan village inside the big city, populated by destitute and free-living artists who'd come there mainly from areas off to the east. Somewhat isolated from the rest of the capital, it was populated by painters, hoodlums, and the lower classes. We'd stop for a drink at the Rotonde or the Dôme, go dancing at Bullier's dance hall, and then go back to Prosper's again, where nothing had changed.

But all that was before we went to the Riviera.

Now I was apprehensive when I went to our usual café. I never uttered my sister's name, but sooner or later people ended up talking about her. Not everyone knew her yet, but the few who'd seen her spent a lot of time on the subject of how beautiful she was. The news had gone around that Lucien and she were already engaged, and no one there really dared say what he thought. I sensed they felt awkward. I was gratified that there were at least a few who expressed reservations about Eugénie's talent—but, actually, they preferred criticizing her dealer, saying he made poor choices, rather than go after Eugénie herself. Keeping their voices low, as if they didn't want me to hear, they expressed their opinion that other, more talented, more deserving artists should have been chosen for the upcoming show. But, listening nevertheless, I came away with a sense of relief and superiority; that they saw the situation this way made me unacceptably happy. My sister lacked vision, discipline, and a good deal more . . . But, even though they didn't seem to have a very pleasant opinion of her, which was pleasant enough for me to know, I realized that, like a curse following me wherever I went, she was *still* managing to have an impact in my world. I'd have been so happy to support and applaud her triumphs on the piano, where she would have had all the lights of the concert hall upon her! She would have differentiated herself from me and we'd have had the pleasure of welcoming each other into our respective worlds; whereas now I wanted, quite simply, to smother her, make her disappear, because she wasn't in our midst to be an artist but to be a thief.

However, I didn't want to expend my energy, dissipate the strength I needed for my work in just any intervention. What could I have done, anyway? What could I have said to discredit Eugénie and make her go away? If I'd had any such power, I'd have lowered myself and used it, I knew. But I wasn't going to interrupt people's conversations to say "it's her or me!" or "don't mention her in my presence!" That would have been ridiculous, even if I could really have made myself do it.

However, I was playing a sort of double game. As if I were just making an innocent inquiry, I was busily picking up details about the steps it had taken to organize her showing at Lamain's gallery; I was trying to find more out about what sort of spirits my sister was in and about her marriage plans. At the same time, I steered clear of even the least indication that she'd been backed up and encouraged by Lucien—since Frédéric might be playing a role in all that. But I just didn't know how to broach the question with him calmly, nor did I want to show just how jealous I was getting. So, when I was with the usual crowd at Prosper's, I had no choice but to pretend. Saying that I encouraged Eugénie's undertaking in a lukewarm manner that might have led them to believe it all was just water off a duck's back—telling them I thought expressing one's talent was the only thing that counted in life. That seemed the best way to avoid any disloyal, hurtful remarks. Really, the best thing would have been for me not to go and join them at the café at all, but that would have left the territory free for my enemy and I'd have found myself alone again. Anyway, I valued being with this band of artists; it had once been my freedom, my happiness.

How would I have felt in this situation if Eugénie had had talent? The thought occurred to me one day and the nausea that came over me was a sign of how relieved I was that she had none. I'd have liked not to obsess over the damned exhibition coming up soon, but it ceaselessly, insidiously occupied my thoughts. Though I turned my mind to its usual preoccupations—that is, my work and our life as a couple—I felt the drumbeats inside my breast rattling a little too fast, pins and needles in my veins, and I had an unexpected sense of being unsteady on my feet—well-camouflaged reminders of my obsession. I had to take deep breaths, straighten up the studio, do some housework, or walk quickly over to the lively scenes along the Seine, taking the broad avenue de l'Opéra, then going through the Carrousel Garden to get out of doors, to get some air. I prayed my thoughts would be drawn to the excitement outside and gradually cease to be so chaotic. And, though I no longer found Café Prosper to be a restful place, it didn't keep me from going there.

The things going on between my sister and me, all the things others couldn't see, seemed to have a logic to itself that was, nonetheless, foreign to my nature. Confronting it would have been an attack on the foundation of our existence: our mother. When we'd had our conversation at Angélina's, she'd sighed as though confronted by an awful inevitability and said, "You now have a little sister, you know. Don't insist." Yes, there she was, my little sister, and there was nothing we could do to change that. All her life, the little girl had looked up to her two elder siblings who'd been unaware of the position they already occupied when they paid their monthly visits to rue Moncey . . .

William was clearly less sensitive than I to the upheaval that was to come; the world of painting was not his. Our lives were different, but we remained close, which made it possible for us to appreciate, complement, and remain attentive to one another the minute he walked through the door to the Café Prosper or came into our studio.

I needed that place of refuge in the rear of the courtyard. I was reassured by its walls, by the usual mess inside, reflecting our existence. There was the little parlor separating Frédéric's area from mine and bringing to mind so many visits, back in the old days; and then there was the big window opening onto the privet hedge that sheltered us from any outsiders looking in and smelled so delicious at the beginning of summer—all gently enfolding me in their benevolence.

We were getting ready to return to the Côte d'Azur for a couple of weeks in July before taking off for Italy. It was time to discover Venice and Rome and be back together, just the two of us, as lovers. We were planning to come back by way of a slight detour to visit Frédéric's family during the first week in September. Already the Lamain exhibit was coming up, to be followed not long after by the show at the Willon Gallery in which we were taking part. Then the end of 1913 would be in sight. Time seemed to be moving more rapidly than it once had.

32

We never drink twice from the same river, I've been told. We were staying in the same little house looking out on the Bay of Agay, as before, when that saying came to mind. The sun beat down relentlessly despite the parasol pine guaranteeing shade at midday. We slept under the living, trembling canopy of heaven, full of gleams multiplied in the sea that swirled down below us. All around, everything vibrated night and day in the scorched grass and shriveled leaves, all of it throbbing with so many tiny lives. There was even a pulse to the repetitive movements of the little waves you could hear soughing on the rocks beneath the endless buzzing of cicadas, which grew louder and louder as the sun rose higher in the sky.

But between Frédéric and me, everything seemed motionless.

I thought I'd detected some change in the way he was acting toward me, including how he seemed to feel about me in bed. Or was it just because I'd become so mistrustful that my own perception had changed? I persuaded myself that I was wrong and forbade myself to waste any more time worrying about it, or even to ask any questions—as if a single word might make the stars rain down on us and set off a tidal wave, or bring on the end of the world. Especially a word of the truth.

I needed to focus on happiness, hoping to bring back our state of grace the way you prime a pump with a pitcherful of water. So I could never get my fill of our three-month-old memories, though they seemed so distant now. I didn't realize how often I was repeating, "Remember when . . . ?" or "This is where we picnicked . . . where you set up your easel," which all came down to the same thing. There was more life in the recent past than in our present. Frédéric, however, seemed his old self when he was with Ernest Ponsal. I tormented myself, thinking it was all in my head—or else, simply, all my fault.

There was something too unruffled and well-behaved about the trip for it to distract me from my anxieties. In Venice I was the one who embraced Frédéric the first time we went under the Bridge of Sighs, which I'd been told had been named for lovers. He let it happen but didn't react, didn't show any of the tender affection he'd had when we'd first seen the Estérel a few months earlier . . . When I found out that the covered bridge, with the two little *mashrabiya* windows in the stone walls on either side of it, connected the Doge's Palace on one side of the canal to the ancient prisons on the other, and that it was the men due to spend the rest of their life in jail who had sighed, supposedly, as they looked down on the lagoon for the last time, having a final glimpse of freedom, I regretted my impulsive gesture. Not because I was thinking about those poor men, but out of superstition. I imagined that the real meaning of the bridge had been the reason Frédéric hadn't reacted. I was prepared to imagine anything that would persuade me that I was distorting my perception—that really, nothing had changed between us.

Venice floating on the water in the brilliant sunlight seemed gloomy to me. Its palaces with façades discolored by their weeping windows over the centuries; its narrow, dark alleys ending in little bridges where, at the surface of the blue waters with their constant lapping, you saw doors opening inside from the back walls of leprous palaces . . . Really, the whole place depressed me. Dark corners suggested crime, betrayals, adultery. On the third day of our wanderings through the mazes between the canals, the alleyways decorated with flowers, the sumptuous palaces now in decay, and the charming squares surrounded by sluggish water, my anguish suddenly became unendurable. We left for Rome sooner than we'd expected.

Frédéric made no comment on my haste to leave.

I was feeling something, something completely unknown to me up to this point, and it began to become clearer with every day that went by. I felt us approaching a threshold at which I would no longer know what he was thinking or feeling. A threshold I didn't want to cross. For almost ten years the way we shared things had been a gift; now, in its place, silence—while not hostile—was settling down on us the way snow falls, covering the landscape . . . Because Frédéric kept on smiling, listening, talking—but it seemed done out of politeness. Gone was his spontaneity, my access to his deepest thoughts. And it worked both ways: he was no longer looking inside me; he was just skimming past me in search of all the other interesting things to look at in the distance. My mind told itself not to form any conclusions about that politeness, but my body already knew what it meant.

Rome and its 2,500 years of history all piled one on top the other, overlapping, interlinked: its Tiber, its Titus Livy, its Romulus and Remus suckling the she-wolf, its Horatii versus the Curatii, its great fire; its hills and valleys blistered with pediments, triumphal arches, ancient columns, the Coliseum, the Pantheon, the Vatican, Saint John Lateran, the Trevi Fountain; its bell-towers, fragrant gardens, winding alleys . . . "Rome, Rome sole object of my rancor!"*

It had become a drug: I had to see old stones and then I had to see more old stones. They reminded me of those impassioned monologues; treading on the stones two thousand years after the heroes and heroines of antiquity had walked there gave me vertigo. The dead were not entirely dead, thanks to the authors who'd made the legends their own . . . Leaving my own reality I was becoming submerged in the reality of the books made eternal by their verses. Memories of my studious youth and evenings in the theater with Aunt Dilys. I could still remember some of the names but no longer knew who was who. Their voices rose up in my memory, as if, after having been shut up in libraries for centuries, they were now, with the aid of my imagination, emerging from between those stones to haunt once again their natural environment . . . Declaiming the lines written, in sorrow perhaps, two-hundred and fifty years before, filling my voice with their fervor in the very places that had inspired them, moved me as deeply as if I were touching the flesh of those who had left us. As long as I took refuge in history, enough bits of which still remained—badly rearranged no doubt, but there to give life to the ruins—I forgot my obsessions and, relieved of their burden, felt lighter. I recited a few alexandrines to Frédéric. When he was able to quote the words that came next, I was happy, for a brief moment, believing we still had much to say to each other.

---

* A quote from Corneille's play *Horace* in which Camille's lover is killed by her brother in a dispute over the control of Rome. Every French school child knows (or, at least used to know) the scene by heart: "*Rome, l'unique objet de mon ressentiment!*"

Over and over, in the midst of the Roman ruins, I recited Camille's curses as I'd learned them from Corneille! But it was too bad that my repressed anger had nothing to do with the conflict pitting the Horatii against the Curiatii in ancient Rome! I needed Corneille's words to set me free of my rage. Ah! I suddenly felt so much love for the French language!

We took our sketching pads and our crayons with us and each of us would choose a different hillside for a model—all their shapes complicated by ancient monuments standing out with their sharp, blunt edges against the rocky background. Just as we used to in the old days in the Louvre, we sketched different angles, capitals, columns, mutilated statues, simple paving stones, or crumbling rock. In our silent concentration we were really together once again, or at least, so I believed. It was now my turn to begin to love the geometry that could be detected in things, monuments, and landscape. But above all thanks to the shadows reshaping them in the dazzling light. I wanted, again, to show all these things on the edge of becoming chromatically unbalanced, the way I had before, showing the point at which the shadow turned into an abyss into which the things of this world were on the verge of falling. I'd been painting this way ever since our first visit to the Estérel landscape. I was hoping to have a series of paintings at Willon's next big show that would demonstrate this new way of seeing the world—that is, on the brink. The way my brush moved in the thick color was to give the impression of an imminent fall into empty shadow:

> "Oh, that it were my lot to see Rome
> destroyed by my hand, and then die
> of that pleasure!"

33

Going back to our usual environment on Rue Chaptal was even harder.

Seeing our faithful furnishings, our knickknacks, the curtains that had been pulled to protect the rugs and wood inlays against the sunlight, brought my heart into my throat. Everything seemed frozen in a state of expectation. The minute I stepped into our place I knew that nothing would ever be the same, and the dam that had held back my tears since the beginning of the summer broke. I couldn't hold back my sobbing question, "What's happened to us since our first visit to Agay?"

Frédéric wrapped his arms around my neck and sighed.

"Try to carry on if you can," he whispered as if he were telling me a secret. "The two of us have something so profound, so rich. Never forget, Mathilde, how deep we go together. I'm going through a tough time. But remember, above all, that we're here together, and that we'll still be together tomorrow and all the days after . . . That's what's most important."

"That doesn't make me feel a bit better. I'm frightened, Frédéric. I feel as though you're no longer with me . . . I don't get to watch you work anymore . . . I don't have you near to give me strength . . . you're so far away, always running around with Lucien, going wherever he goes. And Lucien is avoiding me! You're hiding something from me . . . or perhaps it's some*body*? If only you knew how horrible it is to torture oneself with things that might or might not be true."

His only response was to hug me tightly against him.

Being alone now in the studio felt different from the times he used to go and work in people's homes or meet with friends without me. I imagined what a curse it would be if I were now expecting a child. Without being certain of its father's love, how could I be certain I'd have any love for his child? The two things go together. I was positive of that much, at least.

Now I know how to recognize the imperceptible changes that take place in a man's behavior when he's fallen out of love—the effort he takes, for example, to make his voice sound natural. And then there were his eyes—I'd come up against a new barrier in Frédéric's gaze that held me at a distance. The worst was that I could see this same barrier in his now distant smile. A simple glance is enough to make me fall on my knees or jump for joy, when I love someone; whatever you want me to do, I'll do. My passion for my mother, at least until she married for the second time, had made me surrender to her entirely. It was for her that I "gave in to the child," for her sake I'd said nothing about my distress at being locked up with those nuns; and then, after my mother had left rue Moncey, taking her baby with her, I'd been the person they'd used to make sure my grandmother had company. I'd had no existence of my own, hoping this would make Mother love me more. All that suffering just to have such a strained relationship with her, one that was, perhaps, empty.

But this was different. Frédéric asked nothing of me. Which was worse.

I felt unwelcome. All my fears of abandonment rose up again, making me feel guilty of having done something wrong without my knowing what it was I'd done. It was a time when I'd have liked to be indispensable somewhere in the world. Even to Grandmother.

We went on with our life, albeit not as before, because, despite Frédéric's assertions about the profundity of our attachment, I felt I was dangling over a void—but we went back to our routine, to some degree, thanks to the upcoming exhibition at Willon's gallery just three weeks after my little sister would have hers at Lamain's. "She doesn't know that she's risking making a fool of herself. It's done no good to warn Lucien . . ." Frédéric remarked skeptically, his voice full of a big brother's concern and compassion. It did me good to hear him say that; it made me feel sure of one thing, at least: he respected me, he recognized my work as a painter, and saw that Eugénie's lacked quality. On that subject, nothing had changed between us —quite the opposite. He regularly encouraged, even complimented me. He liked how I was playing with shadows now—those bottomless abysses calling out to the sunlit elements on their brink. That, in the end, was where we were most deeply connected. When he spoke about painting to me, his voice really sounded like his voice; his eyes forgot to evade mine. In the presence of my work and, of course, in the presence of his, Frédéric was fully alive.

But, saying he'd been commissioned to do some *plein air* work, Frédéric hardly ever painted in the studio now. He didn't suspect that I didn't believe his story. The thought that I had a rival haunted me; was it knowledge I refused to know? How I wished I could keep myself from falling into those abysses; how I wished I could keep on hoping.

34

I'd been tempted not to go to the show at Lamain's. But, in all likelihood, I would have regretted being as weak as that. I needed to face my adversary, figure out the extent of the danger she was posing, and be a good sport to boot. Eugénie, however, hadn't invited me. Even so, if I came surrounded by Frédéric and my friends, what could she do?

I did want to see how her painting skills had developed. Also, whether or not she had finally asserted anything resembling her own personality. I felt my heart shrink in reaction to this thought and knew that deep inside I didn't want her to develop. My next reaction, after I'd given some more thought to the question, was to tell myself quietly that if, in fact, she *had* progressed, then I should admit it. Doubts as to whether or not I could stomach my sister's being in the spotlight in my own world continued to haunt me, of course. Might Eugénie, now engaged and on her way into life as an adult, perhaps have gone further into her art than I imagined? Might she not have uncovered some real talent in herself, at last?

In the late afternoon we all trooped over together: Ernest Ponsal, Alfred Molinier, Caroline Mabain, Louise Foucher, Loulou Chevrier, and I. Lucien and Frédéric had gone earlier, and I'd put off going for as long as possible by taking a lot of time to get ready—pretending I'd lost my gloves, then my purse, all in the hope of avoiding my mother, who, for her part, had been keeping her distance ever since our tea at Angélina's. The thought of meeting her again in the very environment she'd been so critical of, my own milieu, where I'd made a place for myself, made me even more uneasy.

But I didn't escape a brief encounter. She was leaving just as we arrived. After we exchanged a few words and I'd hugged little François, who had grown quite a bit since my opening at Willon's almost a year ago, I took refuge in the middle of our party as though I were hiding behind a wall. I needed to watch how each of my friends reacted to Eugénie's pictures, and figure out what their opinions were, their impressions, in advance of their open discussion of it when we left and they had a drink together. Actually, they were mostly curious to see this girl who had cast such a spell over Lucien.

I kept slightly to the side, protected from my sister's eyes by the veil I was wearing. Meant to cover your hair and face when you rode in an automobile, it was made of silk threads that were more tightly woven than a hairnet, which made it possible to see through it but without being recognizable oneself. My heart was beating too fast and I kept looking desperately over at the entrance, trying to catch my mother before she got away, hoping we could exchange a smile of peace: the coldness and accusation I'd seen in her eyes were deeply painful to me. I would never be able to take back the words with which I'd revealed to Eugénie that her father hadn't wanted her, and I was certain now that my sister had confided in her mother; I'd have done the same. How could I be pardoned for what I'd said? I could hardly bear the memory—even worse, I could hardly stand the fact that I'd revealed something so inconceivable to my little sister out of pure malice. But too much raking over these coals might set alight all the resentment I'd been keeping back. As usual, I needed to find some way not to feel so guilty. My thoughts were confused and contradictory; one minute I was still feeling submissive in my relationship to the mother whom I'd loved so much, but then my next thought was to stage an open rebellion against the ways in which she'd manipulated me ever since our return from England. I caught sight of her again now, just in time to see her head lean down to the left as she went out into the street and vanished—probably saying something to her little boy as they went out the door . . . Our relationship was a disaster . . . and I went back in time to the day she'd left me at the boarding school, just after having celebrated her little twins' ninth birthday. In order to survive, she'd had to leave William and me in the hands of others, and had deadened her grief with her mother and her new baby.

It would be better for me to turn toward the future represented by my husband and our friends. They were there among the curious onlookers for whom Eugénie was putting on this show—not only of her so-called art, but of herself, as an object of desire. What an amazing contrast there was between this lively, talkative young girl who was capturing their attention with her myriad seductive affectations, and, hanging right above her hat, her paintings! Two gouaches she'd done at Sainte-Colombe. In the foreground of one she'd shown the terrace wall of dark green painted wood; beyond it lay the golden hayfield dotted with poppies and bordered by the dark woods descending the gentle slope to the Seine. The other showed a three-quarter view of our mother in her yellow dress with sleeves that were slightly puffy from her shoulders to her elbows; she was writing a letter on the little desk on the porch. Behind her I recognized certain plants that had outlived Grandmother. The scene was certainly right, but what was it about the picture that seemed so empty? What was the truth that Eugénie had wanted to express? What emotion? What passion? What warmth or distaste? How did she see these scenes? What purpose drove her to realize these subjects? In a word, where was her soul? After all, the only thing anyone asked of her was that she *be* in her works! Her model wasn't life as it was lived—neither on the veranda nor in the picture. The buttercup yellow plastered on her dress monopolized the viewer's eyes; everything else was very light and airy, apparently there only to fill space. Yes, a fierce brushstroke here and there, always between two weak ones, would make things more solid, but the intensity was never sustained; it never managed to assert any character as a whole; her use of the brush was still hesitant and superficial, incomplete. Was the originality of her picture in the way she'd framed the dress, cutting it off halfway down, so that you couldn't see the folds below the knees or the feet?

Yes, I might have been a poor judge—not wanting my sister to have achieved any nobility, any spirit, no matter how much I said I did. However, I found that her failures didn't make me happy either. All the time we'd spent together in the Louvre! All those hours painting side by side and finally I had the impression that what was essential had escaped her, that her brain, her heart, and her body were sieves! In a sense, it was a terrible waste, and it made me deeply sad. Once again, remembering her hands running up and down the keyboard, I regretted that, perhaps, her jealousy of me had made her abandon that talent.

As my friends went over to her, I retreated and watched her drawing all their attention to herself rather than to her work. As if she'd only exhibited her paintings in order to show off a new dress. She was talking a lot and laughing at things she herself said, paying no attention to the people she talked to, other than to make sure they were still paying attention to her. I stayed where I was, disappointed and ashamed. I watched her lowering herself, and the recklessness with which she did it made me alternately depressed and exasperated. I'd have liked to take her two pictures down from the wall and whisper to her in a conspiratorial way, "Come on, we're going to work on them a little more together and hang them up again tomorrow before anyone else comes in!" But it was no longer the moment to play the role of big sister, who, after her own success, gives a final lesson to the younger. Especially when "the child" was forcing her way into the world I'd found for myself. It wasn't an entirely unattractive notion, that we might find a moment to meet in peace, over colors and lines, forgetting our rivalry. But, no. Her affectations were unbearable. I hated her more than ever.

I felt a shoulder against mine. Without looking to see, I knew it was Caroline Mabain. She laid her hand on my arms and squeezed it gently. I looked at her and we exchanged worried smiles. She almost seemed to have been listening in to the hubbub of my thoughts and feelings. Giving in to their curiosity, all our friends had forgotten I was there; only Caroline had come back to be with me. I simply returned her quick caress to show her how grateful I was. When we were all back together that evening, having a drink or a cup of coffee, she'd say what she really thought, I expected. We'd be there without Lucien, who'd been invited to dinner on the rue du Four by my mother. These days I only learned what my family was up to because of my husband, who heard about about it from his friend.

As for William, he was in a train heading for Fréjus where an aviator was about to do something crazy: fly over the Mediterranean for the first time. Three years earlier my brother had met Roland Garros, a young man then making practice flights over the mouth of the Rance River. The projected flight would be a dangerous and daring feat, and William was determined not to miss the takeoff.

When asked why she'd chosen to sign her paintings with a man's name, Eugénie became more flirtatious still, if such were possible, pulling out her whole bag of tricks, saying she was hoping not to draw attention to the fact that she was a young girl but rather wanted to be seen as a painter, an artist. Swirling and fluttering about with her fan in her hand as she spoke, she'd slip a wink to Lucien from time to time, the poor bewitched man watching this performance enrapt. Lucien whispered something in Frédéric's ear and pointed to the two paintings. I tried to interpret my husband's reaction. He had his hands in his pockets and was listening to his friend indulgently, ironic: "I'd never take the liberty of disillusioning you, my friend . . ." was what I read in the slightly mocking expression on my husband's face. I was sure I still knew him better than anyone, even if something had changed between us since spring. We understood each other in a way that endured.

As the two friends went on with their quiet conversation, I heard—despite the general din—someone asking Eugénie what she thought of the paintings by Mathilde Lewly, her sister. All at once that charming young woman's expression turned hard, her eyes flashing, but at the same time she seemed alarmed, anxious, as if someone had put her in danger, as though someone had started pelting her with rocks. She looked all around in search of support; you could see she was furious, and her fury contained all the intensity, all the art, that was missing in her paintings. She couldn't even continue the conversation she was having and her interlocutor seemed to sense how much he'd upset her. Her knees had seemed to give way for a second, her posture stiffening to retain its balance, then she raised her voice and retorted impatiently: "Yes, yes, it's perfectly clear that she's always there, one step behind me!" Lucien took the hint and stood perfectly still, on the lookout. As for Frédéric, he was laughing, which kept me from hearing what followed, but he told me a little about it later: the man simply replied that he'd asked me some questions at Willon's gallery a year earlier, and so I couldn't exactly be one step behind her. Eugénie then added that I was just thrashing around, making no progress, that my pictures were a waste of time, which was so meaningless a criticism that had made Frédéric thoroughly amused.

Having Caroline by my side didn't stop me from feeling alone. I said that I was going to slip away unnoticed. She went to whisper in Frédéric's ear that both of us were going straight to Prosper's where we'd waiting for the rest of the gang to come soon. Then we left together.

The evening was cool and as we walked along a question leapt to mind: "How would I put up with my sister's achieving an outright success?" I certainly had to admit that it pleased me now to know that she'd very recklessly demonstrated her incompetence, all the while imagining that she was being wonderful. And she *was* wonderful, superb beneath her broad hat, in a dress of almond green, silk chiffon, splendidly complementing the copper highlights of her abundant hair, which was tied back loosely. The curls that had slipped out of their comb made her even more charming. "She should content herself with being pretty!" I exploded as soon as we were in the street, and we fell into a cathartic fit of giggling. I knew intuitively that the differences between my sister and myself would shield me from whatever nuisance she caused. No one could care for us both at the same time—our characters were exactly opposed. Wasn't Lucien proof of this in the way he'd avoided me since he'd fallen in love with her? The things I required could never be satisfied with approximations. Oil and water don't mix. I remembered the unfinished stole she'd given our mother—still the perfect metaphor for her ambitions, personality, life. Caroline interrupted my thoughts; she'd apparently been appalled at what she'd seen and whispered that Lucien must have paid a pretty penny to have Eugénie taken seriously . . .

Hardest to bear was reading interviews with Eugénie soon afterward in the papers. Word for word, what I'd said about suffering, exaltation, and the discipline inherent to creation was all there. She'd even managed to make use of the remark I'd made in the Luxembourg Gardens—the one that had prompted her to wreck my watercolor: "Sometimes all it takes is to add a little touch of color when you're still not satisfied, in order to give the whole picture character and presence . . ." Yes, I read that and I also read that sometimes she consulted her plant albums to immerse herself in the shapes of pressed flowers . . . But, alas, their colors are lost in time, she dared point out, just as I had myself, when she'd visited us in the studio. My sister was borrowing things I'd done and things I'd thought in order to hold people's attention. That was the saddest thing, but it was also the most revealing one—she had no mind of her own. Was I upset now on my own account, or for her?

I knew for sure that she'd no longer be able to face me. She would read the pity in my eyes; she'd see her own weaknesses. And in hers I'd recognize the exacerbated desire to destroy me. Until she was married there could be no final break between us. We would be seeing each other again.

It only took a few days of reflection for me to feel less threatened, because, in the few columns in the art journals that were devoted to her, Eugénie herself was much more the subject than her talent. I, for one, preferred people to criticize or praise my work and forget about me as me. Certain critics had felt the need to point out that we were related. What was the point in that, I wondered. It changed nothing about my involvement in my art, in the life I'd chosen. I hung on to that thought. Friends who fell under her charm would have to make a choice between us, but that didn't worry me. She'd be doing me a favor. She'd be helping me find out who *was* my friend.

35

Neither my sister nor I had made any attempt to see each other over the winter. She hadn't even had the nerve two weeks after her opening to come scoff at me at our show in Willon's gallery, nor in our domain, Café Prosper. She knew what she'd tried to steal from me. In my opinion, she had no hope of succeeding. But she would be the last to admit it.

Meanwhile, on rue Chaptal, our usual way of life was changing.

Frédéric met Lucien often on the Left Bank when the engineer would abandon his work sites, his calculations, and his plans and escape into bohemia. They had begun to make contacts among the painters of Montparnasse. Sometimes my sister would join them without her chaperone; this was probably allowed because the presence of her brother-in-law inspired my mother's confidence. Unless, perhaps, they were just letting her education slide? I'd have a twinge of jealousy when Frédéric would come home and describe the hours they'd spent relaxing at la Rotonde or Café du Dôme. He suggested that I could always join them, but I preferred to hide my misery on rue Chaptal.

For ten years, Lucien had been one of the most intimate friends the two of us had, as close to us as William. Either one could just turn up when it suited him and as soon as they appeared I'd start thinking about what we might have to offer them for supper, because they were always as starved and exhausted as forced laborers returning after a day of working in the rain or heat. I'll never forget the days, the nights as well, when Lucien had come by with the crew working for him on the reconstruction of the bridge at Lurey-Conflans. He described the spectacular effect the storm had had. The heart of Paris was taking on water like an old wreck at the bottom of the sea. For my part, nearer to home, I can remember when the gare Saint-Lazare began to resemble some strange sort of inland port where stone steamships were anchored around the cour de Rome, apparently waiting for low tide. Little boats or makeshift rafts could be seen emerging from the streets that had been turned into canals by the rains. Where did all the animals go? What would be left for them when they returned? Everything seemed to have been turned on its head, the normal become bizarre. The metro was a sunken city; Parisians went from place to place on planks laid as high as halfway up the porte cochères. They had adapted, more or less, to life under these extraordinary conditions. We'd ventured as far as the pont d'Alma on a cold day in January, the same way people on vacation would go out to a lighthouse to contemplate the raging sea whipped by the wind. There's a giant statue of a Zouave there; we liked to watch the current soak his moustache every time it washed against his pillar. William hadn't shown his face all week; he was off in a frenzy of photography, documenting the drowned city beneath a sky heavy with the snow to come.

After my marriage, and before his engagement, Lucien had treated me like his sister. Now I was going to become his sister legally—the wedding would come after the summer of 1914. It was with a heavy heart that I learned this from Frédéric. I knew I'd continue to be shunned; Lucien would forever side with Eugénie against me, despite the fact that it was only through me—because I was married to Frédéric—that he could ever have become his best friend's brother-in-law. Would he move from avoidance to outright hostility once they were officially a unit? Would I never see either of them ever again? Did I even want to take part in the wedding festivities? I couldn't see much reason to do so, to be honest, but it was nonetheless a little difficult for me to accept that my participation, if offered, might actually be rejected. If I could have talked it all over calmly with Frédéric, perhaps I wouldn't have found it all so difficult to deal with. The absentminded way he listened to me nowadays was becoming insulting; it was as if he was taking their side without wanting to admit, definitively, that he was doing so. Whenever I was trying to make a point, he'd interrupt me in a fatherly tone of voice and advise me to be patient, telling me without the least concern for my state of mind that our little squabbles would pass. He wasn't much good at hiding his ambivalence. And the result was that he continued to avoid me; though, in bed every night, he would repeat what he'd said when we came back from Rome: the two of us have something deep, profound, rich . . .

I was finally coming to realize that I'd never share anything with my sister again, that this was a permanent rift. Perhaps for the best. As difficult as it was to imagine what this would be like, and as difficult as it was to believe that I could manage it, the thought was a solace to me, even a delight. I couldn't confess this to anyone, of course, and especially not Frédéric. He didn't know that my so-called "little squabble" with Eugénie went back to when we were children, and was no less deep and profound, in its way, than the "something" he and I shared.

One day I picked up my brushes and painted a picture of that rift between my sister and myself as a geological fault between tectonic plates shown as two massive, red shapes that had shifted and collided. It looked like an earthquake painted in coagulated blood. I believed for a little while that, in painting this, I'd gotten out all the violence and distress I'd been feeling; but all I'd done was to give it a form outside of me, hence an existence of its own.

Frédéric used to join Lucien in that other world, likewise swarming with artists on the other side of the Seine. They met up with poor starving wretches who'd come from central Europe, Russia, or Poland with no more than their brushes and palettes for baggage, but their hearts full of the dream of a great awakening to art in the land of freedom. And they were indeed free, and their new freedoms included that to appease their hunger with alcohol, and gabble at one another without a single language in common. Nonetheless, in a corner of Paris composed of cheap restaurants and hovels built on empty plots of very poor earth, they managed to create a homeland that they could all share, and that would have an international influence. It was a place of disparate structures laid out in a square and crossed by the boulevards Montparnasse and Raspail. What was most fascinating for old Gauls like ourselves was the journey of no return these people had made, and which destined them for a hand-to-mouth, communal life in which they were nonetheless inventing a new form of artistic expression. More and more artists were drawn to their flame, and their work was beginning to be praised even as far away as the New World.

The two comrades, Frédéric and Lucien, were seen less and less at Prosper's. As the weeks went by, our group came apart, some of us caught like moths in the lights of Montparnasse, others absconding thanks to new loves, new fashions, new interests—or simply boredom.

Then, early this year, 1914, some people who'd recently moved into an apartment on the boulevard Berthier had the idea of commissioning Frédéric for a trompe-l'oeil to be painted between the three double windows of their parlor, to make the view of the little garden outside seem continuous.

Frédéric accepted the commission and only came home when he wasn't working on the project or in Montparnasse with Lucien—which wasn't often. I no longer waited for his return before I went to bed.

36

When the jonquils came out in the little parks, I always greeted them as long-lost friends, my dear *daffodils*, from our days in England. They were blooming when Lucien, William, Frédéric, and I joined a throng of onlookers, collectors, journalists, and others interested in art for an auction of some paintings at the Hôtel Drouot. Works by dead painters, painters from the end of the nineteenth century, and then some still young ones who'd only recently begun to paint. A number of the people attending the auction also had a work for sale, sometimes several. An organization founded ten years earlier to help out indigent artists was selling a hundred and fifty canvases that had either been donated to them or that they had bought for very little. The three of us didn't want to miss out on a collection of that sort being dispersed. William, who was just passing through Paris, joined us.

It was exciting to take a close look at works by the greatest painters side-by-side with some by unknowns who had been abruptly shoved into the daylight by the recent and sudden burst of interest in their sort of style. Considering how our own stock was rising, experiencing the excitement of an auction—well, we were all as drunk on that as if they'd served champagne. We looked impatiently at each other in all the excitement, watching the auctioneer pointing first right and then left: one taker, another one, then a third before a duel between two fortunes was ignited, one big spender on either side of the room. At the mere blink of an eye, a slight movement of the hand or head, the price would go up. I thought I'd keel over then and there when I heard some of the prices being paid. Who would have put down this much money for some of those paintings ten years ago? It was entirely possible for these rich men to be throwing money at colors and shapes left behind by an artist who had died starving and freezing. Painters, rich or poor, let go of pictures that represented hours of insomnia, anguish, or joy for them, often combined with the fear that it all was futile. You either do or don't have talent, true, but who then decides whether your talent is sufficient to justify their investment? Artists don't worry about being understood, about sinking away in solitude as they conduct their inquiries into form and perception. No, they worry about no one *seeing* their work. If no one buys it, you go through life in the worst sort of solitude. It was a ghastly business, really.

Abruptly I wondered if Eugénie's gouaches and watercolors, which had seemed so insipid to me, might also become valuable some day, even if absolutely no one other than Lucien had found them particularly interesting when they were new. How could I know? She wouldn't be the first beneficiary of changing tastes. So long as she actually persevered—which was, to me anyway, an open question.

At Drouot, as I watched the prices climb, I felt increasingly unsure of anything at all. Even the value of my sister's work.

I hadn't seen Lucien for a very long time. We said hello to each other, but with such restraint that it made me really sad; we then went to sit down a considerable distance apart to watch the auction. But there wasn't time to brood—the auction was electric with excitement. The prices weren't going up in small increments, either, but in multiples of ten or twenty, even a hundred. We couldn't have been more spellbound if the money were going to end up in our own pockets. And then the next piece to come up for sale was Frédéric's *View of Rome*. Our excitement reached new heights as we strained in the direction of the podium where the auctioneer presided, his hammer already in the air. Off to the side and several rows in front of us, Lucien, eyes blazing with enthusiasm, looked back impatiently at his friend. Then he went back to sitting as still as a churchgoer. My heart was going to leap right out into the aisle—I was going to faint from the tension, the bowstring drawn in my chest . . . Then, down came the hammer, and the auctioneer's voice thundered an unknown name, and the final price: five hundred francs! The organization had bought it not so long ago for less than a hundred. We went completely crazy; Frédéric's stock was going up and up. It had nothing to do with us; whether we painted well or badly had no effect on the market. It was like a lottery.

When the hammer came down on the final sale of the day, I'd thought I misheard the auctioneer: eleven thousand five hundred francs. My nerves were at a breaking point; I couldn't say now how long I stood there without breathing. It was early in March and still cool outside, but I felt like I was dripping with sweat. It was time to go out and get a breath of air.

Some day, I told myself, I'll come back here and sketch some of these bodies, the expressive faces, that arm bringing down its hammer. There was so much power in the room, so much tension; there was such vehement glaring, such rivalries, battles that seemed likely to end with murder. I wanted to set myself up in a corner and fill my notebook with studies of this bizarre way of life.

The auction was barely six months ago. Now it seems to me it might have happened a century ago, a millennium . . .

37

Though I look forward most especially to the return of the daffodils, I also watch for the iris, the lilacs, the wisteria, and paulownia—the time when humble forget-me-nots are already on display both in flowerbeds and in among the weeds. This profusion ushers in the month of May. The mauve and blue shades merging with each other in the public squares and gardens is a gift I look forward to every year as if it had all been organized for my benefit. From the base of butte Montmartre you can watch things changing: the rising hillside takes on tints of purplish-blue before the thick foliage slowly spreads out its many shades of green.

But this year I hardly took advantage of it. I felt as if I hadn't slept for ages.

One evening Frédéric came home late. He went up to the apartment without going to the studio first, which was unusual. I'd never seen him look so gloomy.

"What's happened to you?" I asked. I put my book down on the pillow.

He went into the bathroom without a word. I was alarmed and listened to the few sounds I could hear, trying to interpret them. Then, still without saying a word, he slipped into bed and snuggled up against me, sighing like a child holding back his sobs in the arms of his mother. His arms were around me, his legs across mine, and he was hugging me. A drowned man hanging onto a buoy. My immediate impulse was to help him let loose whatever he was feeling, to empty his sack of anguish by whispering tender words to him and sinking my fingers into his heavy hair.

The dam broke. That great, catlike body I'd so often watched in battle with brush and knife against his canvases, as if he were at war with them, possessed of indomitable strength—that great body which gave us such pleasure—was shriveled up, defeated. Loud, horrid eructations burst from his throat. I reached for the cloth covering our night table, thinking to use it as a handkerchief. It was futile to ask any sensible questions while he was so out of control. I waited, stroking his shoulders, his back, his hair. The same way I used to stroke little François when he was too restless.

Finally he calmed down, his face buried against my shoulder. I thought I heard a thin voice saying, "Forgive me, my love," but the words were still drowned in tears, and my first thought was that I'd misunderstood. Rocking him like a child, I had fooled myself that I was the stronger of we two, but now I too became fragile, frightened.

Still, without thinking, I murmured, "What do I have to pardon you for?"

He didn't reply. I didn't repeat my question. If I could be patient, I knew he would speak. I wondered what sort of revelation would be forthcoming. Unless he just was excusing himself for letting me see him in such a terribly weakened state? Yes, I told myself: why must you imagine the worst?

After a long silence during which I fought off every possible hypothesis, he finally replied that he'd seen Lucien, who'd told him that the wedding that had been planned for the fall was going to take place *before* summer, meaning sometime in the next three weeks. I couldn't quite understand how this had upset him so. I knew the engaged couple had decided last winter to wait until the completion of the construction project that would monopolize Lucien till autumn at the earliest. So they had changed their minds? I was puzzled and my mind wandered off to the Left Bank and on to Sainte-Colombe until Frédéric's voice called me back to reality:

"I'm not best man anymore. He asked Loulou Chevrier to replace me and to play the organ as they go in and out of the church."

All right, so he wasn't the best man—would that reduce a man like Frédéric to tears? But something else about this didn't add up—it simply wasn't logical: why would the fact that Loulou would play the organ mean that my spouse couldn't be his best friend's best man? True, my sister was furious with me, but why punish Frédéric? In the end I ventured, "And because Loulou will play the organ . . . they decided you couldn't be best man? I don't quite understand . . ."

And yet, I'd hit a nerve. He gave my shoulder a quick squeeze, so hard that it hurt. Then, that great body with its arms, its legs completely wrapped around me, a body whose every muscle I could recreate in clay with the palms of my hands and my fingers, turned away and left me feeling alone. For months now all news about my family had come to me from Frédéric, via Lucien; with this latest development, I mused, I was likely to be cut off completely. Oh, perhaps William would bring me the occasional piece of gossip. If he was around. Before going completely silent, my dearest tossed a parting shot over his shoulder, in a tone of voice that meant the subject was now closed: "I'm not his best man, that's all there is to it."

I felt physically ill as all those repressed suspicions I'd successfully fought to a standstill came trooping back.

That night was endless. The sound of Frédéric's breathing beside me made me think he was still awake, but I didn't dare speak to him anymore. I was filled with so many terrible, frightening, agonizing thoughts. I could only get rid of them by imagining myself running away to be alone on the Riviera or the shores of Lac Léman, looking across at the splendor of the Alps. Well, near the water in any case. That lakeside land composed of vineyards and mountains seemed a happy, spacious, and airy place, even welcoming when seen from the depths of night in our bedroom, when Paris, plastered in gray, was stifling me with its stench. I hated Paris. At the foot of the highest wave of the Jura, suspended for eternity by some magician just before he formed its curve and rolled it out at the foot of the Mont Blanc massif—there I would rent an old building. I'd paint far from Paris with its narrow passageways, far from the complications of my family.

How nice to dream of escape. We all do it. I saw myself in the distance, free from pain . . . Sunny landscapes spread out across my imagination: healthy, invigorating, imaginary places, where people are passionate about the land . . . it seems so real, so comforting. In a few minutes we know for certain that we must go there, as though to meet another self, one who is peaceful and serene, not burdened by all your anxieties. But we forget—we always take our torments with us.

Finally, as the day dawned, I decided that, as soon as the post office opened, I would go there to phone my mother and ask her to meet me somewhere. There was no point trying to sleep another minute: I felt Frédéric watching me. We both lay there, motionless, knowing we'd just spent the worst night of our lives.

38

I was struck at first glance by Mme Versoix's sunken features. Seated at a table in the Café de la Paix her wrinkles were deeper, her curls now gray, her face sad; in less than three years now, according to my reckoning, she'd be fifty. That seemed very old to me, especially since she was beginning to look like her mother. I hadn't been able to see time pass, accept how life was changing. The world I invented in my canvases or sketches was still my true reality and it was timeless. Most of our friends still weren't even married. They lived as toys of one passion or another, and as soon as we were used to one, the day would come, and without warning, when there was no further talk of *that* one, because a newer had taken its place. And then, what was inside *me*, for my part, was really much the same as any other year, despite the so-called march of progress. Yet, I could no longer ignore the changes occurring both in the people I knew and in the world around them—if these were still more like scenes in a magic lantern show than anything in which I was to take part. The Versoix had had a phone for a year now, and my brother's photography equipment made our father's seem antediluvian. And then, every day, the machines made by man to harass the heavens were flying higher and longer; likewise the other machines rolling down our roads or rattling down iron rails. But all that might as well have been part of some Jules Verne novel, as far as I was concerned; it had nothing really to do with my daily life, or, if it did, was sneaking in so surreptitiously that I was unaware of any change. My reality was in the back of the courtyard on rue Chaptal, in a neighborhood that seemed immutable.

I still called my sister "the child," but of course she was about to be married. Time was moving on, and rapidly, whether or not I wanted to take notice. But the minute I was back in our courtyard, where the roots of the one acacia had lifted the paving stones, back where our window was hidden by the privet hedge, the static nature of my home had the anesthetizing effect that I needed to apply myself to my work. As for the rest of Paris, automobiles now threaded their way through the tired, old nags dragging carriages or loaded carts, and electric lights lined the avenues: in the place de l'Opéra, even the twelve numbers and two hands on the giant Omega watch had been electrified, and now pierced the night with their glow. But what did I care? None of this succeeded in making me move on from the days I remembered in Saint-Colombe, not so long ago, where the candle and oil lamp created dancing shadows tinged with glints of ochre. Not even our trip to Venice and Rome had managed to bring me truly into the twentieth century. On this point William was way ahead of me, and, as usual, by a good distance. He loved gadgets and owned an automobile with which to convey himself to airfields and racetracks—and to take elegant ladies for a ride. Even Nadar, the first aerial photographer, had been dead for four years now. So for William, all this change around us was good!

No, not for me.

Though I'd noticed that my mother's features were sunken, it hadn't occurred to me that my own cheeks had perhaps grown thin, that my forehead was beginning to wrinkle, and that my hair was less glossy now that I was almost thirty. When I retained things with a pencil line or a stroke of the brush, the things I saw in people, or in the texture of a fruit or flower, or the feel of a piece of cloth, I did it to grant them eternity. That's no doubt why I'd been so deeply moved at seeing how Grandmother remained faithful to herself though she no longer looked the part. What I was after were things that lasted and did not fade or wither: the emotion, the intention inherent in the inanimate world; attempting to give form to what I saw in volume and color, stark contrasts or gentle blendings. I was after the timeless.

But the love I'd felt for my mother? If love is the word. How could that violent emotion that had been the cause of such wonder for me, as a little girl—how could it have disappeared? I remembered it well, but it no longer stirred me, unless it was that same vehemence that now animated my rage when she stood in my way, when she frustrated my aims.

Across from each other, silently stealing glances as though disinterested, we were at one of the tables at which we'd sat so often with William when we used to take our long afternoon rides around the city—I mean years ago, when we'd first arrived in Paris. I had thought, in those days, that the three of us would be a family forever.

Once again Eugénie would be at the center of our conversation. I was tired of it. I was no longer ready to make even the least concession; I'd lost whatever pity had been left in me before the Lamain's exhibit, and it had been replaced with scorn.

My mother finally ordered something to drink in a voice that was an attempt at cheerfulness, though it struck a dismal note. I made my choice in turn and then the midst of all the noise in the café, silence descended on us again. Staring at her staring at the spoon that she was endlessly stirring around her cup without once lifting her eyes once to meet mine was exasperating, to say the least. Not surprisingly, I spoke first: "So? Eugénie's marriage couldn't wait?"

"Please. Don't be vulgar."

"I don't see how my question was the least bit vulgar."

But what my mother had thought turned my own thoughts to the same subject, which is to say the only thing that must never be mentioned, no matter what, and that I hadn't even considered. I recognized that her reaction was much the same as that of the nuns who raised the both of us. I put my hand to my mouth.

"Your sister needs to marry as quickly as possible," she sighed at last. "We'll have a very simple ceremony with only our closest friends present, at Saint-Germain-des-près, where we know fewer people than we do at Villennes." From the way she spoke, you'd have thought Eugénie was at death's door.

"And, in this context, I suppose, my husband and myself are not to be considered 'close'?"

"She has insisted that neither you nor Frédéric be present."

"And so, once again, you've submitted to her whims. Did she happen to give any reason for this?"

"That's all she would say. Don't forget that you've been unconscionably cruel to her."

"She, however, didn't hesitate to ask us shortly after that supposed cruelty whether she could come with us to a party given by an American couple who are making some contemporary artists a fortune selling their pictures abroad. Her first thought was how she might gain by this opportunity, not at all her so-called injury. And then, accompanied by Mme Chesneau, she paid a visit to us at the studio, all sweetness and light . . . But ever since little missy had her paintings in an exhibit, and didn't bother inviting me—the better to appropriate my words more freely!—she's no longer willing to see us!"

"Lucien did try to reason with her, but she became furious and collapsed in tears."

"She spent all her childhood learning that all she had to do was stamp her foot or 'collapse in tears' order to get what she wanted. Lucien is going to learn the truth about his fiancée pretty quickly, I think. This is far from his last capitulation. I do hope you'll pass on my best wishes for his future happiness. He's a brave fellow, my soon-to-be brother-in-law—which is to say, my husband's best friend."

"Thank the Good Lord your Grandmother didn't live to see this!"

Mme Versoix couldn't manage to say anything more; I could tell that her throat was too busy containing who knows what unseemly bleating for any more polite conversation to follow. She took out her little handkerchief and dabbed at her forehead, her eyes.

"How long have I known that girl?" I asked. "And yet I still don't understand her. Unless, of course, the problem is that I understand her all too well, and she knows it! What can I say? Since you've always ordered the big sister to give in to the little one, I won't insist on coming to her little affair—I'm not the expert gatecrasher that Eugénie is! I wish you all a lovely wedding day, and may Lucien raise her to a comfortable place in society that will permit her to mince and simper in all the best parlors—only provided that she no longer trespass on my territory. When it comes right down to it, she's right not to be associating with us anymore—it keeps me from having to repudiate her publicly."

"Sometimes I've thought you were too harsh, Mathilde, but today . . . well, I do wish Eugénie hadn't made some of the decisions she's made . . . It makes me desperately sad to see my three older children scattered so far from me . . ."

"You never wanted to admit that I see Eugénie as the little tyrant she is! What does William say about all this? Is *he* invited?"

"He'll be the one to give her away . . ."

"Marvelous! She'll have her brother all to herself! I'd dearly like to make you feel better about all this, but what can I do? Neither Frédéric nor I are allowed to cross the threshold on the sacred evening! So do excuse me—I've got a great deal of work to get back to. Oh, and do us both a favor: remember that we two have shared the privilege of learning how to swallow our tears in the presence of the nuns of Sacré-Coeur . . . so don't turn your back on our years of training by weeping now in mine . . ."

I couldn't face her, once I'd stood up; her despair would have broken my heart, put me at her mercy the same as it did once upon a time. It would have melted the bulwark I'd taken such a long time to build up, the underpinnings that now kept me standing. You don't stop loving the mother you worshipped. You protect yourself from her, that's all.

39

Before the end of July, I'd never heard of Sarajevo, and would never have believed that the assassination of Archduke Franz Ferdinand of Austria and his wife earlier that summer would soon resound in every home in Europe, and even reach the back of our courtyard in the ninth arrondissement.

Torn from each other in the unimaginable crush at the gare de l'Est and the gare du Nord on August second, the men who'd been mobilized for what was meant to be a brief, hardly noticeable little war said good-bye before being packed into trains leaving for our threatened borders . . .

Frédéric and I expected to see each other again in just a few weeks, no more than that, and yet he hugged me as if he were leaving forever. All around us the din of family chatter and patriotic songs covered up our own voices. You had to speak very softly in order to hear each other. There were women weeping, others waving their husbands', brothers', or sons' rifles around in the air. The men were leaving, yes, but they went off singing songs and making jokes.

It was no place to reestablish our connection to one another. Frédéric, however, seemed profoundly upset; he whispered tender words, to me, serious things he could just as easily have told me the night before. I was going along with it almost thoughtlessly, listening to his monologue as I let him embrace me, without the least suspicion that I would retain total recall of this moment, this moment for which I'd had no time to prepare.

A great many horses were requisitioned the next day, and soon the buses were turned into meat wagons for the troops. Families, towns, and even the countryside soon changed beyond recognition. Already the Germans were beginning to burn villages in Belgium, while England allied itself with the enemies of the invaders. Far away, with the support of France, vast Russia had refused to comply with Germany's ultimatum, and, along with England, now found itself fighting alongside France at the beginning of August. All of Europe was on the move, and with the addition of forces from the New World, their numbers swelled by additional troops from India and South Africa—all allied against Germany and Austria-Hungary, themselves allied with the Ottoman Empire—we were bound to win in a few weeks, perhaps as few as two or three. Husbands, sons, and brothers all counted on being home well before Christmas. Yet, there was more to it all than first appeared: the news was very complicated to follow from one hour to the next. Circumstances were evolving very quickly.

Yes, the word "war" made me shudder, but it was hard to see anything ominous in that summer sunshine. The word itself was more frightening than the reality in which I still lived. I only knew about war through books or from the stories Grandmother told. The sound of cannon fire, bodies lifeless or writhing, towns in flames, women dressed in black, fatherless children, people on the roads heading for unknown countries—starving, thirsty people . . . all those images had the same texture for me as something out of a fairy tale. The one solid fact I still remembered from the things Grandmother had said was that, in 1870, people had eaten rats. Naturally, looking at pictures of war in books always sent shivers through me—especially the ones showing Napoleon's troops staggering through the snow or else exhausted beneath the blazing sun, their heavy boots ripped to pieces or replaced with rags; in the camps, soldiers had limbs amputated while other bodies—living, suffering, wrapped in bloody bandages—waited their turn on stretchers or simply on the ground. But, sheltered by our apartment with its double curtains and thick rug and of course plenty to eat, I was fascinated more than horrified by the horror. Nowadays we had trains, automobiles, and airplanes, as well as considerably more sophisticated weapons—not to mention the telephone. Modern war probably wouldn't look at all like those pictures. Perhaps all this technology was why the new war wasn't supposed to last very long?

Before the end of August, however, the newspapers showed pictures of German prisoners and deplored at great length the number of French dead. Other photos showed dead horses lying by the sides of our roads, and others still the wounded being carted off to hospitals. I began to feel increasingly afraid, wondering how any of them could keep from going mad in the midst of such systematic destruction. I closed my ears to word about what was going on at the front lines—not to mention the diplomatic negotiations, the alliances, the extent of all the nations' financial investment in the war . . . I wasn't ready for the insanity.

Like many other people, I'd put a little French flag in my window. I did it without thinking. A ridiculous gesture, really; and the more I learned about the battles and the burned villages along the border, the more it appalls me to think back on it. What were the men I loved doing out there, surrounded by so many strangers, their lives equally at risk? Soon I could no longer spare much sympathy for the multitudes being slaughtered; I thought only about my two loves, Frédéric and William, and sometimes I woke up in a sweat because I saw in my nightmares the face of one of them on the suffering body of one of those wounded men in the paper. Where was my brother, who had enlisted as a war photographer? His letters were postmarked here and then there, no two from the same place, from one airfield then another: brief, affectionate, but distant. As for Frédéric, because he was an artist, he was assigned the duty of painting camouflage, on canvas or wood and even on cardboard; it was something that had to be done very quickly in trompe-l'oeil to hide military installations that might be visible from a distance, or even from above . . .

As if it might bring me closer to him, in mid-August I asked the concierge to forward my mail and left Paris to give Frédéric's family a helping hand. His village needed workers to harvest the crops in the fields and then to pick the grapes. The old men rallied around the very young as well as the toughest of the women to do the work in the fields and vineyards. There were even some nuns who took up scythes to harvest winter forage for their animals. Along with everyone else, I was healthily exhausted by this hard and unfamiliar existence. I ended up finding that the right place for me was alongside the cook to help her feed the work crews who got up early in the morning and came back famished, despite the snacks they took along to give them an excuse to take a break. At night, without reading so much as a line in a book, I fell asleep completely exhausted.

The Thorins family, just like all of us, now, read the papers and talked endlessly about the news, which was becoming grimmer and grimmer. Worry caught in our throats. Photographs of the battle for the Marne, the destruction of the cities of Senlis and Soissons, the bombing of the Cathedral of Reims—these gave me a clearer notion of the horror reaching through France. Exhausted as I was, I could no longer sleep. Which of my men was exposed to the worst danger? William or Frédéric?

Unthinking as an animal, I knew that I needed to go home to my burrow; as an inducement, I told myself that my husband or brother could turn up any day now, back in Paris. It would have been easier for them to get back there than to some of the provincial cities. I didn't know where my mother was now, but was convinced that she must be with her little family in the safe haven of Sainte-Colombe.

There were also our canvases and favorite possessions to think about. I had to go home to Paris for them as well. If we all died, I wanted our pictures to live on. An additional torment was the thought of Aunt Dilys, who was, perhaps, in even greater danger than we, off in Belgium, which was partially in ruins. Above all: I was incommunicado there in the vineyards of Burgundy, far from home. What if someone needed to get in touch with me?

As soon as the grape harvest was completed and the autumn fruits gathered, promising my sorrowful but dignified mother-in-law that I'd be back for Christmas, if conditions allowed, I climbed onto the train.

40

I'd collapsed in tears on our return from Italy. I'd been completely undone by the loneliness resulting from the mysterious silence that had grown between Frédéric and me. We were, however, together. When I came home from Burgundy to that same apartment—silent now and frozen by the mid-November chill, everything congealing under the sheets protecting it from the dust—the moment I stepped through the door, I felt the presence of the man who'd occupied these rooms far longer than I: the "head of the household," the man who was my love. Everything I saw somehow told me he'd be back; the walls covered with pictures of our friends, the knickknacks and all the furniture full of family history, or else the happy memories of when we'd bought it . . .

I hurried impatiently down to the studio where, with a turn of the key in the lock, I discovered its atmosphere intact, breathing in the turpentine smell still hanging in the air. It touched me, was as pleasant to me as entering a fragrant rose garden. The whole room was bathed in semi-darkness because I'd drawn the curtains across the wall of windows before I left. Now I pulled them aside as if preparing for a happy reunion. The privet hedge had again begun limiting what you could see outside; it reflected a pale green light, slightly diluted and restful. I thought it was time to have it trimmed. More than anywhere else, it was in this place that we'd built our life as a couple and as artists, and where we kept up our friendships. Everything important happened here. I could have left the apartment, yes, but never the studio. I went back up, reassured to find our universe unchanged, reassured to feel Frédéric's presence.

Except, when it was time to eat—which in this case meant warming up the contents of a meager can in our silent kitchen—and, worse, when I slipped into bed—and this even after using my bed warmer to take off the chill—I couldn't help but think that he wouldn't be joining me—not tonight, anyhow; perhaps not ever—and I was gripped by terrible fear, bottomless grief. I could hardly breathe. War, war haunted me, with images of strangers lying face down on the ground or sleeping like hunting dogs under hedgerows or simply exposed in a field . . . Among all the pictures of villages still smoldering after the Germans had passed through, there was one in particular from the previous week's paper that pursued me. There was a dog lying on a gravesite covered with flowers in the open countryside—its head up, like the guardian of a tomb. The photograph's caption told how the dog bared its teeth to anyone who tried to take care of it, lead it away, or even offer it food. The soldier who'd trained the dog lay beneath the freshly dug earth; it was marked by a wooden cross hung with the dead man's helmet.

I envied the dog; I wished I *were* a dog; but the haunting vision prompting this absurd desire was too much like some unbearable premonition of what was to come. I did my best to will it away. But back it would come, no less terrifying. I had to get out of bed and think of something to occupy me, keep me from thinking about it. I folded and put away the furniture coverings then and there, in the middle of the night, and began to collect some especially precious things of ours so I could take them down to the cellar. Only then, finally, was I able to stretch out and doze off a bit.

After a cup of black coffee, I heard the irresistible call of our lair in the back of the courtyard, and responded to it the way a sailor heeds the call of the open sea. I had a lot to do there; the first thing was to put our pictures away safely in the basement, which one reached through a pair of large trap doors under the sofa. It was a windowless space dug out of the chalky rock beneath Paris. Ventilation was provided by two grates embedded at ground level and hidden by the faithful old privet hedge. It had nothing in common with the tenant's cellars in the apartment building, which you reached via a staircase leading down from a door in the entrance hall. Here our hiding place had the advantage of being as long and wide as the building itself. Getting there down the steep ladder was likely to be difficult with our largest paintings under my arm, but I could take them out of their frames and roll them up if need be.

Before I went to Burgundy, I'd already organized my own work and put it neatly under the winding staircase leading to the attic; we had outfitted that otherwise unused space with wire racks that had spacers to keep the pictures from bumping up against each other. Then we'd hidden the staircase itself behind a heavy curtain all across the length of the room to protect us from the draughts that came in between the first floor and the entranceway. I never went up there, or only rarely. The attic was where Frédéric stored some of his unfinished canvases and then countless studies—he'd been doing so for years. Now it all had to be brought down and stored in the basement.

41

There was an old plate on the floor up there with splotches of dried paint on it, and then two brushes. As though Frédéric was in the habit of visiting his abandoned work and touching it up. Seated on an old trunk, I began to sort through them. Daylight fell through two skylights that had been put into the tin roof, while an oil lamp glowed in a dark corner of the gable. I took his boxes of sketches down first. Then the little pictures, then the large ones. I knew some of them already, others I'd never seen. Many of them dated from before our marriage. I liked comparing his present style to his earlier ones. Hard work, not whim, had brought him into modernity. In time I found several classical scenes of our families that had been painted at Saint-Colombe or in Burgundy.

How lively they all were! The least look in a model's eyes, the stance of the humblest person hard at work, or even enjoying a lazy moment, had been captured for eternity. The artist's futile attempt to reject death, I thought again. You can see it from one picture to the next.

A few hours later I put my hand on a painting and then pulled back as if I'd been burned. It was Eugénie, posing in that long, fitted coat that she was wearing when she'd visited us the previous year, although here it was falling off her shoulders. The color of its cloth was the indefinable color one sees in so-called black tulips, which the gentle caress of the sun had diluted with subtle tints of purplish-blue. The wild tumble of her golden hair and the radiance of her slightly pink skin were set off by the dark, heavy mantle trimmed with fur, and her hat of the same color, as if she were in mourning. She was turning her back on a half-open door and pulling on her gloves while, from the height of her young years, she looked me up and down, her eyes somehow uneasy but no less alluring for that. I propped the painting up under the light coming down through the skylight and, knowing how to read Frédéric's brushwork and how he used his palette knife, let it speak to me about the man who'd painted it, despite the pain that fogged my thinking as it became clear to me what it was saying.

The first thing that struck me was that there were no broken lines cutting her face and body up into geometrical figures. No. It was a classic portrait. I almost expected to see my sister step down from the frame and join me as soon as she'd put on her second glove. Frédéric had used his finest brush to caress her flesh, outline her full lips. He'd taken care to give the whole image the passionate, restless, and knowing look that I'd always found so alarming in my sister. All the painter's intentions were there for me to see in his light, skillful, attentive brushstrokes, in the subtle balance of how he'd mixed the paint to render her pale coloring, but also the restlessness in her fresh face, and particularly in her eyes, where you could detect a note of sadness despite the provocativeness of her half-smile. It became perfectly clear to me: the slightly open door behind her and the arrested gesture of her right hand as she put on her butter-colored glove . . . it meant that they'd had a rendezvous. I could almost hear Eugénie's voice saying, "Wait for me! I'm coming!"

I was dying.

I didn't move, however. I stayed put, studying the details that were making me suffer. A morbid fascination with the catastrophe now swooping down on my marriage, on me, is the only explanation I can offer for the reserve of strength that allowed me to face that portrait of my sister, the predator, when I was so alone there in our courtyard. Unless, perhaps, it was a peculiar sense of triumph: the feeling that I was finally getting the answer to all the questions that had been gnawing on me ever since our last visit to Agay, followed by the dismal trip to Italy . . .

In the end, really, I'd have loved to be like her. Forever being rescued by her mother and grandmother at the first sign of trouble, and now beloved by the love of my life! Why should she ever have bothered to follow my advice and discipline herself when everything was always made so easy for her? All she had to do in life was be appealing and launch into gales of laughter in front of an audience, even do a little skillful whining if necessary, perhaps add in a bit of light blackmail, and she got whatever she wanted—in short, she was quite right to sit around waiting to be married, flitting from one enthusiasm to another, while the world was handed to her on a plate.

But Frédéric, ever the excellent observer, must have seen the restless anxiety deep inside her eyes in order to have rendered it so skillfully. Eugénie wasn't radiant, in the painting, but neither was her charm spoiled by her discomfort. She was beseeching him, really—that was what he'd captured; heaven knows he'd had plenty of opportunities to watch her play that game. But there was more: *he* was waiting for his model, waiting for her to be ready, after she had posed, all ready to console her; it was clear from the way he'd depicted her. In showing her about to put on her second glove, he'd caught her just as she was having the impulse to come see him. The picture made me a witness to their disgusting affair—and there was no end to the disturbing things I could imagine their doing together. Her gaze, which plunged into the eyes of anyone looking at the canvas, and hence into those of the artist as well, gave her a majesty that was only emphasized by the burden of grief it contained. Good God, how beautiful she was, how much he desired her, and how much this hurt!

So Frédéric had already been obsessed with my sister before we made our trip to Venice and Rome—if, indeed, he hadn't already possessed her. Now I knew what had been wrong. I couldn't have felt more horrified and guilty at my indiscretion if I'd gone through his mail. Looking at this painting was like having two hands squeeze the life out of me.

The timber rafters seemed to be sinking like the bow of ship in a scarlet ocean. Without a second thought, as if defending myself from a physical attack, I grabbed a palette knife and stabbed at my sister. Screaming at her, I found that the more I tore into the canvas, the more it loosened the vise around my chest. Panting, forehead drenched in sweat, I soon found myself sitting on the floor like a lunatic, systematically lining up the shreds of the portrait according to their size. I opened my hands, amazed at how pale they were against the knife, which was still splotched with pigment, and not my sister's fresh blood.

I was shaken by sobs, cathartic, despairing. My crime, in my eyes, was not that I'd disfigured Eugénie, it was that I'd attacked what, up to this point, I'd always respected the most: a work of art. Frédéric struggling at his easel stood out clearly in my mind, a symbol of the ten years we'd spent together in this studio as partners and collaborators. And I'd just vandalized his work.

Who was I? Whom did I really love?

Now the immense regret I felt over having destroyed one of his works was overwhelmed by an intense euphoria. So many violent emotions had swept over me in so little time—I was elated by the chaos, elated that I'd escaped my eternally well-behaved and sensible exterior. Next came the laughing, no more under my control than the sobs.

Digging around in the dark under the rafters, I set out in search of other criminal acts to perform. I was convinced there were other pictures of my sister hidden here.

Now I knew what Frédéric had really been doing when he was out with Lucien. For months, once he'd completed the work on the fresco on boulevard Berthier, he'd spent all his time away from home on a portrait of Eugénie Lewly! Perhaps he'd painted it while Lucien, in the same room, was tracing out the lines and curves of bridges or buildings that he'd studied. But what were the artist and his model doing together when the engineer went to his construction sites? Was Frédéric capable of betraying his wife and his best friend at the same time? Did Eugénie ever have a chaperone with her anymore, now that Mme Chesneau hardly left the rue du Four at all except to go and sit on a chair in the Luxembourg Gardens?

I moved the frames around, picked up portraits of my family and of myself that Frédéric had painted at the beginning of our marriage. The child at the piano, Grandmother and my mother playing bridge with our cousins from Bazemont, William and I rowing on the Seine. Ancient history. But I lingered over them the way you'd rest beside a fountain in the shade, even if you know you still have miles to cover. Until my hand fell at last upon a second portrait of Eugénie.

In this one, she was wearing the dress she'd worn for the first time on the day of the opening at Lamain's gallery. So, a fairly recent job. Whose red velvet banquette was she sitting on? Which house had they spent so many hours in that he was able to finish this picture? I thought this must be what it felt like to be eaten alive. Behind her, I recognized her thick, flowing, fitted coat, lined in fur, draped over her arm—the same one she'd worn in the earlier portrait. It fell sinuously onto her right elbow before cascading down under her arm and the armrest. Her hand was free, closed on her fan. Her bosom was high and perfectly shaped, enhanced by the low V-neck with white lace ruffles spilling from its collar—the same lace as on the cuffs of her sleeves. She seemed on the lookout for something. I'd taken note of the great elegance of that dress when we were at Lamain's, but it was entirely different to see it now: as if Frédéric had sewn it, stitch by stitch, onto my sister's body. Both of her hands were on her knees, one of them holding her closed fan and the other lying like some useless knickknack over the folds of her dress. Eugénie's beauty was depicted as tragic, here—her face austere, turned slightly left. The painting's frame cut off the banquette and rustling silk satin just below her knees, so that all the viewer's attention was necessarily drawn to her chest and face, the latter of which was haloed by the flowers on the brim of her hat. She had just arrived or was preparing to leave—hence the coat still dangling from her arm. Yes, she was definitely on the lookout for something, and eyes were quite somber. I couldn't help thinking that she was staring at a door outside the frame of the picture. The same door, no doubt, that had been half-open in the earlier picture and through which she expected someone to enter soon. It could only be a man. Her tormented face suggested guilt to me—and bitterness. Or fear. Did she dread Lucien's coming home a little early, as she let the artist admire her? Or, on the contrary, was she *wishing* he'd come? Where exactly did this scene take place? Had Lucien set them up in a new apartment where they all met without me?

And what was the model feeling? Was she in love with the painter or was she simply playing the coquette, teasing him because she liked so much to be the object of an artist's attention—lightly grazed by his eyes, his thoughts, his brush? Ah, but I knew that he wasn't touching her as lightly as all that. Once again I was able to read the truth in Frédéric's approach, I felt the skill with which he was taking hold of her. I'd come between two people whom I knew too intimately, and it was no longer possible to pretend that I hadn't seen, sensed, or guessed what was going on around me.

How he must have desired her, loved her! And how I couldn't bear, how I hated that he did! Every brushstroke revealed his desire.

It was an artistic consumption as much as a carnal one—and vice versa.

I picked the knife up again, but calmly this time, and plunged it into my sister's mouth, as though I could stab down her throat, into her chest, and so be done for good and all with this model posing in the process of departing, coat on arm, on the arm of my husband. I worked on the mouth until there was no more flesh on her gorgeous lips and then I stuck the knife in her eye.

42

How many portraits are there of my sister?

I move the canvases around, scattering them here and there, convinced I'll discover more. I can't feel my heart beating; all I can hear is ringing—not outside, but inside me. My frozen fingers are digging through sketches, paintings, tarps. Soon I'm back at the same canvases for the second time, then the third. Am I going mad? Overcome by grief, I look at the things lying unwrapped on the floor . . . parts of a puzzle, I see, signs there showing me how I've been betrayed, but no longer legible. I hurt all over from crying, laughing, and stabbing.

A name comes back to me now, rising up from who knows what depths. There's only one person I want to have with me, I know—there's only one hand to cool my feverish forehead, one kind gaze. Where are you, Mme Chesneau, in these troubled times? Are you back in the Normandy countryside, or are you still with Mme Versoix and her daughter, Eugénie Morel, whose maiden name was Lewly? At Sainte-Colombe or Divonne-les-Bains? Is the whole family still on the Rue du Four and are you with them? Ah! If my old chaperone could only be here to soothe me and tell me, perhaps, that the baby has been born!

It's time to come down from the loft and inventory the more recent pictures, the ones Frédéric slid behind the heavy curtains lining the second gable to keep the heat in the room. Even if I'd lit the stove I would still be cold; my bones feel as though they'd been carved from blocks of ice. Yes, my teeth are chattering, and yet, every so often, drops of sweat pearl on my temples as though I were standing in front of a blacksmith's forge. Now and then a voice inside whispers that I should stop the hunt and the sabotage, but I'm not listening; this is the voice of reason, I know, and why give that voice another second of my time? It's controlled my every move since we came back from Italy. No, I'll listen to a different voice, the voice of my animal nature, and now that it's caught the scent of blood, it can hardly give up the chase. Lifting one of the two panels of the curtain and laying out the pictures that had been leaning against the wall in a line on the floor—like an enormous card game—I am convinced that I'm about to find another portrait of my sister, caught by Frédéric in the bath, perhaps, since that's an image much in style these days. And then a new vision, worse than all the others, pops out of my imagination, as though simply another step in a logical progression: why not a quick sketch of Eugénie in the rumpled sheets of a bed where the second pillow still shows the characteristic imprint of someone else's head? I'm filling in the wrinkles in a messy bed, drawn with just a few pencil strokes, and it's all so telling, so graphic, that I can hardly stand it. Since no such drawing actually exists, as far as I know, why then does my imagination keep feeding my pain rather than doing everything possible to distract me?

That thought immediately brings to mind something I've probably been pushing away for months; I have to stifle screams in the rag where my fist has been clenched ever since I started in on this hunt. The thing that's just crossed my mind is simply too much, and yet is so perfectly obvious. Why hadn't I thought of it sooner? No, I'm not crazy, no, I'm not out of my mind: Eugénie is expecting a child and the father is my husband, and she will probably be coming to term around now, if she hasn't done so already. I've known it for such a long time, but have been refusing to acknowledge it. How much strength I've been wasting resisting it.

Quick! I have to get to the door before I vomit in the studio! I fling myself at the foot of the privet hedge, my tears mixed in with the bread and coffee my stomach is rejecting. I'm ashamed to admit the things that happen now, against my will: all that filth dribbling out of my body. The cool flow on my legs is the only way I realize what's happened. Soon after, the feeling that my woolen stockings are wet drives me, running into the apartment. Washing and changing my clothes before I finish pouring my tears out on the bed bolster. Visions of Eugénie entwined with Frédéric cast me down into the fires of hell.

Did Mme Versoix know about all this when I'd met her at the Café de la Paix? I can still hear her sighing, "Thank the Good Lord your Grandmother didn't live to see this!" Yes, she was thinking above all of *her* mother, and what she would have made of it all. How much had my mother known about the tricky little situation her "child" had become involved in?

With some distance now, I can see that life was well-ordered in the days when my grandmother ruled. For a second I have a haunting vision of her ghost leaning on her cane. She's crossing the rose garden at Sainte-Colombe with the proud bearing of someone who knows what one must do in life so that everything runs smoothly, with no surprises: someone who has built a domain where one's servants and one's family never diverge from the paths she has laid out for them, as if the unexpected were simply out of the question.

And yet, when we were of an age to become entangled in life, she didn't manage to drag us along to see things the way she did. There was a different blood running through the veins of her three Lewly grandchildren. It was not simply what came from her or from her husband who was a product of the Lyonnais bourgeoisie. Her grandchildren had the blood of an Englishman, a gambler who had ruined his fortune before doing away with himself—not to mention that they shared the blood of a cousin who'd been sent off by her father to live in France, endowed with a pension for life, provided she never set foot again in the land of her birth, because she'd given birth to a bastard son . . .

Nothing in my life makes sense anymore; nothing has any value. I don't love anybody and feel that no one loves me. Nothing is certain. What role could my mother have played in Eugénie's marriage? I will never know. What I need is some solid thing to anchor my reason to, so it won't slip away completely in these dreadful days, when Europe is aflame, when we are perhaps about to lose our men despite how full they are of plans and hopes and love—how full they are, all in all, of life? William, Frédéric, Lucien and so many others sent to the front . . . The madness of a war that I don't understand, the madness in my heart: "May Frédéric never return, since he has divided himself between my sister and me." Looking at our bed, the place where I'd learned to love his body together with mine, I can't keep from imagining a bomb scattering shreds of my husband all over the unfamiliar landscape in Argonne. This thought strips me of all feeling.

Because maybe I'll never see him again—and, if not, how will I ever get over the way we said good-bye? Even the adoring words he whispered to me as, rifle slung over his shoulder, he wrapped me in his arms on the railway platform—even these drum hard enough in my head to hurt. Yes, here in our bedroom I hear those words again, but now they wound me. At the station, when the train seemed to be catching its breath before heading off, laden with merry soldiers, the time for explanations had passed. But that voice which I can't keep from loving goes on and on, repeating itself the way you might tell your most precious secret so that it will never be forgotten—it's saying that it was I who was the diamond of his life, and that if, one day, I doubted his love, he at least would never doubt it again . . . Four months and two weeks later I take apart each word in an indescribable state of anger and hatred. Because, of course, if he wouldn't doubt it again, it means he *had* been doubting it. I could have accepted that much, if it hadn't been my sister who had planted that doubt in his mind . . .

As he left, Frédéric had tried to repair a year during which we'd been trying to find our way, a year that had seen us torn apart, a year full of questions and full of nights he'd escaped me to enjoy distractions I knew nothing about. The last words he spoke as he hugged me to him in the pushing and shoving and all the mingled sounds of the crowd, the railwaymen, and the engines . . . today, as this war trudges on through the horror of trenches already white with snow, his words take on two meanings: "Yes, my love, men are capable of being carried away by passing fancies—even men like me. But these momentary things don't put in question the things that matter, the things they've built . . . Please, don't forget that."

But it had taken the sighs of the departing train for him to give me even that one little hint.

I can't help wanting revenge, cursing him now for his cowardliness.

At his parents' I'd seen photographs of the war and would have had no right to entertain such murderous thoughts. He's in danger. Perhaps he's cold and hungry. His letters describe such terrible things, but never linger long over his mood, aside from reporting, on one occasion, how excruciating it is to hear comrades dying beside you, seeing others already stiffened by death, knowing you have no choice but to go on fighting. His letters always end with variations on the same prayer: that on his return he will find the wife he adores and the warmth of the studio where he pictures her as he saw her not long ago, in the back of the room and smiling at him from her easel. He dreams of embracing me, he loves the way our passion is always the same and always different; he loves our life among all those other people doing their work, making their art . . .

I'm not done with digging through the boxes and Frédéric's secret hiding places.

Trembling as if I expected to find a corpse, I pull the second panel of the heavy curtains aside. I love looking at its smooth flowing lines from my easel. There's a simple joy in seeing the way the shadows play in its velvet folds at a particular moment just at nightfall, when the light is softened by filtering through the privet. It's a painting just in itself, varying according to the season.

Five canvases are lined up against the wall and I think of how much care Frédéric took placing them there so they would be protected from the dust. Remembering the simplest of gestures brings so much life into an empty room! You'd think if I turned my head I'd catch my beloved mixing his paints on his palette. I lay my hand on the first painting and swivel it around to face me.

Now, something I wasn't expecting: I find I'm face to face with myself. Had Frédéric found time to complete the portrait of me at my easel from the sketch he'd made a few weeks before he was called up? Where had he gone to work on it? In Ernest Ponsal's new studio on the rue des Dames, or to Lucien's place?

How different was this woman he painted just before the summer! I feel like centuries have gone by and crushed me between the moment he sketched me and today, when, in the midst of such chaos, I'm finding the completed picture. My hair is braided and put up in a crown on my head, the way my friend Alice used to wear hers; my face is bent peacefully over my work with my eyes focused on the point of my paintbrush. A model who forgot she was being looked at. In the foreground the console table is covered by a long tablecloth with cheerful stripes in shades of Burgundy wine and buttercup yellow, and on it is a vase of peonies just opening. The flowers are bent over my favorite Jules Verne novel, *The Lighthouse at the End of the World*, right next to a bowl of fruit. Behind my stool Frédéric has painted the indispensable screen in its carmine red, faded by the years. I move it around whenever I want to reframe my surroundings. How could I look so serene despite what we were going through when he painted this portrait? You would say I'm totally at ease. Is that how he saw me, despite his mad desire for my sister? Or was he painting the Mathilde of our not-so-distant, happier days, already feeling nostalgic for them? I feel I've aged so much. If somebody told me that my hair's gone white, I'd believe it.

The tranquility of this model, this model who is me, has nothing in common with the distress felt by the woman looking at her. I'm captured in a three-quarter view and the light is falling on me from the side. Was it in order to throw light on my face and hands, one of which is on the edge of the easel and the other holding the brush so delicately, that Frédéric dressed me in black, showing only a restrained bit of white collar dipping slightly away from my neck, and a thin lace ruffle at each of my wrists? Perhaps he wanted to emphasize my austere side—something everyone seems to agree that I have. It must have been warm in the room because I'm not wearing a shawl.

Here, in this particular spot, I've trusted in a benevolent presence for ten years. My husband was able to show this much in the portrait; you'd think nothing could shake me, that if I were to raise my head from my work it would be to smile. He rendered my determination, the rigor with which I worked, the respect I had for what my hands, the tools of my spirit, produced. My lips are closed, but not tight or bitter. Of all the many portraits he painted of me alone, or with friends or family, I've never had the sensation of being so completely seen and known as in this picture, never so solidly established as a painter in her studio. He took great care with the hand lying on the easel's upright, showing my wedding ring sparkling with the same light as that in my hair. His wife, the artist at work. An odd impression to have just now, when I've been thinking I have nothing left, when I've been cursing him, when I feel I've lost myself entirely.

After all the turmoil, silence.

There's no such thing as an innocent brushstroke in a painting.

I've known that for a long time. This is not a mirror that I'm searching so carefully now, it's Frédéric whom I'm approaching, it's our deep bond that I'm seeking here. The painter is there, invisible, is always there just as much as his model. He has meticulously braided my hair and made it shine in such a lively way that you want to touch it with your hand, as you would silk; he has caressed my profile with such a delicate stroke of his brush. No anxiety is apparent in his lines—instead there's the sort of trust that makes it possible to put the best of oneself into a work . . .

The more I examine and appraise the picture closely the more tears blur what I see. You'd think they would wash away the pain I'd felt mutilating me an hour or so earlier. But no.

I prop the portrait on the arm of the comfortable chair in our little parlor before I wrap up in a plaid blanket and stretch out on the sofa. The picture hasn't told me everything about the painter. I need to hear what Frédéric wanted to express, hear it completely, and more than completely. There's always something in a work of art that escapes the artist responsible for it. *That* is what I need to have.

I can see from a quick glance at the privet hedge that the courtyard is flooded with the gleaming mauves of evening. The shadow of the painting I've put on the armchair reminds me of the insane, murderous rage I felt this morning. I light an oil lamp and take a sheet of Canson paper and a soft lead pencil from my box; then I start my first sketch. On the paper I'll set myself free from all I've imagined since this morning—which were the very worst things my mind could produce. I'll set myself the task of turning them into something more.

Let Eugénie take everything away from me. My soul will stay right where it's always been. "The child" will never dry up the source of my inspiration—the place on the little cul-de-sac dating from 1720, where you could look out onto the great lawn and the tall trees in Marble Hill Park, right on the banks of the Thames. There, with the eyes of a loving couple upon them, the Lewly twins were happy and free. That is my inexhaustible treasure, new to me every day, because that was where I learned my way of seeing things. The river continues to flow.

Whether I'm alone or not, it's in an artist's studio that I'm most at home; it's when I use my brush or pencil that I speak to the world and that I truly exist. Who could ever take away from me the one thing giving real sense to my life: the need to touch the world with my colors?

BRIGITTE LOZEREC'H hasn't stopped writing since the 1982 publication of her first novel, *L'Intérimaire*, which has been translated into numerous languages and into English as *The Temp*. Since then she has published six novels and a biography of the polar explorer Ernest Shackleton.

BETSY WING has published, in addition to her own fiction, translations of *Western* and *The Origin of Man* by Christine Montalbetti, as well as works by Assia Djebar, Paule Constant, and Édouard Glissant.

SELECTED DALKEY ARCHIVE TITLES

Michal Ajvaz, *The Golden Age.*
The Other City.
Pierre Albert-Birot, *Grabinoulor.*
Yuz Aleshkovsky, *Kangaroo.*
Felipe Alfau, *Chromos.*
Locos.
Ivan Ângelo, *The Celebration.*
The Tower of Glass.
António Lobo Antunes, *Knowledge of Hell.*
The Splendor of Portugal.
Alain Arias-Misson, *Theatre of Incest.*
John Ashbery and James Schuyler, *A Nest of Ninnies.*
Robert Ashley, *Perfect Lives.*
Gabriela Avigur-Rotem, *Heatwave and Crazy Birds.*
Djuna Barnes, *Ladies Almanack.*
Ryder.
John Barth, *LETTERS.*
Sabbatical.
Donald Barthelme, *The King.*
Paradise.
Svetislav Basara, *Chinese Letter.*
Miquel Bauçà, *The Siege in the Room.*
René Belletto, *Dying.*
Marek Bieńczyk, *Transparency.*
Andrei Bitov, *Pushkin House.*
Andrej Blatnik, *You Do Understand.*
Louis Paul Boon, *Chapel Road.*
My Little War.
Summer in Termuren.
Roger Boylan, *Killoyle.*
Ignácio de Loyola Brandão, *Anonymous Celebrity.*
Zero.
Bonnie Bremser, *Troia: Mexican Memoirs.*
Christine Brooke-Rose, *Amalgamemnon.*
Brigid Brophy, *In Transit.*
Gerald L. Bruns, *Modern Poetry and the Idea of Language.*
Gabrielle Burton, *Heartbreak Hotel.*
Michel Butor, *Degrees.*
Mobile.
G. Cabrera Infante, *Infante's Inferno.*
Three Trapped Tigers.
Julieta Campos, *The Fear of Losing Eurydice.*
Anne Carson, *Eros the Bittersweet.*
Orly Castel-Bloom, *Dolly City.*
Louis-Ferdinand Céline, *Castle to Castle.*
Conversations with Professor Y.
London Bridge.
Normance.
North.
Rigadoon.
Marie Chaix, *The Laurels of Lake Constance.*
Hugo Charteris, *The Tide Is Right.*
Eric Chevillard, *Demolishing Nisard.*
Marc Cholodenko, *Mordechai Schamz.*
Joshua Cohen, *Witz.*
Emily Holmes Coleman, *The Shutter of Snow.*
Robert Coover, *A Night at the Movies.*
Stanley Crawford, *Log of the S.S. The Mrs Unguentine.*
Some Instructions to My Wife.
René Crevel, *Putting My Foot in It.*
Ralph Cusack, *Cadenza.*
Nicholas Delbanco, *The Count of Concord.*
Sherbrookes.
Nigel Dennis, *Cards of Identity.*
Peter Dimock, *A Short Rhetoric for Leaving the Family.*
Ariel Dorfman, *Konfidenz.*
Coleman Dowell, *Island People.*
Too Much Flesh and Jabez.
Arkadii Dragomoshchenko, *Dust.*
Rikki Ducornet, *The Complete Butcher's Tales.*
The Fountains of Neptune.
The Jade Cabinet.
Phosphor in Dreamland.
William Eastlake, *The Bamboo Bed.*
Castle Keep.
Lyric of the Circle Heart.
Jean Echenoz, *Chopin's Move.*
Stanley Elkin, *A Bad Man.*
Criers and Kibitzers, Kibitzers and Criers.
The Dick Gibson Show.
The Franchiser.
The Living End.
Mrs. Ted Bliss.
François Emmanuel, *Invitation to a Voyage.*
Salvador Espriu, *Ariadne in the Grotesque Labyrinth.*
Leslie A. Fiedler, *Love and Death in the American Novel.*
Juan Filloy, *Op Oloop.*
Andy Fitch, *Pop Poetics.*
Gustave Flaubert, *Bouvard and Pécuchet.*
Kass Fleisher, *Talking out of School.*
Ford Madox Ford, *The March of Literature.*
Jon Fosse, *Aliss at the Fire.*
Melancholy.
Max Frisch, *I'm Not Stiller.*
Man in the Holocene.
Carlos Fuentes, *Christopher Unborn.*
Distant Relations.
Terra Nostra.
Where the Air Is Clear.
Takehiko Fukunaga, *Flowers of Grass.*
William Gaddis, *J R.*
The Recognitions.
Janice Galloway, *Foreign Parts.*
The Trick Is to Keep Breathing.
William H. Gass, *Cartesian Sonata and Other Novellas.*
Finding a Form.
A Temple of Texts.
The Tunnel.
Willie Masters' Lonesome Wife.
Gérard Gavarry, *Hoppla! 1 2 3.*
Etienne Gilson, *The Arts of the Beautiful.*
Forms and Substances in the Arts.
C. S. Giscombe, *Giscome Road.*
Here.
Douglas Glover, *Bad News of the Heart.*
Witold Gombrowicz, *A Kind of Testament.*
Paulo Emílio Sales Gomes, *P's Three Women.*
Georgi Gospodinov, *Natural Novel.*
Juan Goytisolo, *Count Julian.*
Juan the Landless.
Makbara.
Marks of Identity.

SELECTED DALKEY ARCHIVE TITLES

Henry Green, *Back.*
Blindness.
Concluding.
Doting.
Nothing.
Jack Green, *Fire the Bastards!*
Jiří Gruša, *The Questionnaire.*
Mela Hartwig, *Am I a Redundant Human Being?*
John Hawkes, *The Passion Artist.*
Whistlejacket.
Elizabeth Heighway, ed., *Contemporary Georgian Fiction.*
Aleksandar Hemon, ed., *Best European Fiction.*
Aidan Higgins, *Balcony of Europe.*
Blind Man's Bluff
Bornholm Night-Ferry.
Flotsam and Jetsam.
Langrishe, Go Down.
Scenes from a Receding Past.
Keizo Hino, *Isle of Dreams.*
Kazushi Hosaka, *Plainsong.*
Aldous Huxley, *Antic Hay.*
Crome Yellow.
Point Counter Point.
Those Barren Leaves.
Time Must Have a Stop.
Naoyuki Ii, *The Shadow of a Blue Cat.*
Gert Jonke, *The Distant Sound.*
Geometric Regional Novel.
Homage to Czerny.
The System of Vienna.
Jacques Jouet, *Mountain R.*
Savage.
Upstaged.
Mieko Kanai, *The Word Book.*
Yoram Kaniuk, *Life on Sandpaper.*
Hugh Kenner, *Flaubert.*
Joyce and Beckett: The Stoic Comedians.
Joyce's Voices.
Danilo Kiš, *The Attic.*
Garden, Ashes.
The Lute and the Scars
Psalm 44.
A Tomb for Boris Davidovich.
Anita Konkka, *A Fool's Paradise.*
George Konrád, *The City Builder.*
Tadeusz Konwicki, *A Minor Apocalypse.*
The Polish Complex.
Menis Koumandareas, *Koula.*
Elaine Kraf, *The Princess of 72nd Street.*
Jim Krusoe, *Iceland.*
Ayşe Kulin, *Farewell: A Mansion in Occupied Istanbul.*
Emilio Lascano Tegui, *On Elegance While Sleeping.*
Eric Laurrent, *Do Not Touch.*
Violette Leduc, *La Bâtarde.*
Edouard Levé, *Autoportrait.*
Suicide.
Mario Levi, *Istanbul Was a Fairy Tale.*
Deborah Levy, *Billy and Girl.*
José Lezama Lima, *Paradiso.*
Rosa Liksom, *Dark Paradise.*
Osman Lins, *Avalovara.*
The Queen of the Prisons of Greece.
Alf Mac Lochlainn,
The Corpus in the Library.
Out of Focus.
Ron Loewinsohn, *Magnetic Field(s).*
Mina Loy, *Stories and Essays of Mina Loy.*
D. Keith Mano, *Take Five.*
Micheline Aharonian Marcom,
The Mirror in the Well.
Ben Marcus,
The Age of Wire and String.
Wallace Markfield,
Teitlebaum's Window.
To an Early Grave.
David Markson, *Reader's Block.*
Wittgenstein's Mistress.
Carole Maso, *AVA.*
Ladislav Matejka and Krystyna Pomorska, eds.,
Readings in Russian Poetics: Formalist and Structuralist Views.
Harry Mathews, *Cigarettes.*
The Conversions.
The Human Country: New and Collected Stories.
The Journalist.
My Life in CIA.
Singular Pleasures.
The Sinking of the Odradek Stadium.
Tlooth.
Joseph McElroy,
Night Soul and Other Stories.
Abdelwahab Meddeb, *Talismano.*
Gerhard Meier, *Isle of the Dead.*
Herman Melville, *The Confidence-Man.*
Amanda Michalopoulou, *I'd Like.*
Steven Millhauser, *The Barnum Museum.*
In the Penny Arcade.
Ralph J. Mills, Jr., *Essays on Poetry.*
Momus, *The Book of Jokes.*
Christine Montalbetti, *The Origin of Man.*
Western.
Olive Moore, *Spleen.*
Nicholas Mosley, *Accident.*
Assassins.
Catastrophe Practice.
Experience and Religion.
A Garden of Trees.
Hopeful Monsters.
Imago Bird.
Impossible Object.
Inventing God.
Judith.
Look at the Dark.
Natalie Natalia.
Serpent.
Time at War.
Warren Motte,
Fables of the Novel: French Fiction since 1990.
Fiction Now: The French Novel in the 21st Century.
Oulipo: A Primer of Potential Literature.
Gerald Murnane, *Barley Patch.*
Inland.
Yves Navarre, *Our Share of Time.*
Sweet Tooth.
Dorothy Nelson, *In Night's City.*
Tar and Feathers.
Eshkol Nevo, *Homesick.*
Wilfrido D. Nolledo, *But for the Lovers.*
Flann O'Brien, *At Swim-Two-Birds.*
The Best of Myles.
The Dalkey Archive.
The Hard Life.
The Poor Mouth.

FOR A FULL LIST OF PUBLICATIONS, VISIT:
www.dalkeyarchive.com

SELECTED DALKEY ARCHIVE TITLES

The Third Policeman.
Claude Ollier, *The Mise-en-Scène.*
Wert and the Life Without End.
Giovanni Orelli, *Walaschek's Dream.*
Patrik Ouředník, *Europeana.*
The Opportune Moment, 1855.
Boris Pahor, *Necropolis.*
Fernando del Paso, *News from the Empire.*
Palinuro of Mexico.
Robert Pinget, *The Inquisitory.*
Mahu or The Material.
Trio.
Manuel Puig, *Betrayed by Rita Hayworth.*
The Buenos Aires Affair.
Heartbreak Tango.
Raymond Queneau, *The Last Days.*
Odile.
Pierrot Mon Ami.
Saint Glinglin.
Ann Quin, *Berg.*
Passages.
Three.
Tripticks.
Ishmael Reed, *The Free-Lance Pallbearers.*
The Last Days of Louisiana Red.
Ishmael Reed: The Plays.
Juice!
Reckless Eyeballing.
The Terrible Threes.
The Terrible Twos.
Yellow Back Radio Broke-Down.
Jasia Reichardt, *15 Journeys Warsaw to London.*
Noëlle Revaz, *With the Animals.*
João Ubaldo Ribeiro, *House of the Fortunate Buddhas.*
Jean Ricardou, *Place Names.*
Rainer Maria Rilke, *The Notebooks of Malte Laurids Brigge.*
Julián Ríos, *The House of Ulysses.*
Larva: A Midsummer Night's Babel.
Poundemonium.
Procession of Shadows.
Augusto Roa Bastos, *I the Supreme.*
Daniël Robberechts, *Arriving in Avignon.*
Jean Rolin, *The Explosion of the Radiator Hose.*
Olivier Rolin, *Hotel Crystal.*
Alix Cleo Roubaud, *Alix's Journal.*
Jacques Roubaud, *The Form of a City Changes Faster, Alas, Than the Human Heart.*
The Great Fire of London.
Hortense in Exile.
Hortense Is Abducted.
The Loop.
Mathematics:
The Plurality of Worlds of Lewis.
The Princess Hoppy.
Some Thing Black.
Raymond Roussel, *Impressions of Africa.*
Vedrana Rudan, *Night.*
Stig Sæterbakken, *Siamese.*
Self Control.
Lydie Salvayre, *The Company of Ghosts.*
The Lecture.
The Power of Flies.
Luis Rafael Sánchez, *Macho Camacho's Beat.*
Severo Sarduy, *Cobra & Maitreya.*
Nathalie Sarraute, *Do You Hear Them?*
Martereau.
The Planetarium.
Arno Schmidt, *Collected Novellas.*
Collected Stories.
Nobodaddy's Children.
Two Novels.
Asaf Schurr, *Motti.*
Gail Scott, *My Paris.*
Damion Searls, *What We Were Doing and Where We Were Going.*
June Akers Seese, *Is This What Other Women Feel Too?*
What Waiting Really Means.
Bernard Share, *Inish.*
Transit.
Viktor Shklovsky, *Bowstring.*
Knight's Move.
A Sentimental Journey: Memoirs 1917–1922.
Energy of Delusion: A Book on Plot.
Literature and Cinematography.
Theory of Prose.
Third Factory.
Zoo, or Letters Not about Love.
Pierre Siniac, *The Collaborators.*
Kjersti A. Skomsvold, *The Faster I Walk, the Smaller I Am.*
Josef Škvorecký, *The Engineer of Human Souls.*
Gilbert Sorrentino, *Aberration of Starlight.*
Blue Pastoral.
Crystal Vision.
Imaginative Qualities of Actual Things.
Mulligan Stew.
Pack of Lies.
Red the Fiend.
The Sky Changes.
Something Said.
Splendide-Hôtel.
Steelwork.
Under the Shadow.
W. M. Spackman, *The Complete Fiction.*
Andrzej Stasiuk, *Dukla.*
Fado.
Gertrude Stein, *The Making of Americans.*
A Novel of Thank You.
Lars Svendsen, *A Philosophy of Evil.*
Piotr Szewc, *Annihilation.*
Gonçalo M. Tavares, *Jerusalem.*
Joseph Walser's Machine.
Learning to Pray in the Age of Technique.
Lucian Dan Teodorovici, *Our Circus Presents . . .*
Nikanor Teratologen, *Assisted Living.*
Stefan Themerson, *Hobson's Island.*
The Mystery of the Sardine.
Tom Harris.
Taeko Tomioka, *Building Waves.*
John Toomey, *Sleepwalker.*
Jean-Philippe Toussaint, *The Bathroom.*
Camera.
Monsieur.
Reticence.
Running Away.
Self-Portrait Abroad.
Television.
The Truth about Marie.

SELECTED DALKEY ARCHIVE TITLES

Dumitru Tsepeneag, *Hotel Europa.*
The Necessary Marriage.
Pigeon Post.
Vain Art of the Fugue.
Esther Tusquets, *Stranded.*
Dubravka Ugresic, *Lend Me Your Character.*
Thank You for Not Reading.
Tor Ulven, *Replacement.*
Mati Unt, *Brecht at Night.*
Diary of a Blood Donor.
Things in the Night.
Álvaro Uribe and Olivia Sears, eds.,
Best of Contemporary Mexican Fiction.
Eloy Urroz, *Friction.*
The Obstacles.
Luisa Valenzuela, *Dark Desires and the Others.*
He Who Searches.
Paul Verhaeghen, *Omega Minor.*
Aglaja Veteranyi, *Why the Child Is Cooking in the Polenta.*
Boris Vian, *Heartsnatcher.*
Llorenç Villalonga, *The Dolls' Room.*
Toomas Vint, *An Unending Landscape.*
Ornela Vorpsi, *The Country Where No One Ever Dies.*
Austryn Wainhouse, *Hedyphagetica.*
Curtis White, *America's Magic Mountain.*
The Idea of Home.
Memories of My Father Watching TV.
Requiem.
Diane Williams, *Excitability: Selected Stories.*
Romancer Erector.
Douglas Woolf, *Wall to Wall.*
Ya! & John-Juan.
Jay Wright, *Polynomials and Pollen.*
The Presentable Art of Reading Absence.
Philip Wylie, *Generation of Vipers.*
Marguerite Young, *Angel in the Forest.*
Miss MacIntosh, My Darling.
Reyoung, *Unbabbling.*
Vlado Žabot, *The Succubus.*
Zoran Živković, *Hidden Camera.*
Louis Zukofsky, *Collected Fiction.*
Vitomil Zupan, *Minuet for Guitar.*
Scott Zwiren, *God Head.*